Meet Polly. Kind. Car... what she seems and ... her.

In a leafy, quiet part of the suburbs of north London, it is a girl called Polly's sixteenth birthday. Her special day is not celebrated and is mostly forgotten, this leaves her feeling unloved by her family. They also let slip that she is adopted.

A series of strange happenings take place that Polly is unable to explain and there is an encounter with a mysterious woman, on her birthday, who knows her from when she was a baby. The woman gives her a gift that unleashes within her special powers to save the planet from Armageddon.

A secret organisation known as the Inner Circle are looking for a book of powerful magic called the Tome of Herne. Within its ancient texts is a prophecy foretelling the destruction of the surface of the planet. The book also contains long forgotten pagan secrets of how to invoke unnatural long life. The Inner Circle are seeking this knowledge in order to be the chosen few that survive and shape the new world post-apocalypse. Polly and her friends, Chris and Toni, must protect the Tome of Herne from falling into the wrong hands at all costs.

Unbeknown to Polly, her true destiny is part of the prophecy and is waiting to be discovered in the crumbling pages of the Tome of Herne.

Polly and the Tome of Herne

Polly and the Tome of Herne

by Peppa Aubyn

Polly and The Tome of Herne on Amazon.com:

A fantasy story about a girl with magical powers who uses them to save the planet, humanity and all living things from total annihilation

Book Cover Design by 100 Covers

ISBN: 9798393833473

EAN

Fiction > reference > Independently published / self-publishing

Contents

I dedicate this book to my big sister, Debsy,

who learnt to find love in all the light places from a very early age.

I miss you

Chapter One   What the summer brings.

Thursday

It was a day like any other, in July, in north London. There was a faint breeze, which was warm, with a slight hint of begonias. This was a part of London where pale grey pavements are quaintly uneven. Where little tufts of grass and dandelions sprout through cracks in the concrete slabs and in places where uniformity is preferred, by the neighbourhood residents. This is the suburbs. The tree-lined streets look picturesque with branches overhanging the pavements. The leaves are lush and green. Everything is in bloom. Peaceful. The faint hum of insects can be heard, as well as birds chirping in the trees. Everything is calm and still. Everything is ordinary. Nothing unexpected every happens in places like this. Except, sometimes, and this is one of those times, this is where a sequence of truly extraordinary events begins, and, they happen to ordinary people. Looking back, it is a good thing too, as these events save the world from total annihilation.

It is the end of the school day and the best of weekdays, which is Thursday. Polly has an inset day at school tomorrow, which means teachers go in for training without pupils present, so it's a day off for her. This is fortuitous, as it is also Polly's birthday tomorrow, sixteen years old and leaving school for good next week – the finality of this is daunting for her but she hides it well.

Polly is scuttling along at a seriously fast pace and not paying attention, she is feeling overwhelmed by the prospect of her childhood coming to an end. Usually, she is seeking to be mindful and present, taking her time to stroll through these streets. Her love of nature is so compelling that she is easily distracted by the flowers and small creatures and trees that she sees on her way home. It would take the average person ten minutes to walk the distance from her school to her house, but it takes her thirty to forty minutes, much to her mother's and father's annoyance. Yet, in all fairness, it does not take much to offend her parents and they are always actively seeking ways to be annoyed and criticise poor Polly. Only the other day they had entered the living room in the family home and criticised her for having the TV on. It was not loud and they had never told her not to do this before. Both of them took turns to yell at her for over an hour or more. Berating Polly is some kind of sport to them with each parent taking their turn to criticise her. Polly was upset at that time but she sat there agreeing and smiling until they left then fought to hold back her tears. It's a good thing that Polly spends a lot of her time outside in nature and away from home with these two as parents. Her disposition is naturally kind hearted so she does not notice all the slights from them and she has grown accustomed to the harsh words.

Polly is different from her family. Being thoughtful, kind and caring are important qualities to her. She is aware that she possesses a cognitive type of strength that means she does not seek out external approval, being very in control of her own mind like she is. Most people, including her family, find this difficult to understand and she is often a target for bullies. Polly does not mind so much, reasoning that this means the bullies are occupied with her and give less fortunate people some respite. If one were to describe Polly in terms of her physical appearance, it would be to note that she is tall, with a lean elven look to her. She has hazel-coloured almond shaped eyes and she wears her chestnut brown hair long. However, the most remarkable thing about her is often why people with ill intentions become wary of her. She possesses an inner strength and can catch the makeup of people just by looking at them. People often do get the impression that she is able to see into their soul. This gift makes people who have something to hide feel uncomfortable.

Considering this remarkable skill, it is a good thing that Polly is inherently good and wants nothing more than to spread happiness in the world and protect the ones closest to her, otherwise she would be quite a frighteningly powerful person if she had ever developed any sort of darker traits. We will never quite know for sure why some people are surrounded by evil and remain wholeheartedly in the light; whereas others are bad from the start and have been raised, surrounded by people with good intentions.

Polly abruptly skids to a stop to admire the pink dogwood tree at the corner of her street. It has stunningly beautiful crested white flowers with pink tips and veins. She leans forward and inhales the scent of the petals and blows out the perfume of it into the hazy summer air. This action makes her gloriously happy. She twirls around and around while doing this. She starts stumbling and tripping over her feet. Her chestnut auburn wavy hair swings after her and her hazel eyes are crinkled in the bliss of this free-spirited abandonment. Her Breton t-shirt is scrunched into the front of her light chinos; she looks rather unkempt apart from her gold chain swinging round her neck. The necklace is elaborate in design, an antique and is formed of a circle within a circle with a compressed letter 'g' within. Polly doesn't recall when she received it, as it has been with her since she was a very small child.

Smiling to herself as she starts to walk again, suddenly, her instincts are roused, she hears the faint rustle of a hedgerow nearby. Polly stops, heart pounding in her ears and immediately crouches down. There, peeping out of the bush, is a beautiful pure white dove. It majestically takes flight through the greenery before gliding in circles around her head. The dove then gently drops two feathers above her, before flourishing its wings and flying away. Polly watches as the gentle breeze catches the brilliant white feathers, they twirl downwards, and land gently in her outstretched hand. She is still in the crouched position looking up at the last traces of the bird, when she catches a glimpse of Mrs Arthur and her scratchy woollen, green cardigan-clad arm. And then, the beaky and piercing face of Mrs Arthur appears over the hedge. Her neighbours narrowed eyes and arched eyebrow indicate to Polly that she is suspicious and suspects the poor girl of doing something distasteful. To Mrs Arthur having fun is definitely distasteful and not part of Mrs Arthurs' repertoire or indeed her life.

Polly picks up the two feathers and stands up, straight backed, quickly realising that her crouching is being observed with disdain. 'Good afternoon to you Mrs Arthur, why, I was busy admiring your marvellous pink dogwood tree and didn't notice you standing there in your big green cardigan. By the way, your cardigan looks like part of a tree, it's beautiful just like the colour of moss.' Mrs Arthur squints at Polly, she is busily checking if the exchange is an insult before she responds 'Well, Polly dear, of course you didn't. Head in the clouds as usual.'

Mrs Arthur sighed and tutted, pursing her narrow lips 'Your Mother has just driven past in that gas guzzling big blacked out SUV of hers and you better get home. You know she likes you being there before she gets in.' To the average passer-by, this comment sounded like a friendly neighbour reminding a fifteen-year-old girl of her mother's care but to those that are initiated in the ways of this neighbourhood, the comment was made to scare Polly and Mrs Arthur thoroughly enjoyed the power she exerted by these few words. Polly immediately picked up her school backpack. It was laden with library books that Polly loved to read. She pushed the feathers into a gap in the zip and she bolted down the street. Not now noticing a single leaf on a tree or a butterfly flapping its delicate wings or a luminous blade of grass in her haste to get home. One thing was for certain, Polly would be in trouble. Her mother had arrived home before her and Polly's birthday is tomorrow. Mother wanted Polly's help with the dinner party preparations for tonight's celebrations, for want of a better word.

Polly is running at full speed now and beads of sweat are dripping from her forehead. She manages to keep this out of her eyes by running the back of her hand over her face and pushing the dampness into her fringe. Beads of sweat are also dripping down her back. Wheezing and panting, she skids to a halt at the new garden gate made from limed oak and jumps over it, not wasting anytime on the finicky latch mechanism that conspires against her. She catches her trousers as she vaults over the gate and a huge smudge of dirt catches on to the material. Polly has not noticed the splodge of dirt in her haste to get to the front porch. Trembling now through exertion and wariness of spirit and mind, she lifts her arm ready with the front door key and takes a deep steadying breath before she enters the melee that she envisioned is waiting inside.

She steps into the Farrow and Ball painted hallway. The walls are painted a fashionable sage green to complement the black and white mosaic tiled floor. The air is cool from a small window being open and this, coupled along with the fact that the front of the house is currently in the afternoon shade. The general aesthetic of the reception area is very chic and precisely the same as in the decorating magazine that Mother reads. It is expensive, therefore, the best and most admired. Well, in mother's view, anyway.

Polly pulls at her laces to undo the top of her converse boots, cursing under her breath that she had not taken them off in the porch before entering. At the same time, she is hastily grabbing at her satchel and she tries to loop it over one of the hooks on the matching green coat stand. Doing these two things at once, inevitably, causes her to lose her balance and she starts to tumble to the floor. She tuts and sighs "I know that rushing always makes me clumsy, but I'm anxious to make everything perfect so my parents don't have an opportunity to criticise me" Polly thought to herself. She is in a heap on the floor when mother enters the hallway. 'Oh, I'm so glad that you've decided to join us, Polly. How kind of you to arrive on time to help your poor mother with the shopping for YOUR birthday dinner party.' Mother said this in her pitchy, nasally voice, using the most sarcastic tone she could muster, she continued 'My back is aching now so I'm not sure I'm going to be able to make Uncle Jack's favourite summer fruits pudding but what do you care, hey? It's not YOUR favourite pudding, is it?'

As Polly lay there with tears of frustration in her eyes, she reflected that she could never quite keep up with both her parents' logic or figure out why she was at fault most of the time. But on this occasion, she was particularly confused. Why would Uncle Jack not receive his favourite summer pudding due to Polly being late for her curfew? The other part of the mystery was that mother was not actually making or cooking anything. The party was being catered for by a prominent London chef and an army of cooks. Polly also scrunched up her face to give thought to exactly what shopping Mother had carried into the house. She settled on a guess, that it was most likely from Chanel and not necessarily for anyone but herself. There is a curfew and it is set for 3:30PM on school days even though school finishes at 3:25PM AND Polly usually helps Miss Langley, her favourite teacher, tidy up after class. Her parents refuse to take this into consideration, which is somewhat befuddling. She had explained to her parents on a number of occasions, that helping after class usually takes about 20 minutes. The answer is always the same. Polly is informed that the time set is the time set and Polly needs to make this work. Following these discussions, she often hears them walking away together whispering 'sneaky little teacher's pet'.

Her Mother continues her lecture and grows more passionately venomous as she goes on. Mother stops dead in front of Polly and looks down at her, suddenly realising that Polly is on her back staring up at her in a dishevelled state from the floor. 'Good grief girl, get up off the floor and clean yourself up. You have got mud on your new trousers and you are sweating like a pig. if the neighbours look in, they'll be concerned.' Polly noted Mother did not express concern for Polly at this point, moreover that she was worried that the appearance of the situation be observed.

Mother switches off the passive aggression and changes to acting more like a purring cat that has noticed a lame bird under a thicket of thorns. A cat will not put themselves in harm's way but will, most likely, relish the situation knowing that the poor defenceless bird must come out at some point or die of dehydration. Cats are superior in every way in terms of their hunting instincts, yet are adorable and loving at the same time. Polly loved cats for these unusual polar character traits, but her parents' unusual behaviours were not as adorable and Polly often found herself drawn to the forensic and evil criminal material at the local library, trying to understand them better. 'Polly darling, please do fetch mummy her special drink.' she batted her eyelashes furiously, which made her look slightly deranged and then added in a harsher tone 'with a queen olive on a cocktail stick this time. Please do remember clumsy clod as you forgot it last time and it really does ruin mummy's day. You don't want to ruin mummy's day, do you?'

Polly hesitated, still laying on the floor. She was worried. Mother became quite 'over-excited' when imbibing too early and the dinner party needed preparing. Father walked in at that precise moment; he was home very early due to the dinner party. Mother had called his executive assistant to arrange it all months ago to fit round his schedule. Father strode passed Polly, placed his luxurious leather briefcase on the polished side cabinet, loosened his silk tie while unclipping his gold cufflinks from his shirt. Mother squealed and launched herself at him, they both kissed each other, arms and legs intertwined. They have the same deep orange spray tan so working out which arm was whose was like a puzzle one really didn't want to try to solve. Polly felt queasy observing the scene, the discomfort scratching at her throat. Mother came up for air and announced 'Chop, Chop butterball, off the floor, the special drink is calling my name and you'll need to help out to set up the party too.'. Polly sighed and rolled her eyes. She automatically knew that this statement was Mother-code for helping-means-doing-all-of-it. Polly heaved herself up off the floor and made her way to the cocktail bar in the living room. She would make the cocktail and then get on with setting up the party – fully aware that no one else would do it.

The afternoon waned into evening, with Polly doing lots of chores. She started with putting up the fairy lights over the trees in the garden, and stringing glowing lanterns throughout the house, and getting champagne buckets ready with ice from the walk-in freezer, and arranging flower displays for the dining hall, and then lastly, readying the guest suites.

The dinner was being catered and Polly was working through the menu with the Chef when the party organiser, called Bunny, walked in. Bunny is an old school friend of Mothers and the daughter of an oil tycoon. She is a trust fund holder and owns the catering company, but she tends to stay out of the general running of the business preferring to host charity events and go on holiday, which she refers to as 'business trips' for tax reasons. Oftentimes, she refers to herself as creative director, paying herself an eye watering salary and her staff a pittance. She arrived after her team had done most of the preparations and cooking. Grabbing a glass flute from one of the trays placed by the entrance and pouring herself champagne, she barely acknowledges her team before sitting down on a barstool in the cavernous kitchen. The household kitchen doesn't get much use apart from when Polly cooks for herself and for dinner parties. Mother and Father barely eat, preferring a skeletal aesthetic or 'heroin chic' as they often refer to it as. Either way, starving themselves appeared to make them both ill, angry and miserable.

Hearing that Bunny was in the house, Mother glided down the stairs in her midnight blue organza cocktail dress. It had heavenly tiny sequins twinkling all over it in a very subtle way. It had a Breakfast at Tiffany's vibe and her hair was in a chignon a la Audrey Hepburn. Her bleached blonde hair was rather dry and this, coupled with the deep orange fake tan, broke the spell of the look somewhat but other than that she was perfection personified – if one ignored the constant scowl on her face. Around her bony neck a new diamond necklace was clasped. Bunny bounded over instantly when she noticed the piece of jewellery and gave out a loud gasp. Mother took hold of the diamonds and with a throaty laugh declared them to be from Father to match the recent bracelet, earrings and smaller necklace gifted this year. These were all separate presents and each one given as a gift when Father had been caught out in some indiscretion or another. Bunny, knowing this was code for 'he's been at it again', grabbed a bottle of tequila from the side and proclaimed 'next time get a bloody yacht sweetie. I've been telling you darling, cruising around Croatia would be much better and you've got tons of jewellery out of him now'.

Mother looked up at Bunny and tartly replied 'we are not alone here' moving her eyes sideways, indicating the chef and the rest of the team. Polly was not mentioned, she went unseen as usual. Polly often wondered if her parents knew that their relationship was unhealthy because Mother sometimes did show a glimmer of sadness while looking at her diamonds, but it happened so rarely that Polly may have been mistaken and was probably projecting her own sadness onto her mother. The sadness of not being connected to her parents and feeling constantly in the way and misunderstood. Polly let out a sigh while watching the exchange between Bunny and Mother, she could not comprehend why the two women were friends, but never voiced her view.

The thing is, children who grow up in a home where they are unloved will learn that they are on their own, their very survival is based upon reading a situation, looking for risks and learning to hide their feelings. They will learn to wear a mask and fit in. They will also become hyper resilient and some even will parent the parent. Polly had learnt to do all these things from a very young age, but she had been lucky enough to find two very good friends which stopped her from becoming too self-sufficient and a loner, they were Toni and Chris.

Now, for a party allegedly being arranged to celebrate Polly's 16th birthday, it was remarkably light on invites being sent to Polly's actual friends. To such an extent, that in fact the dinner guests were very close family and associates of Mother and Father. Yes, Toni and Chris were not invited.

Uncle Jack and Aunty Gladys arrived with the usual fanfare and bellowing greetings. Polly ran to welcome them in the hallway. Uncle Jack and Aunty Gladys saw her enter the space and threw their coats into her arms and strode by without a second glance. Polly lowered her eyes, her face stung red with the indignity of it and that no birthday greeting had passed their fleshy lips. Mother and Father cooed over Mothers' brother and wife, remarking at how well they looked, and Uncle Jack jiggled his third chin with delight. Aunty Gladys' chubby fingers grabbed a menu and enquired after the food which was as usual, a sumptuous and rich feast of buttered, caramelised and generally overstuffed and unnecessarily trimmed food. There were seven courses in total tonight. Mother and Father never partook in any of the meals but did ensure that all the guests' individual tastes were catered for.   This was in consideration that both profiteered from each guest in some way.

Several more guests arrived; air kisses abounded and Polly did not bother traipsing to the hall after the embarrassment of the first greeting. She doubted very much that anyone had been told that it is her birthday tomorrow.

The evening wore on with many compliments to the hosts and chef for the excellent food, as course after course arrived. The champagne and Chateau Neuf Du Pape, along with vintage wines and special reserve brandy, continued to flow all night. Overindulgence continued with cigars for the men and pretty gift boxes of illegal slimming pills for the ladies to take as a course tomorrow.

 Polly had dressed herself in a simple white tunic dress with her hair in a gold alice band, she looked effortlessly chic and didn't realise how stunning she looked. After some food, she started to feel sleepy yet uneasy surrounded by the bullish and drunken crowd. There were the usual discussions about who bought the best cars, holidays, houses, brands, kitchens, designer clothes etc, one upmanship always being the key theme of the group. This was rather dull to listen to.

There was a lull in the discussion and then it turned to how good housekeeping staff were hard to find because they were all lazy. There were comments about live-in nannies demanding not to work 100 hours straight. This was 'appalling' was the word most used by the group. Bunny thought this abhorrent and spilt quite a lot of wine down herself when, rather too enthusiastically, telling the group how disgusted she was. Mother looked on at her friend murderously as she was spilling wine everywhere - these same nannies were also daring to mention employment rights too, 'for goodness's sake!'. The politics of the day were discussed and each guest giving insider views on the functioning of society and its apparent decline, there was noted silence on the fact that political policy setting may be the cause for this, as it was usually designed to favour the few. The boorish group went on to exclaim how climate change is 'preposterous' and environmental issues 'fabricated' and there was indignance expressed at industrialisation being at fault in any way.

After listening to the conversation for hours, Polly becomes weary of the disdain being projected, especially towards nature. "It's hard to watch the over farming of the planet and the impact that this is having on its fragile ecosystem, knowing that I can't do anything about it and these adults haven't got a clue". Polly's sadness became weariness and she rubbed at her itchy eyes. She started to notice her necklace was getting rather warm which was odd. It was 11 PM. 1 hour to go before her birthday. Guests started to periodically depart.

At 11:41PM Mother, Father, Uncle Jack, Aunty Gladys and Polly were the only people left and had taken themselves to sit in the vast conservatory which was Polly's favourite room - it had a huge skylight that opened out onto the sky. Polly was sitting in her favourite chair where she usually read her books, which is set further back and

17

away from the other members of the group. Looking up, she was taken aback and mesmerised by the night sky that night. It appeared to be twinkling at her and the stars and moon were all much lower, closer than ever before. It was breath-taking and made her feel very small.   Mars shone bright red and appeared to be descending, bowing and lowering its underside directly over the skyline above her - she got the impression it was shining just for her and it was so close she could touch it. Polly reached out as she realised that the planets, moon and stars were very close to one another and in alignment. They crowded into view and lit up the room in a dazzling display. Although, this was not natural, yet, she did not feel alarmed and continued to gaze in wonder at this cosmic display. Eventually, Polly tore her eyes away and looked around at the guests, none of the others had noticed anything odd, being rather drunk like they were.

Polly heard the word 'Birthday' mentioned by her father and Uncle Jack's response stunned Polly into paying closer attention to the conversation in the room. 'Not being funny old chap but how do you know it's her birthday tomorrow, oh heck, look at the time, I mean today, oh no tomorrow, still got 5 minutes to go', Uncle Jack said looking at his watch in a befuddled manner '.... you don't really. She's rather scrawny and measly so you don't know how old she really is, do you? I mean, that woman did not give you a real birth certificate, did she? Told you she was a newborn baby but let's face facts she could have been any age', said Uncle Jack. Father chuckled like he was reflecting on buying a car and potentially the mileage clock had been turned back. 'You have got a point there, Jack.' said Father, while lifting his whisky on the rocks in agreement and nodding his head.

 Jack continued to bumble on 'My dear sister is so very maternal, bless her soul' Jack patted Mother's knee and she nodded with a weak smile on her face 'and was desperate for a baby right there and then. Understandably, you see her two good friends had just had their babies and she wanted all girls, all at the same time for photos and whatnot, she would have taken any old thing presented. I know that the adoption agency was not giving you options in the timeframe you wanted and that this woman presented you with this one but by God you don't know anything about her really, do you or how it's going to turn out?' Uncle Jack hiccupped and ended his tirade with 'Not really one of us, is she?'

'Well,' Mother slurred unbecomingly and belched, her hair had come out of its chignon and was sticking up at all angles and her mascara was streaked on one side of her face. 'THIS woman' Mother mimicked Uncle Jack with a great deal of malice and jerked her head upwards 'is still around if you would like to ask for your money back Jack. She lived in or near Glossop at the time and is called Lady Cadmun-Herne, a very reputable and respected Lady of the British Realm, of old empire lineage. Connected to royalty, someone from the village told us. In all honesty, he was a bit of a crackpot if I recall. It wasn't like we were purchasing the child from a roaming circus caravan band.'

Polly cleared her throat at that point. All of them looked round horrified, dropping glasses and gaping their mouths open. They had completely forgotten she was still there. Polly uttered with a painful emotion in her voice 'are you talking about me?' an awkward silence fell over the group and this was confirmation enough, alongside the furtive glances between them. Polly's neck was very hot now and she was deeply distressed and felt ill, mostly due to feeling like the air had been removed from her lungs, this being a result of what she had heard tonight.

When all of a sudden, Polly experiences a blinding light behind her eyes and, simultaneously, the lights go out in the house leaving everything in darkness, including the lanterns and the fairy lights in the garden. This was rather odd, as these particular lights were not connected to the mains or the same power source. A faint glow gradually surrounds Polly and she notices it is coming from her necklace. She looked down at it and was alarmed further by the fact

19

that her feet were lifting off the ground and she was floating upwards, towards the skylights in the room. Her necklace was steadily growing more brighter and the sky above her was pulling her closer and closer, reaching for her in a way she could not explain. Reeling, Polly held her necklace and she suddenly felt a comforting connection to a great power that she wanted to hold onto, before she gently started floating back down again. Gasping, she looks around at her family, sitting over the other side of the room and none of them seems to have noticed this strange occurrence, so, Polly put this down to her mind playing tricks on her.

The stars above and the galaxies beyond, that were once so far away, were now very close to the earth and to Polly's house. They were illuminating the sky. Mars glowed brightly leaving a burning red hue in the room. Polly did not notice any of these peculiarities at the time as she was feeling very ill and her necklace was steadily starting to heat up, glowing again. She also was worried she was going quite mad. "How could I have floated off the ground like that?" She whispered to herself and to the darkness.

An aroma fills the room of some type of forest fauna, the embodiment of the smell of grass and woods, yet, there were hints of lavender, chamomile and night shade mixed in too. Mother, Father, Uncle Jack and Aunty Gladys grew sleepy and their eyes started to droop heavily. Each of them in turn, fell into a trance like slumber. Polly felt a calmness descend around her as the group fell to sleep and the night sky rescinded, seeping back out of the room as seamlessly as it had drawn in. Polly was very confused. She had suffered from flashing lights behind her eyes at times, which she was told by the school nurse were migraines. She often kept her eyes closed when these fits took over her but this time she had not. She was frightened, she knew it was odd, but she felt like the recent incidents were connected in some way. She wanted to run away, into her bedroom and lock the door but she knew she would need to check her family were okay first or otherwise she would worry about them. The instinct for kindness was inherent in the girl even when it definitely wasn't deserving. She went over to the group that was her family, to make sure they were still breathing, then put each of their heads to the side lest they vomit and placed covers over them. They were sure to have a lot of questions tomorrow.

She walked out into the cool darkness of the hallway and started up the winding stairs. With each step, her way was becoming more illuminated by the glowing sparkling light of her necklace. She fumbled and staggered up the stairs. Her vision was becoming blurred too, so she held onto the banister and put her foot on the last step, levering herself up onto the upper hallway landing, which was covered in a thick carpet pile. She immediately and without thought, wriggled her toes into the fibres for comfort. Having done this since she was a small child.

 Polly felt confused and alienated from herself and her environment. Everything she heard and saw tonight made sense but also was too painful to comprehend. Her thoughts were spiralling around in her head. A dread filled her very being and felt like a lump of ice in her stomach.

What she thought she knew as her truth was not, yet, it did not really matter in a way. She still knew who she was at her core and there was a bonus to a certain extent; it was a relief to know that she was not related to her parents. She felt a pang of guilt for thinking this particular thought.

Everything looked strange and disjointed as she walked down the shadowy hallway. She felt different, distant, walking along. The hallway looked deconstructed in her eyes now and back to raw material; blank plaster, bricks, paint and floor covering, with no memories or emotional attachment. She passed by her mother's bedroom, and stopped and turned round with a compulsion of purpose. She knew where her mother kept important documents, but was not sure if this particular document would be deemed important

21

enough to her mother to keep; after all, it did relate to her. Polly needed to find out and right at this moment – she needed to know the details of her birth and wanted to look for her real birth certificate.

Entering the bedroom quietly and stealthily was a habit. She had never felt welcome in this room. Stalking silently through it even though she didn't need to. She went over to the cream cashmere dressing table and touched the smooth surface with her hand. Pushing the concealed button under the dresser table and a small document drawer slid open with a light coming on underneath. She reached inside and brushed her hand through the various documents. There were a number to sift through, such as, legal deeds, Last Will and Testaments, an old leather-bound book that had two stars intertwined with an embossed '$\mathcal{G}$' on. Then she found what she was looking for, her birth certificate.

 She had seen it before, a very long time ago. It had all her details printed on it, her birth date with the name Polly Hanscombe and Mother and Fathers' names. The details reflected her current life and were all there. She folded it up and put it back. Then she noticed a smaller folded document that she had not seen before. It was another birth certificate with what looked like a star chart pinned to it and, although the date of birth, weight and gender were exactly the same as the other certificate, the name was not. This certificate had on it the name Pollux Willow Luminkaida. There were symbols that she could not read after the name.

She heard herself gasp and instinctively took this document and reread it through, what felt like a thousand times, standing there, alone.

The Father's name on this certificate was Alexandre Cadmus-Herne and the mother; Tabitha Illuminere. Her head started whirling, trying to explore the different possibilities of what this could mean. Her emotions were wild and exaggerated and her head spinning with ideas, she was feeling out of control. Her hands were trembling over the document. She felt sick and angry, and scared, and relieved, and happy and tired; all at the same time, emotions consuming and overloading her. "I knew I was different but seeing it here in black and white makes me worried, what will become of me?" It all felt impossibly complicated. The need for sleep came crashing in on her all of a sudden, her body had quite literally run out of adrenaline. She took the documents and the star charts, closed the drawer and walked unsteadily out of the bedroom, through the landing hallway and into her room.

Polly slipped into bed fully clothed and fell into a dreamless sleep, for which she was certainly grateful for. Polly needed respite from her mind and from the possibility that she was not who she thought she was when she woke up this morning.

Polly and the Tome of Herne

Chapter two The Beginning

Friday

Polly woke up with a start, emerging from a blackness of sleep straight into the reality that someone was walking around in her bedroom. Her body responded instinctively, arching and flipping upwards from a sleeping position, to kneeling on the bed. She then rolled silently towards the side table; her taekwondo lessons from the age of five years old and natural athleticism gave her an advantage to do this move without much effort. Her right hand grabbed for her bedside lamp and the left was balled in a fist and she pivoted forward, flipping onto her feet and onto the floor below. Assuming an attack stance with the right side of her body anchored to the ground for stability.

She noticed her first floor window and balcony door were open and the curtains were blowing inwards like billowing sails in a rough sea, hinting that a storm was coming. Polly is staring at the curtains when a voice fills the room. 'Hey girl, what's got you all riled up this early in the morning and why you still dressed up and holding a lamp?' Polly instantly relaxed, her friend Toni was in the room and let herself in using the window like they used to in the old days when they were kids.

'I thought I'd surprise you. Happy Birthday Polly', with that Toni pulled out a confetti popper and showered her with it before pulling a present wrapped up in cat patterned gift wrap from behind her back. Toni was wearing her ash blonde weave today that looked stunning against her dark caramel skin. She was wearing a Nigerian wedding guest outfit which did usually include a matching headdress called a Gele, but Toni had popped over to see Polly first before getting fully dressed for her cousin's wedding. 'Why did you climb up through the window and in that beautiful dress too? Your mum is going to kill me' Polly said laughing, quite confident that Mrs Adeoye would hug her more than kill her.

She was so grateful to have Toni as a friend, her family was so amazingly warm with loving kindness that they almost made up for her own horrible family, almost but not quite, obviously. Toni laughed and strode over to Polly in two strides, the bedroom was the size of a penthouse suite, but Toni's legs were long and lean from gymnastics and taekwondo. Taekwondo is where the two friends met and had been firm friends ever since the first day. Toni and her family lived in the same upper-class neighbourhood as Polly. The family had experienced subtle prejudices and micro-aggressions over the years from certain parts of the community. Toni's parents were solicitors and owned a prestigious Holborn law firm and their family members, who were barristers, were also Partners. The family was strong together, united, bonded and proud. For generations, adversity had given them strength and bonded them further in their love for one another.

The girls attended their first taekwondo lesson enlisting, unbeknown to them, at the same time and on the first day of new enrolments. The two girls were both five years old at that time and were left out for being different: one for being shy, unconfident, gangly and awkward and the other for being different in a sea of white faces. They were paired together and were firm friends from that day forward. They enjoyed taekwondo and both had a natural aptitude for the sport.

Their instructor, a black man named Sam, was an ex-soldier with a decorated military background. He trained his son, Christopher, at the dojang three to four times a week. Sam saw the potential in the two girls and encouraged them both to work together, led by Chris, who was a little bit older at six years old nearly seven. Chris objected to this at first, he did not want to hang out with the two 'dumb girls' as he phrased it at the time. As the years went by the three competed in regional and national championships together and became best friends, inseparable. They fought as a unit and were taught to look out for each other first and foremost. Sam's philosophy was unit first, enjoyment of the competition second and trophies came last - Sam's view being that silverware is desired by the ego and does not satisfy the spirit.

Polly pulled at the string around the wrapping paper and unfolded the gift. It was two gold bracelets, with each one having both girls' names inscribed in a loop with 'Forever' written inside. Polly pulled open the box and pulled out one of the bands and slipped it onto her friend's wrist. She then did the same with the other on her own and leapt forward to hug her friend, so tightly and for a very long time, until Toni started laughing and pretended to gasp for air. They broke a part and both girls had glistening eyes from their happy tears. Both them blinked them away and started sparring with each other trying to dispel the emotional tension with the disciplined moves of their chosen sport.

'Hey, what are you doing today and sorry we can't do something together, but Maami says I need to go to this dumbass wedding. I could always sneak you in if you've got nothing on, huh?' Toni said. 'Mothers given instruction' Polly said rolling her eyes upwards and mock saluting 'I'm to help her at her beauty and hair shop today then I'm free this evening if you wanna hang after the wedding?' Polly added. 'Are you for real, girl?' Toni said looking mock offended ' You know how long Nigerian wedding parties are. You'll have to meet me at the reception in Park Lane. We can dance and flirt with some bad boys for a while. Get our teenage kicks and runaway. Call me, ok?' with that Toni giggled, blew her a kiss and dashed out of the room towards the hallway stairs and started to run down them. Looking back, she said 'Don't let them get to you today. It's your birthday so only good vibes are allowed in that brain of yours, okay?' She pointed towards Polly's head to emphasise the brain part of what she was saying and ran down the stairs two at a time.

Polly put her hand to her forehead and then started to remember last night. She had forgotten in all of the excitement of seeing Toni in her room and, of course, opening her present. 'Hey, I've got to tell you something', Polly leaned over the banister and shouted into the atrium below but Toni was already at the bottom of the winding staircase and mouthed silently 'WhatsApp me' moving both her thumbs in a tapping motion together which is universally recognised as the signal for WhatsApp. Polly let out a long sigh and then went back into her room to change into her pyjamas and dressing gown then went downstairs, unsure of what she was going to find.

A flamboyant interior house designer had supported Mother to 'unleash' her creative tendencies and the kitchen had several of these 'artistic' pieces. One of them being the garish and quite frankly, humongous chrome kitchen clock, which at this precise time said showed as 8:32 AM. Mother and Father were nowhere to be seen downstairs and Uncle Jack and Aunty Gladys were also not in the conservatory. Polly guessed they must have woken up and gone upstairs to bed at some point in the small hours of the morning. She must have been completely out of it to sleep that deeply, not hearing them coming up the stairs.

She opened the door of the double fridge and pulled out a bottle of sparkling water then stretched and yawned before closing it. On observation, the fridge light was on, and the kitchen appliances were all working, humming away gently so the power must have come back on at some point. But on closer inspection, the clocks on the appliances were not flashing nor in reset mode of '00:00'. "So, there couldn't have been a power cut and its proof I'm bonkers" Polly was actually starting to doubt that any of it happened at all and maybe she fell asleep at the table and had dreamt it. Did she still have the birth certificates then and star charts? That part seemed real enough to her at least. She would go upstairs to check. As she closed the large and cumbersome fridge door, Mother was standing behind it, with a green face mask on. Polly jumped backwards and yelled.

Mother's eyes widened and she jumped back and yelled too. 'What in the world is with you, Polly? Have you gone utterly bonkers? Why are you not ready and leaving for the shop you little lard bunny' Mother said without any remorse. Polly stood upright and stared open-mouthed for a while. It wasn't the fact that her mother had not wished her a Happy Birthday, this was in keeping with tradition; to ignore any special occasion for Polly. It also was not anything to do with the fact that she had expressed no concern that Polly was frightened and had screamed upon her arrival or that she had called her daughter a little lard bunny. No, it was more the fact that she had not mentioned about the family having collectively fallen asleep, the strangeness of the stars and planets last night or that Uncle Jack had blurted out that she was adopted.

Polly furrowed her brows and asked tentatively what Mother thought of last night. Mother took a deep breath, pouted her overly filled lips and said, she had been really excited about receiving the diamonds and how everyone looked so gorgeous but suggested that maybe Polly could do with losing some baby fat before wearing white in the future, and then ended the diatribe with pointing out that Bunny was secretly jealous of her new dining room.

Polly just stared at her mother in shocked disbelief, then quite simply and without saying another word, spun around and resignedly marched upstairs, convinced the whole thing had been a dream.

She quickly jumped into the ensuite and showered, brushed her teeth while towelling off and went to her walk-in wardrobe to put on a black shirt and trousers. This was the staff uniform in Mothers salon. In a rush to get downstairs, as she did not want to be late, the balcony window and door were left open. The documents from last night were caught by a breeze and gently glided onto the floor and were blown under the bed. Later that day, Ellie the housekeeper came in to tidy up after the family had left the house for the day. The light showers from the rain and the wind had sodden the carpet from the balcony door being left open. Ellie pushed it shut and towelled down the handmade sheep wool carpet dry, not noticing the documents under the bed.

The day at the salon was incredibly busy and dull. Winchmore Hill and The Green is very pretty in the summer even when it's slightly windy with rainy showers. Polly spent most of the day sweeping up hair in the front of the shop, while gazing out of the big glass-fronted window of the place. The shop was decorated in bold colours of orange and hot pink with black fittings. It was very eye-catching and often drew in customers with its vibrant decor and loud pumping R&B music. The managerial staff were recruited by Mother and mostly in her own image.

All the part time staff, mostly Saturday girls and boys that work on inset days too, wished Polly a Happy Birthday and presented to her a branded lip gloss that they had bought and all contributed to. The other permanent staff did not. The present was very touching as the branded range selected was Polly's favourite. It is an organic brand, cruelty free with very good environmental credentials, all the things really important to Polly. Mother had convinced the salon team many years ago that Polly was unstable and had in her words 'special needs'. She had mentioned numerous times that her daughter was volatile and could go off at any second so best to stay away from her altogether. They did better than that, they would ignore her completely, only talking to her to give her mundane or disgusting jobs; like, unclogging the hair from the plug holes in the basins or clearing away the hair-filled wax strips. They seemed to think she must be spoiled because Mother was the boss and super rich. They had proactive strategies to keep her in line. Mother supported this approach with glee and relish, often encouraging them to give her more tasks to do.

Towards the end of the day, when everything was being packed up and the staff were switching everything off and leaving, an older lady slipped into the salon quietly and asked to speak to Polly. Gracie, the team manager, came into the back of the shop and told Polly there was some old bag asking for her and quickly added that the older woman had refused to book in for Botox, fillers, hair extensions, mani or a pedicure, waxing or bleaching or any general hair styling requirements of any kind (Gracie had checked this several times with the lady as she looked a bit too 'au natural' for Gracie's liking) 'she came into a salon and just asked to speak to you Polly and wouldn't give me her name, the cheek of it', Gracie added.

Polly was baffled she didn't know any older ladies without Botox or fillers as Mothers' own Mother and all of her friends, that were of the same age, were enhanced to the hilt with Botox, fillers and facelifts as a minimum.

 Gracie flung the shop keys at Polly and told her to lock up afterwards 'get rid of the old bag' Gracie said. Polly was mortified as she was sure the woman could hear every word of the conversation. As Polly approached the front desk, her WhatsApp pinged with a message from Toni saying 'get glammed up and here pronto, tons of hot guys x' Polly had put a pair of leather leggings, shoes and a halter neck in her backpack. She would get ready at the salon and then she planned to jump on the train at Winchmore Hill Station to Finsbury Park and then onto the Piccadilly Line to Hyde Park Corner. The reception was being held in one of the lavish five-star hotels there.

Polly was twiddling her necklace, something she did when she was nervous and saw the lady in question waiting in reception. The woman was strikingly attractive. She was wearing a black travelling cape made out of thick woollen material and this seemed strange in the summer heat. The Lady had beautiful flowing silvery-snow white hair and very keen ice blue eyes. Her eyes stood out, they were astonishingly vibrant and also, kind and crinkled round the edges from smiling a lot. This, immediately put Polly at ease. It was easy to like the older woman, a sunny disposition permeated and glowed from her.

Polly introduced herself and automatically asked if she could help, this was her natural disposition, to help even if it was not understood exactly how. Some see this as a weakness of human nature, but

31

community and kindness are at the very core of our survival instincts, a mammal that has been expelled from the group knows the real threat of the wilderness, and isolation, being one of death.

The woman looked at Polly for a long time with a questioning and assessing gaze, before explaining that she could help her by accepting a gift for her birthday. Curiosity got the best of Polly, surprised, she asked if one of the team had mentioned it was her birthday. 'Of sorts, yes', the silver haired woman had replied with a secret, knowing smile. Rifling around in her cape, she then produced a green glass ointment jar, no bigger than a mobile phone and put it in Polly's hands. It had a small cork stopper and a rather charming silver Celtic coin tied to it with a piece of string. 'Please use this to bring forth your glimming' said the older woman. 'My glamming up do you mean? Polly did not want to question the older woman as she most definitely respected the wisdom of her elders. 'Is this a product that I need to test for Mother?' Polly went on to say, holding it up and looking at the little glass bottle closely. Her reflection was warped in its gnarled and mottled surface.

They were in a beauty shop, so the little glass bottle started to look like a tanning solution to her. The lotion inside was mud coloured and smelt earthy when Polly unstopped the topper to smell it. The mixture was odd, steam curled off it, yet it was not hot to touch. 'Must be a chemical reaction of some kind' Polly thought to herself.

Polly excused herself and ran to the back of the shop to get the sales representative forms, stored there. This was a must do whenever a new product was being tried in store - well, that's what she assumed the older woman was, a sales rep. When she returned, the silver haired woman was nowhere in sight. Polly looked through the window resuming her usual position of hands either side of her face and nose scrunched up against the glass, trying to see if she could spot her. It meant that the moistness of her breath would soon obscure her view within seconds, but she tried anyway.

Not wanting to get into any trouble, Polly decided to use the solution in the HD spray tanning booth and not tell anyone about the product, unless it was brilliant then, she would figure out how to contact the sales representative. Polly looked at the bottle, it glistened under the salon spotlights. She might keep the bottle after she had used it. What was strange was the bottle had changed to look like a very pretty and expensive refillable perfume bottle with a top to dab on the skin and exactly what Polly had hoped to receive for her birthday.

Polly turned on the tanning machine. It made an awful noise, chugging and churning away. She loaded the mixture into the compartment, put the bottle in her rucksack, disrobed and stepped in. The plastic floor was ice cold against her naked feet and her toes flexed involuntarily. The lights came on and the spraying machine moved across overhead on a tracking system. The spray gun nozzle zipped forward and settled in front of her face, ready for action. The music in the salon was loud and club beats were pumping out of the sound system. Polly felt giddy with excitement because it was her birthday and she was having a spray tan, AND was getting ready to go out in a couple of hours, to party with Toni and Chris in Central London. Plus, she wouldn't be seeing Mother and Father for a couple of days which immediately made her feel happy and relaxed.

The machine started spraying the solution onto Polly's skin. The liquid felt strange. It was hot and not spraying but streaming out of the device in strings, like cobwebs. On contact with Polly's skin, it started to move by itself, latching on and encasing her, moving autonomously to cover her entire body. It laid on top like a second layer of skin, gliding and slithering along the surface. Polly started pulling at it to get it off her. It had a liquid rubber type consistency and snapped back into place, like latex washing up gloves. It was swarming all over her body; with more joining it from the spraying machine. It started glowing and glittering with a blinding iridescence. Little bubbles were popping up and getting bigger and bigger. Polly started to panic and pull at the door, which was now locked - Polly had not done this herself.

The machine started beeping, signalling that it had run out of product and the pumps were still blowing out. It would start overheating soon. However, Polly's focus was on more of an immediate problem at hand. The lotion had completely encased her body and was moving upwards passed her neck, towards her head, her eyes, her nose and then lastly enclosing her mouth. She could not breathe, she gagged for air, her lungs were painful from not being able to draw in oxygen. The liquid swirled within her mouth and down her windpipe, gasping for air, she slumped unconscious to the floor where she lay, still, for a couple of hours.

Polly's eyes opened with a start and adjusted quickly to the complete darkness surrounding her. She was in a prone position on the floor and her neck was at an awkward angle, and quite stiff. Polly could hear movement in the shop outside of the door. Polly thought that it might be Toni or Chris wondering where she had gotten to. It felt like she had been blacked out for ages, her neck muscles and limbs were stiff and cold. Feeling around the floor with her hands, she concluded that the lotion was nowhere to be found, not a drop, anywhere. There were small patches of grass inside the cubicle and, rather oddly, snowdrops had rooted into the grass and there appeared to be earth on the plastic floor of the booth. A lot of it. Polly scratched her head, bewildered and was starting to seriously question her own sanity. The events over the last two days had been odd and a little frightening. It made her worry that she was imagining things happening. The dirt under her fingertips was reassuringly real to touch yet, equally, as difficult to explain.

She got up and opened the cubicle door slightly and stretched her arm around to reach for the hanger, to get her clothes. There was no residue on her skin, so she opted not to take a shower as she was already late. Rushing now, she automatically put her leather trousers on first followed by the halter neck, then necklace and heels. Each

34

person has a system for getting dressed and Polly's was bottoms first. Once she was dressed, she started applying her make-up, feeling a bit more normal again, she remembered that someone was outside the room. Whoever was in the salon would most likely come over to the cubicle soon. She shouted out 'I'm in here' and the noises abruptly stopped outside. That was odd she thought, momentarily and then carried on finishing getting ready. She applied her lip gloss and puckered her lips at her reflection in the mirror and whispered "Happy birthday" to herself. Opening the door, she stuck her head out first to see who was there. "WHACK" she was hit over the back of the head with such force that she was knocked to the ground by a man all dressed in black military gear. He was not alone and accompanied by another man that was identically dressed.

Stunned by this turn of events, Polly lay still for a few seconds and then felt the back of her head for any blood, instant relief flushed through her as there was none to be found. She did note to herself that she was not in any pain either. Perplexed by this, Polly reasoned that her attacker had obviously not hit her hard enough. There was no time for any further analysis, she was under attack and needed to take action. Flipping up using her legs to spring forward, she was in the middle of adopting a defensive stance, when the man punched her in the stomach. His hand rebounded off her like a hard object hitting a rubber surface and his knuckles were bloodied, broken bones protruding underneath the skin. Shocked, he flinched and then stammered out a wary 'W-where is Eleanora? Where is the compound she stole?', he was saying this while tentatively feeling his knuckles for damage.

'What, what…what's going on here' Polly stammered. He crouched down and this time, landed an uppercut that connected with her jaw. It was like hitting solid granite and his knuckles split open with blood pouring out of the gash. He looked down at his hand, bewildered, and looked at Polly in wonder and amazement.

Shocked into silence, her eyes wide open with pupils dilated in fear and disbelief. Firstly, because she was being attacked in her place of work which was usually a very uneventful space to be in and secondly, because she had not felt a thing, not one tingle or anything. The man was tall, at least six feet. She reasoned that she should have felt something at least. He started backing away from Polly like she was a dangerous animal and that was when the other man stepped forward. He had presence and was much bigger, broader and muscular. Smart too, he had waited for the other man to attack first, allowing him to assess the situation. He readied himself, slightly turning to the side and went to kick Polly to the ground, trying to hook her leg and take it out from under her. Before he could do this, Polly ran towards him faster than she had expected and she stumbled into him, instinctively grabbing him by both arms in the confusion of the fight. She slammed him into the wall, knocking the breath out of him and leaving an indent in the plaster and bricks with his body. She let go and he slid down the wall, gradually.

This was when the first attacker ran at her and she picked him up fully, circled round and threw him over the reception desk with barely any effort at all. She watched herself do this with astonishment, as he flew across the shop, straight through the front window pane. The window was treated safety glass and broke into tiny pieces on impact. The man lay on his front sprawled over the pavement outside, covered in glass and bleeding from his hands and his head. Polly was in shock by the realisation of how astonishingly strong she was and could not move, rooted to the spot with fear and bewilderment. The other man stood inside the shop peering at her in open disbelief.

The shop alarm started going off, as did numerous car alarms down the street and the other assailant instantly reacted, bounding over the reception desk, onto the pavement and he hauled his companion onto his back ready to take flight. His companion's foot was twitching and his hand was bleeding heavily, his tongue was lolling from his mouth. The assailant turned towards Polly and shouted 'we will meet again' before he ran away towards the residential area. Polly stood in a shocked daze. This was not necessarily due to the fight as she was used to competitive sparring but moreso, because she was frightened that she had done something terrible, by using inexplicable strength. She shook herself and whispered "pull yourself together Polly" for now all she could do was tell herself to run and get the hell out of there.

The Agents breath was laboured, his lungs and hamstrings burned due to the weight of his companion on his back. He was running, he needed to be fast to get them both away from the scene undetected. The operations van was parked down Arndale Road which was a sleepy little residential side street setback from the main road.

The large blacked out surveillance van, with aerials on the top of the roof, was eye-catching wherever it was parked. There was a drone-launch hatch on the roof. Its doors were opening up at this present time and he guessed that the drones were being recalled back to dock. The van will leave within minutes of the last drone locking down as per protocol. He had about two minutes to get back or otherwise he would need to find an alternative place of safety, somewhere to touch down and embed for the night.

He knew that the other agents would be connecting with their system control centre and they would be hacking into the parade of shops CCTV system to delete footage, within the incident window, by now. This would wipe out all digital information of the incident. He was under orders to leave no physical traces behind either, but blood had been spilt. He had no time to clean up as the alarms were very loud and had drawn attention from the pub goers across the street. Hopefully, the police would assume acts of mindless vandalism instead of an organised and coordinated attack, but he must remember to put in a report to request that the control centre delete police DNA records from the crime scene.

The company supported the metropolitan police with its IT infrastructure. This meant that access was easy and evidence even easier to erase.

The Company in the last 10 years had strategically outbid other contractors to provide infrastructure and technical support to government agencies, such as, the police, military, education, environment, central government, social media and health IT systems. This means that one global system of intelligence and access has been created by The Company. They had identified countries that they wanted to infiltrate. The Company had a very targeted and Top-Secret strategic plan to take control of global resources and infrastructure from individual Governments. They were able to do this under the radar, using distraction techniques on a global scale. Streaming into the population's collective consciousness divisive content on media platforms and through news networks. The company was focused on excluding certain groups and inciting hatred towards those groups and the lower classes. Consumerism is the most important thing nowadays, the strategic thinking of the corporations that he worked for is if you can't afford to be a consumer then you are a drain and your resource allocation will be diminished and inevitably, you will be too. It is no coincidence that life expectancy is decreasing for poorer parts of society.

The general population, given the chance, will express their views on the current climate emergency and are often highly critical of governments not having a plan to combat climate change quick enough. People are mistaken, there is a global and strategic plan for the environmental crisis, but it has not been developed by governments, Moreso, Boards of corporations. People who can afford it will be protected and the other half of the population of the planet will be wiped out leaving an abundance of resources behind and potential to grow back even stronger. It will be a time for setting a new world order.

The company agent was hot and sweaty from the physical exertion of carrying his companion on his back, but his sweat turned cold, and he shivered just thinking about all this and the devastation, yet to come.

The tracking and communication device in his neck that The Company had injected, flashed and beeped twice which is a signal to return to base. Little did the Company Agents know that the devices also had the ability to inflict an electric shock or to detonate, this would be used as a control function if the need arose. The devices had been installed for Armageddon-type-scenarios and the controls were held by Top CEOs who were part of a billionaire consortium called The Inner Circle. The Company Agents were their dark operations organisation that enacted their terrible plans for a price. The Agents were all highly qualified ex-military personnel. A mixture of Seals, and SAS and Special Forces. The Agents were highly paid, but in the event of Armageddon, what use will monetary systems have at that stage of the plan. A different power hierarchy will emerge and the agents would have the advantage; being in prime physical condition coupled with brute strength, combat and survival skills, tactical training and muscle, will be highly prized. The Inner Circle have planned for this inevitability and devised a way of retaining their control with the devices otherwise they would not be able to remain on top. That is unless they find a way to be superhuman themselves.

The van was a couple of seconds away and had already started to move silently forward. These vehicles are powered by solar energy and renewable atom technology not released to the global market. The agent reached the van door handle and heaved it open, throwing his companion in the back as the van came to a standstill once more. He ducked into the van, which took some effort due to the size of his frame. Just as he was doing so, he heard a dog bark close by and a man saying 'Toby, no, let's go now' in a panicked way, sensing the danger of the precarious situation they were in.

The agent paused and reversed his huge bulk out of the van in a heartbeat and moved his hulking frame around to look behind him. The golden Labrador barked again, turning its side to the stranger and sensing danger for his owner and friend.

The dog's companion had turned white and started telling the agent that he hadn't seen anything as his assailant bore down on him. The agent removed a gun with a silencer from the inside of his bodysuit and shot the man twice in between the eyes and once in the heart with ease. The dog began to bark and whine, the assailant went over to reassure the dog into submission. He had always liked dogs, so, loyal and trusting. The whole exchange had taken seconds but had ended with a man losing his life and the dog being taken in to the company's programme – both vanishing in a blink of an eye never to be seen again.

The agent returned to the van with the dog and muttered a code and two Agents jumped out to pick up the body for disposal, not hesitating once to fulfil their instruction. He got in and closed the doors.

'Well, that was all a bit............. unexpected,' he said to all present in the van. A guy in mirrored sunglasses sitting in the front of the van said, 'No Eleanora or the Product?'. He took off his hood and mask and replied shaking his head 'No, Eleanora must have been there as the product was on site and consumed by someone either by mistake or we have another Grade 1 status problem.' Mirror Glasses responded by lifting up one of his eyebrows and asked, 'Grade 1?' 'Grade 1' confirmed the assailant and banged on the top of the roof to signal to go. The two Agents had returned with the body in a bag, slinging it into the back. The dog began a low whine as the van began to slowly move away.

Polly and the Tome of Herne

Chapter three   The Company you keep.

The Company van travelled North and joined the M25, and then onto the M4. They were driving further North to a secret location. People on the motorway innocently drove their vehicles next to The Company van, not suspecting that the crew inside were part of a secret organisation supporting a network of billionaires to plan for global dominion, in order to secure resources for the elite classes.

This had all started as a result of climate change and the environmental impact of the systems that these big corporations had profiteered from over decades; mostly driven by greed. The Company Agents did not notice a small white van following them from afar as they were not expecting anyone to know about their plans or about the Company's clandestine activities. This was a very secret organisation guarded carefully indeed. The company agents were being paid vast sums and were also being promised a place in the safe havens and bunkers being built for when society collapsed and Armageddon begun.

 The van left the motorway and pulled into a big industrial warehouse site. Within the middle of it was a rather large compound structure with security detail on the gates. To the outside, this would look like a delivery depot for Premiere, a global internet -based business enterprise largely focussed on e-commerce, digital streaming and artificial intelligence (AI) including expansive product delivery networks. The industrial warehouses and compound were at ground level and there were secret subterranean structures underneath.

 The van pulled into the compound area and all the agents got out. Two were carrying the black bag and moved off from the group to throw it into a section of the sprawling site ominously referred to as The Tank.

 Toby was barking all the while and seemed to want to follow his friend's body, but he was being led away into the centre of the compound and into one of the warehouse buildings. They all got into a big functional, industrial lift and pressed '-4'button on the panel. With a jolt, the lift started to descend and Toby started to whine again. The lift eventually jerked to a halt and the steel doors opened onto a vast white chamber with clinical cubicles dividing the floor area. The space was very brightly lit and scientists walked around in lab coats and some in sealed boiler suits with masks. There were others in wetsuits too. It was a hive of activity with people bustling around and going about their business. Eventually, the squad came to a glass room with an air lock chamber. The chamber was connected to another side of the building. It was a security measure and a precaution to reduce the risk of dangerous contaminants getting in or out.

The squad walked through the airlock chamber and then unlocked the second door to another glass room and entered.

A middle-aged man in a decontamination suit was standing in the centre of the room, talking to a younger man on a screen who was dressed in a black T-Shirt. The man in the suit was reading from a report. He looked round, nodded and continued talking. ' Miles, shall I continue, Sir?' The younger man on screen nodded. 'Thank you, Sir. the burial site has been completely excavated and we can confidently report that we could only find the one female skeleton and a few animals, that appeared to be wolves, buried next to her. The examination has indicated, Sir, that she died in childbirth. Expert historians and archaeologists have conferred and are advising that the child must have survived or otherwise it would have been buried with her. We could find no evidence of cannibalism or sacrifices in the vicinity which would imply that the people, at the time, buried and not consumed their dead' the report continued with lots of details of land evaluation, historical context and behavioural analysis of the culture at that time.

Each detail was very important and the reason for this being; the owner of Premiere, currently on the screen, is looking for ways to develop transhumanism products and for solutions, both scientific and mythical, to extend human life and the human anatomy beyond its current limitations.

This research is mainly driven by the compulsion to stay healthy, wealthy and live through any global climatic catastrophic event. Miles Luxemburg wants to be in the best position to shape the world after society's collapse. The CEO has become obsessed with ancient civilisations, symbolism and artefacts, believing them to hold the key to eternal health, immortality and planetary recovery following a global crisis event – he believes understanding this better will help him speedup the recovery process.

His team have been analysing a plethora of ancient texts and transcripts from previous civilisations. They had been instructed to develop an algorithm that would detect references to immortality and descriptions of climatic catastrophic events. This, enabling The Company to study these closely to understand recovery phases better. For example, ice ages. Miles wanted to know how some mammals and human civilisations had survived previous climate events and how they recovered their resources post-event. The current climate emergency is estimated to be irreversible in eleven years-time and it is predicted that sea levels will rise, the planet will heat up and possibly trigger a global ice age, wiping humanity out. Billionaires and corporations are seeking to understand what the planet will look like and the environmental impact, in order to model survival and recovery scenarios. Some, billionaires are already developing underground networks of bunkers and these are being excavated under parts of Alaska, America and Africa – the Triple A sites as these are referred to amongst secret organisations.

The software programme that has been completing the meta-analysis of these ancient texts, uncovered a code or more accurately, a set of complex language systems and repetitive patterns that have led to the discovery of a tribe that appear to have achieved immortality. The code leads back to pagan times and refers to a network of caves in

Wales, part of the United Kingdom, where a tribe of humans survived a climate event on a global scale, and each of the tribal people lived for thousands of years underground.

 Archaeologists followed the instructions in the ancient texts and found one of the burial mounds, that was located next to an underground Pagan Temple. This was where some of the humans remains were noted to have been buried. Nearly a year ago, a team of scientists and archaeologists started excavating the site and recovered a female skeleton. A study indicated something baffling that scientifically could not be explained. The female, herself, had lived to be at least two thousand years old and her bones Indicated that she lived in optimal health during this time. Study of her skeleton showed signs that she had lived underground during one of the Ice Ages but also had evidence of vitamin E absorption, no mutations and her DNA registered as receiving energy from the sun. The other factor was that there was a compound in her system that was not identifiable to any organic matter discovered or recorded on earth.

There was a set of scrolls buried with her and a book was found in the pagan temple. The scrolls and the book had been scanned and studied extensively. Hidden within the text of the scroll was reference to another scroll that could not be found, therefore, assumed missing. It would appear that the missing scroll held the details of the process to invoke long life. The wording that kept repeating in the scroll that was found was:

The masters will drive the children to maim and destroy nature in [21st century?]. The Planet weeps and no one hears her

100 years of drought and famine

Followed by 100 years of floods.

And 100 years of ice will right the wrong that will be done.

Some of the texts had faded but the software algorithm estimated that the remaining text read something like this:

The Children of the forest are loved. The Goddess will send forth a champion with extraordinary gifts. Two [dragons?] eggs will open to save the twin planets and start all anew with a rebirth within 7 days and Mother will smile down on her children of the [forest?] as they will be with [her?] bringing her the strength to save all Mothers Children great and small. The potion of The Goddess will protect the chosen few.

It was difficult to understand the texts fully, but it was believed that a code lay within them that would shed light on the extraordinarily long life of the human whose skeleton had been found and a means to heal a planet in climatic crisis. This information is now guarded very closely By the Company and is referred to with the code name Phoenix.

'Well, I do hope you have got some better news for me, Kane,' said the young man on the screen to the lead Agent. 'We've still got no idea how the female lived to over 2000 years old and was still able to conceive a child. The Phoenix scrolls don't make sense when deciphered so we need to retest the algorithm. At this time, we are no closer to finding anything out and our lead pagan expert, Eleanora, was trying to delete all our information and sabotage the only sample of the compound that we had manage to extract and isolate, then she chose to run off with it and the book from the temple to North London. Please tell me we have Eleanora. She found something and I want it back'. The room became tense.

'Yes, Sir, we tracked down Eleanora to a place called Winchmore Hill. She was staying in a rental. We traced her debit card activity to a local ATM. We decided to put her under surveillance to understand why she was there. She was watching a hairdressers shop for 3 weeks then tonight, for some reason she chose to interact with a girl in the shop and then vanished. She has not returned to her rental. A girl was in the hairdressers when we went in to see if Eleanora or the product were on site and the girl took me and Able out with ease.

She was strong. Like superhuman strength. The girl and Eleanora exchanged the product, that I am certain of.'

The guy on the screen broke into a wide smile placing his hands behind his head and said 'well, done guys, this is super great. We are finally getting somewhere. Do please get me Eleanora and now it seems we need the girl.'

Polly and the Tome of Herne

Chapter four   A Power emerging

Running frantically away from the salon, Polly did not realise she was running at superspeed. The trees, plants and streetlamps were streaking past, leaving behind a blurred line of white with green iridescence in her peripheral vision. The greenery slowly began to fade out the closer she got to inner London.

While she was running, Polly was distracted and her brain was trying to work out the events of the last couple of days. Trying to find a connection but failing miserably. The streets were dark and recent rainfall had made the tarmac shiny and a little slippery with petrol that had risen to the surface.

Polly had been running blindly, not taking in her surroundings, yet, she had been cautious not to be seen and had been running down quiet side streets, avoiding people. She lifted her head to see where she was and thought she noticed Shoreditch high street on her left. This confused her slightly as she couldn't have run from Winchmore Hill to Shoreditch in that short space of time, so she came to a complete stop and estimated she had been running for about three minutes straight after leaving the salon. This too was baffling her. Usually, she could only run for a couple of minutes at full tilt before having to slow down and catch her breath, even then she would feel quite sick.

Polly was not sweating or breathless or wheezing, she didn't really need to stop in fact she felt super-charged and dare she say, elated and fantastic. She spun around and jumped in the air, touching the top of the roof of a six-storey office block and landing softly on the ground. Astonished by her new ability, she stopped and stood still, wanting to test herself further , so decided to jump up and down on the spot again. Her head banged on the underside of a rather tall London lamppost. She gasped as she came tumbling down. Another

49

two things she noticed was that her head did not hurt and also, she didn't feel cold even though the evening air was crisp, and she was wearing a light satin halter neck top.

She looked down at her heels and closely inspected her feet, marvelling at how these were not sore and blistered, given that she had run in high heels. She then looked back up at the lamppost and while she gazed up trying to work out how tall it was, an older man started watching her from across the high street. He walked into the quiet cobbled side road called Blossom Street and silently moved slowly and carefully towards her. Polly was absorbed in her thoughts about the events of the last couple of days, but something, a sense of some kind, made her notice a change in her surroundings and she soon spotted the shadowy figure walking along the road towards her. Polly did what all women and girls do during the dark evenings in London, and pretends that she does not see the man but all the while, casually searching for her phone. She soon realises that she does not have it. 'Bloody well damn it' she mutters under her breath. The shadowy man starts walking more obviously towards her and says in low soothing tones 'what's a lovely girl like you, doing here and on your own, beautiful'. Relieved to a certain extent, as he was not one of the men she had encountered in the shop and fought with earlier but equally apprehensive, as this guy seemed a bit creepy.

'Are you lost sweetheart? I can be your knight in shining armour and come to your rescue. Had too much to drink, have you?'. He looked about thirty-five or forty years old and had a very eager look on his face for someone that was trying to be truly helpful. Polly turned and started walking towards the noise of the city and the well-lit area of the high street.

He started following her along the road, so she quickened her pace. He shouted behind her 'hey, I'm only seeing if you're okay love. Let's go to the bar on the corner and talk over a drink, what do you say?' Polly carried on walking and he ran up to her and made a grab for her left arm. 'Hey, what do you say, you look like you've already started drinking......' he said with a false chuckle, then got angry and shouted 'you're being pretty rude.' Polly swung round instinctively, putting her right arm forward in a defensive stance. The man got in the way of the block and he was hurled to the ground. 'Why, you little b....' he growled from the floor, all pretence of being nice, dropped. 'I am 16 years old, Sir, and I would advise you to stop what you are doing as this is harassment and I've had a really bad night so far.' Polly tried to explain this calmly but failed miserably. The guy sensing the desperation in her voice, mistook this for her being frightened of him, when and in fact, she was frightened of what she could DO to him. 'Yeah, apology accepted, let's forget about this and go for a drink, beautiful, just you and me' he said getting up and trying to put his unwanted arm around her. Polly stood still, bewildered. 'Did you not hear me say I am 16 years old?' Polly pointed out. 'Yeah, you're right. Let's skip the bar and go to my flat instead, it's close by.'

Polly was angry now, not just for herself but for all the girls this guy had clearly accosted and frightened in the past. She could feel the heat and light rising behind her eyes again and her heart was hammering against her chest with anger. She breathed out and looked down at herself, and noticed a green energy emanating from her into the night air and into the ground. All of a sudden, the man was knocked sideways onto the pavement in front of her. 'Oooof' he gasped. There were spindly looking green vines, poking out of the ground and they were rapidly entangling themselves around his arms, his legs and his neck. He was spluttering now and screaming 'what the hell is going on, help me, help me please'. Tighter and tighter they gripped him, with more winding themselves around him and larger vines started to drag him along the street. In the distance, a drain cover blew up in the air, pushed up by more vines from inside. Gripping him tightly, they pulled him underneath the streets of London. His yells that were once loud, were now becoming muffled, until nothing left could be heard of him. The drain cover fell back down to earth and sealed the opening shut.

This happened in the space of seconds and Polly stood there the whole-time gaping and transfixed to the spot. She was trembling now from the shock of it all. Her thoughts were racing with confusion, disjointed images of creeper vines flashing through her mind. She had questions and lots of them; "what was that and how could roots and vines suddenly appear and carry a man off." She was starting to think there was something wrong with her and it was very easy to believe, Mother and Father always said she was crazy. When you're told something enough it's easier to start believing it about yourself. Polly, up until this point, had believed that there was something odd about her parents but now, she was starting to believe that maybe they were right after all and there was something really wrong with her.

Polly searched her back pockets and found her debit card. It was a miracle it had not flown out while she was running but it was there. She held it to her mouth with relief and felt a little safer knowing she could use the London underground or get a black cab anywhere now. She stared for a while longer at the drain cover and then shook herself, deciding to leave. She would go to the wedding reception being held at the JW Marriot Grosvenor House Hotel, Park Lane. The wedding reception might not be the right word as there were three ceremonies and parties to celebrate the happy couple. This was the second one of them, the payment of the bride ceremony had already taken place and the White Wedding was today. The family were Hausa Christians and the third ceremony was a women's only event which Toni was really looking forward to, the women of her family alluded to special magic being shared.

Polly went out onto the high street and spotted a black cab to get her to the hotel.

After what felt like thirty minutes driving through the streets of London, the cab pulled up outside the JW Marriot Grosvenor hotel. Reassuringly and in keeping with tradition, the black cabbie had chattered away quite happily about all things London like football,

Tottenham's fall and rise again in the premiership, politics, the Conservative party's latest environment policies, that impact cabbing, and the Mayor of London's latest proposal for cleaner streets in London, the Queens funeral 'gawd, rest her soul' and the cost-of-living crisis 'bloody greed crisis and crooks taking liberties, is what I call it'. Polly had sat quietly in the back, closing her eyes and trying to get the image of the man being dragged down a drain hole by plants out of her reeling mind.

'Thank you' Polly called over her shoulder as she exited the shiny black vehicle that is the epitome symbol of London, glided away into the evening Mayfair traffic, with a slight hum. Polly stepped out onto the moulded stairs of the hotel that were sometimes decorated with red carpets for events. Her hand slid over the cooling rich cream brick of the magnificent Georgian building. She was in awe of the structure and the vast expanse of natural stone, leaving her feeling like she should whisper in its splendour. Polly also had a thing about Claridge's. She would often find herself outside the building and feeling at complete peace within The Library. It made her feel humble, like the feeling one gets from being in a cathedral, Polly had this very same feeling from being in Claridge's for some reason that she could not explain.

In the hotel foyer, on a golden stand decorated with beautiful white orchids, a notice was placed that announced the room that hosted the wedding reception of Mr & Mrs Chukwu. Polly followed the corridor and went into the banqueting room. It was a beacon of activity. Decorated in white and pale gold with hangings of white silk from the ceiling. There were ostentatious flower displays, and waiters serving champagne flutes to guests who were sitting down on golden chairs to eat Nigerian food that smelt delicious. Polly's favourite was Jollof rice. It was amazing and tasted so moreish that when she first tried it and couldn't stop eating it, she thought it might contain a drug of some kind. Maami Adeoye would laugh and say 'only love, only things cooked with love taste this good Pol Pol.'

The extravagance of the event was astounding and mesmerising. The sheer numbers of people at the function were too many to count. There were twenty-five people at each table and there were over a dozen tables. Polly was looking around trying to spot Toni in the crowds but there were just too many people in the room to discern her. Polly started to walk around the dining room, painfully aware that she was in her skimpy party outfit and the group were still in formal evening attire and Nigerian ceremonial dress.

She was getting a lot of stares and some of the men and women were pouting their mouths to show their disapproval and signalling to other people that she was not dressed appropriately for a wedding. A disapproving murmur rippled throughout the banqueting hall and Polly stood there, devastated. At the top table the bride in her full white dress and tiara glowed with health and beauty. She did not notice Polly but Maami Adeoye, who was serving the bride Champagne and a small glass of traditional palm wine, suddenly did. Putting down the bottle, she excused herself from the top table, as she was the Aunty of the Bride after all, and came straight over to Polly. She looked over Polly, somewhat alarmed. 'My dear' she said, widening her eyes with slight incredulity but kindness Why are you in this state? Go over to Toni and go upstairs to get dressed' she hissed out of the corner of her mouth, barely moving her lips, while waving and smiling at the guests as she passed by. She was mouthing 'no problem here, no problem here' to the concerned women at the tables.

Polly apologised and whispered, behind her hand, that she had been in an accident. Catching a glimpse of herself in one of the ornamental wall mounted mirrors, she looked down at herself, and realised what others were seeing through their eyes. Her hair was sticking up all over the place and her trousers were all creased. Her make-up had run and she looked dishevelled like she had been partying all night; her tears stung the backs of her eyes as she slowly realised, she was embarrassing her closest friends.

Maami's stiff body language softened as she took the opportunity to really look at the girl's face; realising that Polly was in shock and she soothed Polly by pulling her in for a cuddle and rocking her backwards and forth. She wiped the young woman's face with a damp napkin. 'Ma' she clucked 'I am sorry to hear about your accident Pol Pol. Please go upstairs and we shall help you.' Polly could see Toni's concerned face bursting through the crowd, her magenta Gele and matching dress swirled around her, and she took Polly by the hand and guided her quickly out of the bustling banqueting room and upstairs with Chris in tow, to the suite she was sharing with her Maami and Papa.

The suite was beautiful. All cream with a mixture of soft and raw edged furnishings. There was a boutique feel alongside the opulence and grandeur. Toni realised quickly that Polly was in shock and pushed her friend into the bathroom and turned on the taps to run a bath. Toni busily, started putting into the warm water aromatherapy oils with rose, geranium and lavender to soothe her friend. She got Polly out of her clothes and into the water and started washing her hair. She then quietly left her friend in the warm and steamy room and said to Polly 'Come out when you are ready and we will talk'. As soon as the door was closed, Polly started crying, big thick tears slid down her cheeks. "I'm alone with this sense of dread that something bad is happening and I'm going crazy". She rested her forehead on her knees and let her tears mingle into the warm water and she did this for a long while – until it was too cold to sit there any longer. Polly would have been reassured to know that people who worry that they are going crazy tend not to be the ones that should worry about such things after all.

Once the crying ceased, she stirred and started to wash her limbs with a natural sponge and thought through the events of the night. It was inconceivable to her that anyone would believe her, she didn't even believe it herself and it just felt unreal. How would she tell them about her powers and the guy who followed her in Shoreditch and tell them about the tussle and the vines? There was nothing else for it, she would have to keep this to herself until she had a chance to think it through and she understood it herself.

She got out of the bath and into one of the big white fluffy robes on a hook and then walked out of the bathroom into the suite. Both Toni and Chris stopped talking and turned towards her. "This is going to be tricky. They'll want answers and I don't want to have to tell them I'm slowly going mad. What if they don't understand and leave me"? Polly thought to herself.

Chris had green eyes and light brown skin. His hair was curly and brown with golden sun-drenched tips. He was very tall and gangly. Lots of girls had a crush on him at school but he never seemed to notice them, preferring to read books and carry out scientific experiments rather than get entangled with the female of the species, is what he would say with a perplexed and scared look on his face whenever he was grilled by Toni. Chris was quite a serious, solemn and a bookish kind of person. He wanted to save the world and found girls his age quite annoying he would say, well, some girls. Polly and Toni being the exception.

'So, what happened?' Chris blurted out. Toni dug him in the ribs. Polly pulled the collar up on her bathrobe and sunk further into it and down into the sofa. She sighed. Chris and Toni came round to join her sitting on a sofa opposite to her own. Polly started explaining 'I finished work, got changed in the shop. I used this new tanning spray in the booth and I think it's had a bit of a bad reaction on me because I don't feel, erm, very well. I forgot my phone. I then went out walking and a guy followed me and wouldn't leave me alone. He grabbed my arm and then I accidentally pushed him and then he.........then he......sort of left.' Polly peered over at the two of them, Toni looked concerned and Chris looked questioning and then Polly carried on 'I hailed a black cab here and that's it really. There you have it. I'll be alright.' Polly said this all in a rush, rather rambling, with an anxious inflection in her voice. Toni and Chris both looked at her, then Toni got up and hugged her friend. 'I'm so glad you are ok. Your mum called to say the shop had been broken into and your rucksack, phone, keys and coat had been found in the shop and no one could get hold of you. The police reported that the CCTV wasn't working so we didn't know where you were or if you were alright. I told your Mother that I thought you might be on your way here. I am so relieved you're ok. We were really quite worried' and with that, Toni hugged her friend again with relief shining out of her face.

Chris had a puzzled look on his face 'where were you when the guy followed you?' he questioned. 'Shoreditch' Polly mumbled not looking him in the eyes 'Why'd you stop off in Shoreditch and how did you get there from Winchmore Hill, bit of an odd journey to Park Lane isn't it?' Polly was flummoxed; she hadn't meant to say Shoreditch but she was feeling fatigued and her brain was muffled from the exertions of the evening, it was in survival mode. She had not thought through her cover story. She was stuttering and stammering to answer.

'Alright, Sherlock, what's with the interrogation .... Leave it out, Polly has had a tough evening, let's get into the details tomorrow.' Toni took Polly by the hand and led her into one of the three bedrooms off the main part of the suite. She helped Polly to get up on the bed and then tucked her in, whispering to her goodnight and that she needed to re-join the party or Maami would stop her allowance for being rude to the wedding guests. Toni also told her that she would text Mother to say Polly was okay and here for the night. Polly told her to please herself and betted that Mother would not really care either way.

Chris poured himself a water and mused again on what he had just heard. He cared a lot about Polly more than he would like to admit, but he wondered if shock had affected her memory because there were quite a few inconsistencies in Polly's story. For instance, did she leave the salon before the incident and if so, why did she leave the keys, her phone and her jacket and why did she travel to Shoreditch because it's certainly not the easiest way to get to Park

Lane. Also, why did she get off the tube to walk about in Shoreditch? She also did not include the incident in the shop in her story. None of it made sense. Chris thought back on the many times during their childhood when they got into trouble together and this one time in particular stood out.

When Toni and Polly were twelve years old and Chris was thirteen nearly fourteen, they conspired to play truant from school so they could watch the new Lord of the Rings film in Leicester square on the day the film opened, which was one Thursday, ready for the weekend box office rush. They were all three, huge LOTR and fantasy genre fans. They made a whole day of it in the centre of London; playing the arcades in the Trocadero, eating a buffet in Chinatown and then gorging on pic 'n' mix at the Odeon in Leicester square, before the film.

They had a day of fun, laughter and freedom, which was particularly exhilarating for Polly and Chris, both had parents that were quite overbearing. The next day back at school, the teacher had asked for their absence notes from their parents. Chris had typed up and signed all three, perfecting each of their parents' style of writing and signatures.

Part of the fun was the planning of the truancy as well as its execution. The teacher read through the notes and then looked at all three of them resting her eyes squarely on Polly. She then asked the trio to follow her and marched them to the headmaster's office. 'These three students played truant yesterday. Please call and speak to their parents and think of a suitable punishment. I am too disappointed in them to even look at them right now.' The teacher had said this with utmost certainty. Chris remembered feeling very indignant as he was sure his handiwork was exemplary and faultless. He shouted to her before she shut the door 'how did you know?' The teacher replied 'Your work was fantastic, Chris, top marks for you dear boy, but you see, Polly has a tell, she can't look into my eyes when she's making something up or lying, haven't you noticed?' Yes, Chris had and she showed this to him again tonight.

Toni came out of the room quietly, holding the door with her palm as she closed it shut. She bounded across the room to Chris and planted the flat part of her right hand on his shoulder with a force, intent on showing him her frustration. 'OOowww, bloody hell Toni, what was that all about?' with which Toni shushed him to be quiet.

'She was not telling us the truth, you know her tell as well as I do, Toni' Chris said abruptly.

'Some friend you are, I'm sooooo glad you've got your friends back,' Toni said with thick sarcasm in her voice. 'I've always got her back but somethings up. Do you not feel it?' Chris said in a concerned way. 'Look whatever it is, she'll tell us in her own time......now get up and come dance with me and Maami.' Toni said, pulling him playfully by the arm.

' You know I don't dance, so what are you asking me for?'

'For punishment' Toni replied with a huge maleficent grin on her face. Chris groaned as Toni pulled him out of the sofa and out of the apartment to dance to the deafening but rhythmic beats downstairs.

Meanwhile, In Winchmore Hill, the security response team had attended to the shop alarm and then called the police when they saw the window had been smashed and the place was insecure. The constables who responded to the call thought it was an inside job. There was no sign of a forced entry, nothing had been stolen but it looked like someone had turned the place over trying to find something. The glass was on the outside not the inside of the shop. The CCTV had been wiped. From that point on they had taken an interest in the staff. One person had come up as having a record of selling stolen goods in the last 6 years and she also had associations with some nasty undesirables known to the police. It was the manager, Gracie. Her details were recorded on the incident log, along with her address details, which was very convenient for the Company as they read through the police files.

The van waited outside the block of flats in Tottenham Hale; it was part of a new development called Meridian Water to regenerate the whole of the surrounding area. Tottenham Hale was identified as an area of deprivation and had attracted redevelopment funding due to its established transport links to the City of London and it was going to be the next Knightsbridge – a very prestigious area.

There was a lot of construction going on all around the vicinity. These apartments stood alone and back from the site slightly which would make it much easier to carry out the abduction. Kane had a huge grin on his face as he gave the order to bring the van to a stop. He rolled down his black mesh mask over his big smiling face and chin and growled 'I'll do this alone to make it easier for me to carry the team manager down the stairs and I doubt she's going to give me any trouble'. He jumped out of the back of the van landing lightly on his feet for someone his size and proceeded silently towards the apartment block with a syringe full of a serum that places a human into unconsciousness.

Polly and the Tome of Herne

Chapter 5 Eggs will make up for everything.

Gracie, the team manager of the salon that Polly's Mother owned, was a person who had street smarts, a smart mouth and quick temper. She had grown up in one of the seedy parts of London and had to fight and hustle for everything since the day she was born. 'Don't hate the players, hate the game' was her favourite saying. So much so, that she had it tattooed on a place on her upper arm that she could easily conceal under her work clothes. Street kids like Gracie can climb the proverbial social ladder, but they tend to give themselves away by not being able to relate and fit in. Always looking out for the catch, this being due to extensive trust issues, so Gracie was vigilant and careful about what she revealed about herself. She was desperate to climb the ladder out of the poverty that she had witnessed from a very young age.

The flat that she lived in was modest, but she had carefully selected it and purchased it at a rock bottom price knowing that the area was being regenerated and was soon to be gentrified. Her plan was to refurbish it and then rent it out using the capital to raise a mortgage to buy somewhere she wanted to live. Her job was pretty well paid and interesting too, but she was there to learn the ropes and then open up her own salon soon. Gracie had big plans for life and would stop at nothing to make them a reality.

She heard a van pulling up across the road and she went to the window. It was 11:45 PM so there usually weren't any noises from cars at this time. Her old East End London instincts kicked in. She couldn't explain why she felt threatened. Maybe it was the way the tall guy jumped out of the van door, or maybe it was the way he had a military gait or maybe it was the way that he casually looked all the way around looking for witnesses before he moved into her block of flats. Maybe it was all this information that triggered her to run to her bedroom and pull out her heavy, solid wooden truncheon from under her bed. Her old man had given it to her when she moved out. Well, he didn't exactly give it to her in person as he was in prison at the time, but he had his good friend deliver it to her. The message read 'knock their teeth out first Princess, take care Dad PS I'm so proud of u's x'

Kane cut the lights so everything went black before he unlocked the door with his key kit that could mould into any opening and spring the lock. As he strode through the door, he slipped on oil that Gracie had, had the wits to place there and as he started toppling over trying to steady his core, Gracie hit him once in the forehead and then once in his nose breaking it with a satisfying 'crunch' on contact.

Gracie swung down the long truncheon holding it to his neck and squatted down to see who had broken in. Kane's eyes were closed. Gracie felt for a pulse and as she touched his neck, Kane's hulking arms shot upwards and grabbed both of her wrists. In one continuous move he pulled her to the ground and snaked one hand around her and over her mouth before she could let out a scream. He hauled her onto his back, she was very light with a small frame, but she kicked and punched with all of her might and was slippery like an eel. He had trouble restraining her so couldn't administer the serum. This little fighter was not giving up and he had no choice but to seek help, which meant concentrating on getting her to the van, so he had to risk being seen.

He dashed out the front door, down the flight of stairs, as quick as lightning. He threw her into the van and jumped in. Only, now taking the time to mop up his nose that was splattered all over his face.

Gracie did not make a sound, but the Company agents felt uneasy in her presence, as her eyes were ablaze and her gaze like white hot rods of fury. Kane paused before he administered the serum. He didn't know if it was enough to quench that kind of burning anger, but he need not have worried as she went out like a light.

Gracie woke up the next day in one of the basement areas of the Premiere compound. There was no natural light. She was being held in a white room with smooth surfaces made from plastic. There was a moulded plastic bed with a linen cover and the temperature and lighting were controlled by AI, so therefore, just perfect.

On the wall was a speaker and two buttons. One for the agents to use and one was a speaker phone.

'Good morning, Grace' said a bodiless female toned AI voice. 'I hope you slept well' It went on and when Gracie did not respond, it continued with 'Would you like some breakfast? We have a large range of choices to meet your every need' silence. 'We have tofu scrambled eggs, eggs and asparagus, eggs benedict with spinach, omelette with mushrooms, Spanish omelette…….' The AI continued to list the never-ending breakfast combinations while Gracie hopped off of the bed and ambled over to the panel. She felt a little heavy on her feet and her brain did not feel too great either but other than that she seemed ok.

She peered into the panel box and tried to open it with her fingers, but it did not budge. She looked around her, scanning the environment to take in every detail. '……….Fried eggs, organic beans on toast with smoked tofu and kimchi with a poached egg…' 'ahem, hello' Gracie spoke into the room, interrupting the breakfast menu list because she was keen to see how she was meant to communicate with the AI. '……..egg white omelette, egg white waffles with cheese, boiled eggs with sourdough soldiers like mother makes them, spinach, tomatoes and garlic omelette, egg…….'

Gracie rolled her eyes and moved over to the panel again. She held the button down and said 'hey, hello robot.'

'Hello Gracie, what can I get for you this morning?'

'You can get me the hell out of here for a start.'

'That is not possible Gracie. Please order your breakfast. You will need your strength for what lay ahead' said the AI without a tone of threat in its voice, just surety.

'Well, in that case, I'll have a bacon sandwich with a sharp knife,' she grinned. The AI said 'we are a vegetarian ethos-based company driving towards a synthesised plant-based lifestyle establishment. We would invite you to take part and experience this way of living with us. I will order you vegan bacon on- rye with tomato sauce from our own polyphonic crops grown underground' with that, the light turned red, and the lights dimmed low.

A while later the vegan bacon on rye extravaganza arrived. Gracie was ravenous but before she demolished the sandwich, she sniffed it to see if it was poisoned. This was futile because firstly, she did not know what poison smells like and secondly, she did not know what vegan bacon smelt like either so how would she know if it was contaminated with anything.? She decided to risk it and bit into the sandwich. It was surprisingly good, but she had read that vegan imitation food was highly processed and probably would harm her with the amount of chemicals in it, but she was happy with those odds at this moment in time.   She put down her plate. A white disc shaped cleaner robot spun out of the wall and cleaned it away along with any crumbs it found. 'Now you have eaten, we wish to ask you some questions.' Gracie jumped off the bed and pulled a sharp pin from out of her hair, ready to fight. She stood still focussing on the door frame readying herself for an attack. None came. A vent opened slowly and gas was piped into the room. The gas was powdery and heavy when inhaled. Gracie took a huge gulp of oxygen in and held her breath, and then placed her arm sleeve over her nose but this was futile because eventually she had to take in breath. When she eventually did, she felt warm, at ease and mellow. In a haze she started singing and giggling to herself.

The AI voice started asking questions and Gracie had no choice but to answer them. She could hear her own voice but did not feel connected to it.

AI: 'How long have you worked for Mrs Hanscombe?'

Gracie: '2 years'

AI: 'Do you know Eleanora?'

Gracie: 'Who?'

AI: 'Tell us about the day that the shop got broken into and tell us about the 2 hours before you left'

Gracie: 'It was a busy day. We had on a promotion for three areas of Botox and 0.8 ml of lip filler for £499. We were booked up with appointments back-to-back. The part time staff were all in a really idiotic mood because it was Polly's birthday. She is the daughter of the owner. They kept singing happy birthday and hugging each other, giggling away like they were at a party or somethin' so I had to break it up a few times. Towards the end of the day, I was cashing up, the other staff had gone home, and Polly was in the back clearing away when a lady with long white grey hair came in asking for Bollux or Pollux or somethin'. She had on a woollen coat and she had really blue eyes. It was odd because seriously this woman looked like she had never stepped foot into a salon before, not that she looked bad. She actually looked really good but really natural.' Gracie sniffed her disapproval 'I mean she could have done with a little touch up or some........'

A man's voice filtered into the room and he cleared his throat and gently interrupted her. His voice was soothing and polite but still had an edge to it, like he was holding his anger in, and it strained his voice to do so. 'Gracie, please continue. Please tell us why the woman was there.'

'I told you she asked for Bollux or Pollux but I said, 'do you mean Polly?' and she said "Yes, of sorts" which again I thought was odd but I went and got Polly anyways. I had finished cashing up, so I told Polly to close up the shop when she had finished with the old bag. I left Polly with the old girl.

'Please clarify what is meant by the old girl' queried the AI.

Gracie blew out her cheeks with a sigh of impatience 'Old lady, old woman you know it's like an east end term for older lady'.

The man's voice came through the speaker again. 'AI pause learning algorithm. Hey, Gracie, you are doing super great. Can you tell us where Polly is and her address, please. Does she live with her parents?'

Again, Gracie tried not to speak by holding her mouth shut and clenching her teeth together, but it was difficult to do. She didn't have any control and began to tell them everything about Polly. What she looked like, how annoying she is, how old, her address, her friends, what her parents thought about her, her love of nature, her political views. Gracie thought that Polly was irritating but she did not want any harm to come to the girl and she sensed that these guys were talking sweetly but their intentions were no good.

Her voice started to dry out and she felt sick and dizzy after 2 or 3 hours of being relentlessly questioned and responding. The voices carried on asking her questions, but she slumped forward and fainted and was unconscious from that point on.

Two of the Company agents were deployed to pick up Eleanora's trail. She had gone to ground after surfacing in the salon in Winchmore Hill. The company had secured the flat she had rented. The owner was approached via the estate agent and the agents were told Eleanora had not left a forwarding address but had served notice. For a hefty fee they had taken over the flat 'as is' and one of the agents posing as a tenant said that he would clear out Eleanora's personal effects into a skip and the estate agent was grateful that she did not have to do it so immediately agreed. They had swept through the lounge, bathroom, WC, bedroom and closet under the stairs over a two-day period. Nothing turned up that would indicate what she was doing there, who she was planning to meet or where she was heading next. She had not used the Wi-Fi to connect a phone or laptop, so they had no records of email accessed, websites or searches, which was odd. When Eleanora had worked for the company, she demonstrated excellent tech skills so why would she choose to go off grid and how was she communicating with anyone? They needed to find answers fast.

One agent went downstairs to the flat below to see if the neighbour had any further information about Eleanora and the other carried on searching the kitchen. The kitchen had a slate grey tiled floor with a pale pink rug over it and pale terracotta pink wooden kitchen cupboard doors. Very Scandinavian looking, modern and light. There was hardly any trace of Eleanora in the flat. There were no personal touches at all which most probably meant that she had not spent much time there. The agent pulled open a corner cupboard and he noticed a pair of very small silver candle holders with wax drips down the sides from white candles and the wax looked new, it was not discoloured or covered in dust. He pulled over one of the chairs to stand on, to look deeper into the cupboard and found a scrunched-up piece of paper no bigger than a post-it note. It was the fire-resistant charter mark sticker from a tent and underneath was a small piece of paper which read '*Trent Park?*' and crossed out was '*St Albans?*' Eleanora was or had been planning to visit Trent Park recently. The Agent jumped off the kitchen chair and, in his haste to update his partner, tripped on the rug and it flipped over. He saw a semi-circle etched underneath in white chalk. Leaning down to investigate further, he could see that it continued and two metres in circumference. He fully removed the rug to reveal a pagan Pentagram, also called a sacred space. This one had been drawn in the shape of a circle. There were ancient runes inside, candle drippings and what looked like a big scorch mark in the middle. The agent pulled out his device and requested The Occultist.

Eleanora breathed in the sweet clean air and sighed in absolute happiness. Her energy was being restored surrounded by the trees, grass, plants and small creatures.

Her tent was pegged into the ground and she was shaking out her sleeping bag in the crisp, clear morning air. Two squirrels twirled, whirled and chased each other playfully, at complete ease in her presence. One of them sniffed at her feet and ran up her leg and perched on her arm. Eleanora laughed and fed the squirrel a walnut from her pocket, delighting in stroking its head as it ate. 'Now, down little one as I need to put a glamour on the tent to hide us until Pollux arrives.' The squirrel jumped off and Eleanora closed her eyes, imagining a circle around the tent and holding this image in her mind's eye. She called to the wind, the earth, the sun and sea to cover the grounds within her circle to remain unseen by people and that they would instinctively walk round the circle not wishing to enter this place. A soft gust of shimmery air from the sky above blew and it looked like fine spider webbing, floating through the air and settled around the circle. The place would be invisible from now and it would hold in place as long as Eleanora held the circle in her mind – as an accomplished witch, this was easy to do. She crouched down low in a cross-legged position, while holding her amulet of power depicting the goddess, close to her mouth; waited for Polly to arrive.

Polly woke up from a deep sleep on Saturday morning. She sat up and sleepily rubbed her eyes. She was surprised to see that she was in the suite in Park Lane but then she started to remember the events of the last couple of days and held her head in the confusion of it all. Whatever was in that bath oil was really good because she had slept really well and felt perky, well rested and buzzing with energy. Her legs were restless, and she shot up out of bed and started jumping a little from foot to foot. She jumped higher and faster, and then higher and faster, then she bounded a little too high and hit her head on the high ceiling. Leaving a dent with plaster pieces falling off and dust in her hair.

She stopped and touched her head. No pain once again, she observed. She went over to the mirror and her eyelashes, face and hair were covered in a smattering of fine white dust. She let out a loud laugh and Toni came running in. 'Pol pol, you, okay? I heard a crash and....'. Toni pulled her head back and to the side to see the scene before her in full. She looked at Polly covered in plaster dust. There was a piece of plaster hanging from the ceiling and then she looked at Polly again. 'You got a football in here or something?' Before Polly could answer and incriminate herself, she gave her friend a smile and said 'what's for breakfast?' as she passed by Toni, she casually mentioned something about a pigeon and it crashing into the ceiling and she had helped it out. All this she said while looking the other way. Polly then left the room. Toni noticed that there were no windows open or any other mess and let out a 'huh' to herself before exiting and closing the door behind her.

Maami and Papa were acting like a newlywed couple on their honeymoon. They kept whispering to each other and giggling. They held hands and gazed at one another adoringly. Toni kept wincing and rolling her eyes and Chris was pretend retching whenever the lovebirds were looking the other way. They had been married for over twenty-five years and were still like love-struck teenagers together, so the real teenagers in the room were quite relieved when they announced that they would be going out early for a walk around Hyde Park leaving Chris, Toni and Polly to have breakfast together alone.

Despite the behaviour of the adults, everyone was in good spirits and Chris and Toni were indulging in a friendly ribbing session over whose dance moves were better last night and how Toni stayed upright considering how high her shoes were.

'Balance and poise of a Kw-ueen' Toni said with a flash of her huge smile and then Toni exclaimed that there were tons of girls gawping at Chris last night and with that, Chris fell into an embarrassed silence and glared at Toni. He tentatively peeked over at Polly to see if there was any reaction, then explained that Toni didn't have to say everything that goes through her head and Toni replied, 'oh yeah, is that so?'

Polly was quiet and enjoyed listening to the debate and the raucous banter, feeling happy to not be the centre of attention. The distraction was welcomed. She ate her almond croissant with freshly squeezed orange juice. She looked at her two friends, and felt completely comfortable in their presence. She didn't know what she would do without them and their unconditional care for each other. Toni didn't quite get it sometimes, as she had a huge family with lots of love and devotion expressed by her parents. Chris did get what the three of them shared, and cherished it just as much as Polly did. Chris's own Mum had died in a car crash and his dad, Sam, was emotionally withdrawn from the ordeal and being an ex-military man. He was still grieving for the family life lost when his wife passed away. Sam was so wrapped up in his own grief that sometimes it appeared that he didn't notice Chris's pain either. Not that Sam was a bad Dad, he just was really disengaged and distracted most of the time.

Polly sat there in quiet contemplation, with glassy eyes, giving away how emotional she felt. Toni was laughing really hard and scoffing down a pain au chocolate, while Chris was doing an impression of her dancing on her high heeled feet last night 'oh, ow, oh, ow' Chris was scrunching up his face pretending to be in pain while dancing tentatively on his feet with his bum exaggeratedly sticking out.

Toni was literally crying with laughter now. She swung her head round to share the merriment with Polly and caught the pained look on her friend's face. Polly immediately squeezed the tears from her eyes and smiled, faking a yawn and stretched her arms out. 'What shall we do today guys? It's too beautiful outside not to be doing something special.' Polly said. Chris immediately suggested the British museum without hesitation and started to talk about an exhibition that he wanted to see. Toni interjected with a wicked laugh and a disgusted look on her face at Chris's boring suggestion and proposed shopping in Knightsbridge for a pair of shoes for the third ceremony. 'Maami said we have to wear traditional tunics whatever that is, so I'm going to get a fabulous pair of shoes to wear underneath'. While Polly put forward a walk around Hyde Park then Green Park then onto Selfridges for chocolate melting dessert in the Brasserie of Light.

They jokingly negotiated for over an hour, mocking each other's suggestions in turn. Eventually, they came up with a compromise, they would go for a picnic in Hyde Park then onto Selfridges for shopping and then Chris could look at some dusty old books in a shop called Lyme's, one of the oldest bookshops in London. While Toni would wait outside admiring her nails.

Chris pushed back his chair with a 'harrumph' and they all went off in different directions to start to get ready. Polly shouted after Toni, she needed to borrow some clothes and Toni agreed on the basis that she could do a makeover on her friend. Chris rolled his eyes and looked at his watch. It was 10:30 AM. Knowing that now they would not be leaving until at least midday. Maami and Papa came back to pack up and start checking out. Chaos ensued as all the people in the suite were catching up at different times, getting ready and grazing on leftover food together. It was noisy but Polly loved each and every minute of it, it was these ordinary moments, taken for granted by most people, that she cherished the most. She picked up Chris's red and gold Hoodie and put it on. He loved this hoodie. He had won it in a kickboxing tournament last year and it was very distinctive with the words Champion on it. She snuggled into it and absentmindedly inhaled his scent.

Maami and Papa called everyone to get ready and downstairs by 11:45 AM just before checkout. Papa had said he would deduct any late check out charges from Toni's allowance if she made them late so Toni finished her makeover of Polly in a feverish whirlwind. Sulking slightly as they stood together in the checkout queue at reception because Toni felt like everyone did not appreciate her make-up artistry.

Polly was talking to Maami in the queue. Maami paused and rummaged through her handbag and eventually drew out a small box. Holding it out and exclaimed 'Happy belated birthday to you dearest Pol pol' and gave it to her. Inside was a small gold ring with a tiger's eye stone. It was beautiful and very unusual; it had a tiny crystal embedded within it The crystal seemed to glow and projected a light onto Polly's face. Maami was watching her intently. Polly went to put it on and a gust of wind blew through the reception area, knocking over plant pots and throwing Polly off her train of thought. 'The weather, it behaves strangely around you Pol pol' Maami said, lost in her own thoughts and looking around the atrium. Polly hugged Maami and put it on her finger and she appeared not to notice Maami's keen and knowing face.

Once the checkout was complete the group said their goodbyes in a flurry of kisses, hugs and cuddles then the three friends headed off into Hyde Park in the afternoon heat of the sun, leaving Maami and Papa to get an Uber home with all the luggage.

Polly and the Tome of Herne

Chapter 6   A glimpse of a Goddess

Saturday afternoon

Hyde Park was an oasis of green and vibrant coloured plants and flowers that day. The Park is located in central London and very large, covering five-thousand acres. It is the last remaining part of an ancient forest. The space is lovingly tended to, kept structured and is currently in full bloom. The three friends went into a local deli on the way to the Royal Park and ordered a mixture of ham, cheese. hummus and tomato croissants and a cake each with tap water for their refillable bottles. They walked along the street to the gated opening of the Royal Park and went in.

It was a balmy Saturday in July, and lunchtime, this meant that the park was a hubbub of urban life and activity. There were groups of runners all in the middle of doing something running related like warming up, cooling down, some were jogging or running on the spot. Other groups were just finishing up an exercise, looking sweaty and relieved, whereas others were just getting started and stretching.

There were yummy mummies in their Pilates and Yoga outfits on their way to the hip and uber trendy Glass Room Studio. Weaving in between the running groups, were the family and toddler groups with the requisite Mamas and Papas, one wheel running buggy and immaculately groomed dog in tow. Mostly, these dogs were poodles with freshly preened and puffed coats. There were also a range of Alsatians and bigger domestic guard or hunting dogs. In amongst the crowds were the tourists, who just kept stopping dead in front of people on the paths to pause and look at something, admiring the views. The runners, who were mostly Londoners, would shout 'sorry' to everyone as they ran past even though the tourists had caused an inconvenience to them rather than the other way round.

Chris looked on at the chaotic scene 'Why do you think us Londoners do that?' Chris asked Toni and Polly thoughtfully as he watched the crowd and this particular interaction seemed to perplex him. He went on 'we say sorry for everything, you know when someone barges at us we say sorry and when a person has dug us in the eye with their umbrella, we say sorry. It doesn't make sense, right?'

'Yes, it does, ' said Toni with a sniff of defensiveness because she really detested anyone talking about her beloved London in a negative way. 'We are pointing out that the other person should be more careful or should say sorry by, well, y'know, making a point of saying sorry' Toni scrunched up her forehead realising that now she had said it out loud that it did not really make a great deal of sense at all, but it was a costume to the people of London and is an inherent part of the city's culture now.

Polly laughed and Chris did his lope-sided grin, running his fingers through the front of his hair. He did this whenever he was nervous. He looked sideways at Toni wondering if she was in a conciliatory mood and was going to leave the debate there or not. Toni pushed out her delicate chin and said 'see, that makes perfect sense' with a not too confident manner.

Polly stopped walking and took Toni by the shoulders and gave them a squeeze, while she smiled knowingly at her stubborn friend. Toni hesitated, and then broke into a grin 'You know, if I didn't know that you are a really super kind person, I'd think that was a little bit patronising' as she laughed warmly and the other two laughed along too. Sometimes, Chris and Polly had to let Toni's ego run its course before they could laugh at some of the things Toni said and did. Toni was a really good person but sometimes she let her emotions and pride get the better of her. This was most probably because she had been sheltered and given her own way a lot in life.

They walked up through the winding path of the park, soaking in the scenary. Past the flower beds and the bees and the lake then onto the more wooded area and could hear the birds as they called to one another. It was a beautiful day. The summer sunshine shone brightly and the day was becoming hazy. Polly started to feel very lightheaded. She smiled at her friends and lifted her hand with the ring on up to brush her hair out of her face and noticed a faint light glowing around her hand. Her necklace was shimmering slightly too. Polly thought to herself that it must be the mid-afternoon sun playing tricks on her. Polly had gotten preoccupied and fallen behind. She heard Chris and Toni in the distance and some way ahead. They walked on oblivious to Polly's strange predicament and had not really noticed that something was wrong. Polly felt a butterfly softly brush her neck. She turned to look at it. There before her was an exceptionally large and lilac in colour and it was flapping and flying backwards. There was an ethereal singing in the air, very faint but Polly could hear it like it was just out of earshot, on the periphery of sound.

She followed the voices and the butterfly was leading the way. Another butterfly circled the larger butterfly. This one was a cabbage white butterfly but as fragile and beautiful as the lilac one. They twirled and ribboned around one another but still guided her further onto where the singing was coming from. She pushed her way through a manicured hedgerow and into a wide expanse of grassland. Out in the centre was a huge and ancient Oak tree.

Its branches were gnarled and twisted, and its trunk knotted and thick. Its majestic magnificence left Polly utterly astounded and speechless. She drank in the sight of the tree and her gaze was transfixed by it. It was a tree of special prominence and power. In olden times, villages would have been built around a tree of providence like this and named after it, such as, Oaks Hollow. Polly, guided by the butterflies, with several more joining, walked the pathway to the tree in reverence and felt more and more soothed of spirit with each step forwards and towards it she took.

Polly approached and placed her palm on the trunk and immediately a surge of energy shot through her hand, up her arm, through to her core and a pulsating light shone throughout her body. Polly threw back her head but did not feel scared or concerned. The Tree was giving her life from all the energy it had stored beneath it; within its root system and centre. It communicated with her in slow rhythmic pulses of light that translated into words in her mind. It was showing her a vision.

It showed her the ancient forests of the world when its ancestors were young; when, there were no pathways trodden and before humans had populated the planet. The vision expanded out further and went back in time. It showed her the earth in the chaos of the beginning and in its newness. It was brutal and frightening on a grand scale; with tectonic plate collisions, with colossal ruptures and volcanic eruptions and it showed her earth. Another planet was very close behind it that looked the same but with more land and less water. The planets were both forming and had been in orbit together. The cataclysmic activity was due to the two great planets, splitting apart from one another. Two giant worlds both with the promise of life. An extremely tall woman walked in the middle of the chaos, dressed in white with flowers woven into her hair. She was maternally holding her belly. Her eyes were a violet purple colour and her hair was a striking platinum white. She was youthful and had on her head a crown with a glowing gem at the crest. She looked up at Polly, she seemed to see her in the dream and slowly started to walk towards her. She was urgently mouthing words to Polly that she could not understand. The vision was becoming less blurred and sharper in focus. It was linked to the woman being able to see Polly somehow and Polly felt like she would be able to reach out and pull the woman into her world. Polly's heart started racing and she felt panicked. The woman could see her and Polly did not know how to break the connection. 'Please let me go.' Polly begged, the tree whispered back 'Yes, return to the place where you were young and talked with the Willow.' Polly pulled her hand away from the tree. Her legs felt weak and she slumped to the ground. The grass sprung up to soften her fall and moss grew rapidly to make her seat comfortable.

'Hey, where did you get to? You kinda just walked off' Toni was running up to Polly with Chris not too far behind. Toni looked up and whispered 'wow, what an amazing tree' and gazed up adoringly at the leaves and branches. 'Let's lunch here' she announced while she began to busily get out the picnic food. Chris did not say a word. As he drew nearer to the tree, he noticed that Polly looked flushed and her eyes were gazing into the distance like she was seeing more than just the expanse of the park. He couldn't quite put his finger on it, but he had noticed a change in his friend. He could not stop staring at Polly, his eyes were not seeing any difference in Polly but in his heart, he had noticed something was very wrong.

Chris and Toni had finished the savoury part of their lunch and Polly had hardly eaten. Toni was looking through the biodegradable bag for the cakes. She threw a cake to each of them and Chris and Toni began scoffing them down hungrily. Chris was staring at Polly and she fidgeted under his gaze, it felt kind of awkward, hiding a secret from her friend. She felt drained by it, mostly because she knew that he could tell something was wrong. The only one who seemed oblivious to the tension and shift in atmosphere was Toni.

They finished their lunch, clearing away the mess. 'So, are you going to tell us some more about what happened to you last night then?' Chris tentatively opened the subject up that he really wanted to talk about but tried to sound nonchalant like it was a throwaway comment, that didn't mean anything. Polly was laying on her stomach on top of the soft moss with her hands supporting her face and her ankles crossed behind her in the air. She immediately stirred. So much had gone on that she had not had the time to think about her cover story. What with the strange and bodiless singing in the air and the vision the tree had given her. In truth her mind was a bit of a jumble and she was struggling to form a response in the fogginess of it all. Polly said curtly 'I told you last night, what else do you want to know, Chris?' Polly's tone was abrasive, brittle and she did not look up from the ground. This was very unusual and out of character for

Polly, to such an extent, that Toni abruptly stopped daydreaming and snapped back into focus to understand what had riled her usually mild-mannered friend.

'You haven't explained anything Polly and I could be wrong, but it feels like you don't want to talk about this.' Chris flinched at the way he had been spoken to. He was shocked at the way Polly had snapped at him and now felt upset, he was defensive in his response. His neck tense and shoulders raised.

 Toni looked between her friends and was wondering where this was coming from. Polly pulled her legs round in front of her and stood up, poised, defiant. 'I told you what happened Chris. Is there something you want to say?' Polly challenged back. Her eyes were wide and staring with anger.

 'Yeah, there's something I want to say alright' Chris stood up too and he was a lot taller than Polly, aware of this he respectfully maintained the distance between them, he continued 'like why did you leave the salon without your phone and did you know about the burglary before you left and also why did you end up in Shoreditch when you was on your way to Park Lane and……..' Polly interrupted him mid-sentence and crossed her arms and leaned her hip to one side in a jaunty way. She hissed 'what are you saying, Chris? You seem to be implying there are gaps in my story, so why don't you just tell me what happened because you seem to know more than me?'

The silence that followed was icy and Chris and Polly stood glaring at each other. Polly had turned white and was trembling slightly and Chris was red in the face with the effort of trying to not show how angry and bewildered he was at the way Polly was reacting to him asking these questions. Didn't she realise it was out of concern for her.

Toni jumped up, her usually thick skin had been breached, she had a queasy feeling in her stomach and felt uneasy, unsteady in the uncertainty of the situation. This was the first time the three friends had been involved in a genuine argument and if it was going to be anyone that argued and became emotional, she thought it would have been her not Polly and Chris, they were both usually stoic and stable.

'Guys, do you think we may have had too much sun today and you've got a bit of heat stroke or something?' Toni said in a cheery voice in an attempt to break the tension. She got up on her feet slowly and twirled her plait round her left index finger. This didn't get an immediate response, so she carried on playing the peacemaker. 'I read that too much heat makes teenage brains shrink and that there is this documentary on YouTube about teenagers turning into zombies and eating their teachers' brains. This one guy....'. Toni went on a tangent monologue to fill the silence. Both Polly and Chris reacted at the same time but in their own unique way. Polly started laughing while holding out her hand to her friend to reassure her that she would stop arguing and Chris furrowed his eyebrows and gave an exasperated sigh and began with 'I've told you before not to watch that conspiracy theory channel on YouTube by Balan Holmes. Zombies, werewolves, vampires and bloody swamp things that live in the sewers under London, it's all just plain old nonsense...he's just doing it for the likes.'

Toni started giggling and wiggling her tongue at Chris and Polly giggled too, and then Chris understood that she was saying all this to stop them arguing. He began laughing too. 'Very funny.' Chris conceded. Toni pushed him and started running off towards the exit and Chris ran after her trying to catch her up.

Her two friends were hyper competitive and were very fast runners, being both physically fit which helped too. Polly knew she could beat them now with these newly found abilities she possessed. She would need to hold back and give them a head start. Polly stared off after her friends, with her hand over her eyes as she watched them go. There was nothing else for it but to tell them when she knew more about what was happening to her. She knew she wasn't going mad now, something was definitely happening to her but until she knew exactly what it was, how was she supposed to explain it and who would believe her if she did? With a sigh she took off running at a safe slower pace to not arouse any more suspicion.

The trio got on the number 390 double decker bus at the Dorchester hotel bus stop. The route ended in Archway, but they were getting off at Oxford Street, the shopping mecca of the heart of London. They had to wait for ages to get off the bus outside of John Lewis as there were a lot of passengers alighting and boarding the bus at this busy part of town. It was Saturday afternoon and the crowds of London were in good spirits due to the summer sunshine.

 The Hare Krishna faith group members were chanting "Hare Krishna" in happy song and ringing small bells in the streets, handing out leaflets in saffron-orange robes with an abundance of glassy-eyed smiles. There were street performers of every kind; steel pans playing. Lone buskers on acoustic guitars and X Factor hopefuls with keyboards and sound systems, singing chart toppers in their own style and showcasing their talents. The hot dog vendors were shouting the prices of their delicious food and perfumiers trying to spray people in front of department stores, with this season's latest trending scent. Crowds formed around the street artists, happy to be taken in by the performers. London was a vibrant mix of culture and the people on the streets could not help but to get swept up in the colourful and diverse rhythm of the street scene of this metropolitan city. London in summer is warm, friendly and beautiful; the city of the young and the bold, and it is thrilling to behold.

Polly led the way through the people flowing in a constant stream on the pavements and made a space for her friends to regroup near a shop front. Then they crossed the busy road to get to the other side and headed towards one of the biggest department stores in London, that was housed in a large Georgian building, it covered a vast footprint of prime real estate in London with an ochre themed inside.

As they headed towards the entrance, Polly's senses started to tingle and her focus was shifting to a side street where a smaller entrance to the building was located. This iswhere cars and limos could pull up and uber wealthy customers could dismount their chauffeur driven cars and be ushered into the couture section of the store by escort. Polly was staring straight through the crowds and noticed two young boys dressed in black pulling on hoods and masks over their mouths and noses to obscure their faces. They were standing behind a column made of stone. The two youngsters were no older than Polly, at a guess. Chris and Toni had already been swept into the department store by the thronging crowd. Polly dashed forward and threaded in between people, to cut across and into the side street. The two boys were watching a limo signal right to swerve into the holding bay, on the road. As this was happening the two boys put their heads together and one of them yanked out of a small pocket, what looked like a gun. They looked around the streets nervously with a grim determination in their stance. One of the boys looked tearful and Polly wondered what had led them here to this juncture of their lives. They both did not look like they wanted to be there, at all.

Silently, Polly moved closer to the building and walked quickly along the building edge hugging the wall, staying as close as possible to it until she was standing behind the boys. They did not notice her as they both stood facing out onto the street. The boys were arguing. She heard snippets of the conversation as words came flying towards her. 'How else we gonna make money for mum to have her treatment? Please let me know if you've got a better plan. No? I didn't think so, so enough of yer snivelling and let's get on with it.'

Two women dressed in expensive couture clothes stepped out of the blacked-out limo. Both the women were carrying personalised Birkin bags and had copious amounts of diamond jewellery on; bracelets on their wrists and rings on each of their fingers. The boys were tense now and preparing to run at the two women. As they went to take flight and hurl themselves forward, Polly grabbed each boy by the shoulder and dragged them both backwards to the ground, simultaneously, Polly cartwheeled over them, turned in mid-air to face them both and pinned them to the ground in one seamless move. She was surprised at how super strong she was and got the urge to test this further without hurting anyone though, something she would think about later.

The two boys yelled out 'Geroff' and this drew the attention of the two women and their huge bodyguard, who was at that moment, getting out of the vehicle behind them. The women screamed and dashed inside the store, just as the doorperson inside was opening the gilded golden store doors for them. Polly shouted 'what the hell were the two of you thinking. Just going to walk up to people with a gun and demand they hand over their expensive stuff in broad daylight, were you?' with a pivot, she moved and pulled off both of their hoods. One of the boys was crying and the other was close to tears too. Looking closer she could see that they were no more than twelve years old and she guessed the younger one was about ten if that. The infamous gun was a toy made to look like a real gun with some details drawn on with a black marker pen. She grabbed it and with one hand broke it into smithereens. Both boys stopped crying straight away and noticed how strong she was.

'W-w-who are you?' the older boy ventured with a stammer. Polly knew what she had to do. She did not want to get the boys into trouble with the police, but she also knew that they had to be too scared to ever try something like this again. She put on a deep, grown-up voice 'No one to be trifled with, do you hear me? I've been following you for a while. I wanted to see if you two boys were going to go through with this plan. You did. This is your final warning. If you do this again then I'll stop you and hand you over to the police, do you get me?' Both boys' eyes were wide and they both emphatically nodded their heads in agreement. They looked starved and emaciated, with a hopeless look on their tiny little faces. 'We promise.

on our mother's life' they both chorused together, one rubbing his nose with his sleeve. She stared down at them with a glare.

'Oh no, that's not good enough for this scum'. A deep bellow came from behind her. It was the humongous bodyguard. He had drawn out his silencer from his gun belt under his coat and had it pointed at the eldest boy. Polly jumped up, arms splayed out in front of the boys.

'They do not have a gun. It was a toy, they are just desperate kids, they are starving,' shouted Polly. 'I did not know that, when I shot them' the bodyguard smirked. He had an evil gleam in his eyes.

He was very tall and must have weighed about sixteen stone, which meant that he should have had the advantage over Polly. He took aim at the boys and Polly knew he was going to pull the trigger, without a second thought. She grabbed hold of the man's arm and twisted it behind him. She was so angry that she lost control of rational thought, and was not paying attention to her actions or to who may be watching. Polly bent down and grabbed the back of his leg and with a heave hoisted him above her head. She then spun around and threw him to the ground. He was knocked unconscious. The contents of his pockets spilled out and a money clip with a large number of £50 pound notes fell onto the pavement. She turned around and could see the chauffeur of the limousine was on the phone, presumably, to the police. Polly grabbed the money and picked up the boys and dashed off towards the crowds.

She ran at lightning speed with the boys down the back alleys between Oxford and Regent Street, across the busy main road of Regent Street where it merges into Carnaby Street. She realised what it had looked like; that she was with the boys, not trying to stop them. This is why she had to get them and herself out of the way. There was a chance that the police would not have believed their version of events and the boys were too young to suffer the consequences of what that bodyguard was intending to do.

She found a quiet side road and put them down gently. 'Hey, are you ok?' They both stood and stared at her for a while without saying anything, then the youngest one blurted out. 'Are you a superhero or something? How did you lift that man above your head like that? He was massive.' They both peered up at her in awe.

'Never mind how. Just know that I'm watching you from now on, ok?' Both boys looked scared, especially, when they heard the police sirens blaring in the distance. 'Look, take this money and get yourself some food and give the rest to your mum, ok? Now, get home and don't ever let me catch you doing something like this again. You could've been killed.' The Older boy said sorry and went on to explain that their mum wasn't well, and they hadn't eaten in days. He couldn't just watch while his little brother starved.

Polly crouched down to talk to the children at their eye level and told them she could understand why they were planning to do the robbery but that it still did not make what they were about to do right. 'Crime isn't the answer'. She made them both promise to tell a trusted teacher about their mum and the home situation the family found themselves in, and ask for help. She hugged both boys and then walked with them to the tube station. They went east and she went North. Wondering the whole time throughout the journey home, if she had made the right choices, if the boys had learnt anything from the incident and if she had done the right thing. She realised that the powers were a heavy responsibility and everything in life was not always black or white. This weighed on her throughout her journey home and, in truth, every day since Polly had gotten her powers.

Polly opened the gate to her house. The spare keys were in the key safe. She used them to open the door and walked through to the Farrow and Ball hallway. She paused, looking around, Polly realised that the hallway had always created a sense of anxiety in her. She was always expecting Mother and Father to treat her badly in this house. Today, however, the space looked smaller to her somehow than it had yesterday. She stood in the stillness of the reception area, taking in deep breaths before she walked into the main part of the house. Her rucksack was on the side table, presumably one of the shop staff had dropped it off as it was impossible to think that mother had picked it up and done something so considerate.

The TV was on and Polly followed the sound into the cream-coloured living room. Mother was sitting on an oversized and overstuffed soft cream leather couch, drinking a glass of rose malbec lighter summer wine. Mother was watching a documentary about dangerous criminal masterminds in the British forensic services system 'completely misunderstood' was one of the phrases being expressed by Mother. She looked over her shoulder and gave Polly a disapproving glance. She didn't get up and ask how her daughter was or if she was okay following the burglary at the shop. She simply mentioned that one of her staff had dropped off her rucksack and that Mrs Adeoye had dropped off her clothes earlier, and had tried to have a conversation about Polly and the events of yesterday. Mother said she had tried really hard to explain to Mrs Adeoye that she wanted to watch this documentary, but Mrs Adeoye didn't listen and insisted on being a complete bore and carrying on. 'I suppose you do it for the attention. My therapist often says that the teenage years are the hardest for any mother'. Polly wanted to shout that she was not her mother but bit down on the inside of her mouth instead, lest she say something she regret later.

Polly decided to completely ignore her mother's indignation and asked where her phone was. Mother pointed to the limed oak sideboard in the hallway and motioned Polly out of the room and that was the end of that. Polly ran for her phone and immediately WhatsApp's Toni and Chris knowing they would be looking for her and worried. She told them that she had gotten lost in the sea of people trying to enter the department store earlier today and could not call them or anything as she did not have her phone at the time. They both expressed gratefully that she was safe and that being all that mattered. Polly, with relief, put her phone in her pocket and started to walk slowly up the stairs and thought that she might have an evening of quiet contemplation in her room to think about the events of the last few days. There had to be a pattern or a thread to tie everything together. She was most definitely missing something.

Doing some practical things too like getting her taekwondo suit ready for the class tomorrow, would help keep her mind off things. She was feeling pretty confused now, but she was grateful that she had plans tomorrow to prepare for. It stopped her from really thinking about how she felt about being sold as a baby to Mother and Father and wondering about her parents. As Polly wended her way upstairs, she was lost in these thoughts and did not hear the news come on downstairs in the lounge below. There were two main stories featured on London Tonight. The first of them was about a hair salon manager who had been reported missing from her apartment and it was a suspected kidnapping due to the crime scene evidence recovered. 'The young woman cannot be named at this stage in the investigation, as the Police are actively following leads of criminal gangs operating in the area who had links with the victim's family' the broadcaster reported. The other main news story was of an attempted robbery in central London today outside one of the capital's most prestigious department stores and there was grainy CCTV footage of a very slim person easily lifting a much heavier person over their head like a helium balloon and then swinging the person to the floor. It was reported that 'The police believe that someone had hacked into the London Street CCTV system and loaded this fake footage as a prank. This is a very serious crime and the Metropolitan Police are asking for any information and witnesses to come forward at this time, and in other news, the Thames barrier…….'

Chris was in his small, terraced house in Palmers Green watching TV with his dad, in the living room. They were talking about the taekwondo lesson plan for tomorrow and generally catching up about

Chris's day, college and discussing potential university placements. Sam, Chris's dad, brought in a cup of tea and chocolate biscuits for them both. He slumped down in his battered old brown leather armchair and flicked through the channels. Eventually, settling on the news and the London Tonight Programme. Chris was staring at the TV but not really watching when he took a swig of his very strong tea then accidentally, spit the contents out with aghast onto the floor. 'Chris! What the hell' his dad yelled. Chris's eyes did not move from the screen, watching the news report with the CCTV footage and learning about the incident that took place that day outside of the London department store that he, Toni and Polly were visiting that very afternoon. Chris stared at the screen not quite believing what he was seeing. There was no mistaking that the alleged perpetrator was wearing his hoodie and what was even more concerning was that it was the one that Polly was wearing when he last saw her near that very same building that day.

Polly and the Tome of Herne

Chapter 7   Truths are revealed in anger.

Sunday morning

Chris arrives at the dojang very early on Sunday morning. He had not slept last night and was up until the early hours of this morning. He had stayed up to watch and rewatch the CCTV footage of the incident. More so because he just could not quite believe what he was seeing Polly do. Yes, he definitely knew it was her. He had studied the footage but it was still too incredible to believe. He attempted to look for more details of the incident. There was no footage to be found on any mainstream media sites on line, which led him to look through London Street view CCTV footage on the dark web. It was odd, he could not seem to find any around that time. This was perplexing in of itself but what baffled him further, was that the CCTV footage between Oxford Street through to Regent Street and the surrounding area appeared to have been disabled too. Face recognition technology had also been taken offline for an hour or more following the incident.

 It was bizarre and piqued his interest no end. It was like someone, or something was covering it up, but why and who? He then went on a number of social media platforms to find out what was being reported by the public and if there were any eye witness accounts recorded on phones and then loaded to their own personal platforms. He found quite a large number of memes and rather begrudgingly, laughed out loud at a particular one of a gangster cat superimposed into the clip, with the cat lifting the man over its head and saying 'that's the last time you don't get me a diamond collar, fam' it was ridiculously stupid but the cats face was really grumpy and made Chris laugh no end. It was much needed light relief.

The only full coverage of the story he could find was on a subversive YouTube channel operated by Balan Holmes. Balan Holmes was an unknown London teenager who kept his identity hidden from the public. Balan tended to interview the witnesses of crime that the police would not investigate. Presenting details and stories of interest not picked up by the media, such as, police brutality and slum landlord activities – real life situations perpetuated by deprivation or exploitation of the most vulnerable. His coverage aims to give Londoners a platform to air views away from the influence of the mainstream press and media.   Giving a voice to the under-represented people of London, who are a part of the more urban-jungle parts of London. Balan generally does his reports wearing a mask. He is extremely likeable and charismatic, and has cult-like status amongst London's teenagers. He's become like a robin hood type character which has drawn a lot of interest from people from all walks of life, trying to uncover his identity. This has been going on for months but no one seems to be able to find him.   Even his hp address is untraceable.

 The coverage of the incident included Balan's deep analysis of the footage, frame by frame. He points out that there are two small boys on the floor. He also focuses in on the hand of the large man being thrown in the air and makes out the black blob in his hand, that he speculates, is a gun that has been pixelated out of the shot. He goes on to reason that the person at the centre of all of this is trying to save the two young boys and that it must be a woman. He opines that this is highly likely because she is trying to save the boys and maybe enraged enough to demonstrate super strength to prevent the man from shooting them. He exclaims that in his opinion the footage is real and has not been tampered with so why would it be reported as such? This is the question he puts to his viewers. At the end of Balan's report he leaves his audience with a rap of caution -

'don't believe all that you see, two youngsters being disrespected, Po Po being ordered to take sides and the young 'uns being neglected, the person trying to protect; gets suspected, ain't it obscene that society sees what's being projected, them say don't question, see what we tell you to see, believe the stereotypes that we've created, parts of our society automatically slated, that's what we are told, but

the woman, my hero, who saved them kids going on bolddddddd. Sister, we respect you.'

Balan kisses his two fingers and holds them up in the air. He looks directly into the camera and goes on to plead to the two young boys in the footage to come forward 'young uns' he says, 'we want to talk to you, to hear you're okay and hear your version of events, call me ya hear.' He flashes up a number and its burner phone. 'Peace out' and the shot fades.

Chris had to admit that Balan's analysis of the event added up and he also thought that the report was really well put together and thought provoking. It was a gritty news piece and a way of looking at society's underlying problems but in a really accessible way. Stylistically, it was grainy footage, urban landscapes in the backdrop. It was well made with really good high-tech equipment. It had a gangster's edge but a gangster with a heart of gold.

Meanwhile, somewhere in Central London, Eleanora and Balan discuss the incident caught on camera over their telepathic link. It was definitely Polly and her powers had grown. Eleanora asked Balan to use his gifts with technology to find out all that he could about Polly and where she was. 'Also, please stop drawing attention to yourself with this YouTube channel of yours. Magical folks have no business being in the public eye and taking part in celebrity culture',Eleanora warned. Balan shrugged, 'I think we do. We have a duty to protect the more vulnerable people of the world because we are stronger' Balan explained.

Chris and Polly

Chris has an old battered broom in his hands and he is sweeping the herring-bone wooden floor of the dojang, getting ready for the classes of the day. Sweeping the floor of any dust before he puts out the mats, face guards and punching mitts. He sprays disinfectant on all the equipment and wipes it down again, even though, it was disinfected before being put away yesterday. It is giving him something to do while he waits.

He is feeling apprehensive. Barely able to swallow and his breathing is ragged. He has sent Polly a WhatsApp message asking her to come to the dojang before class starts and help him set up. His phone pings with a reply 'sure, be there in 10 mins' it's from Polly.

Chris finishes setting up then he takes himself through a meditative tai chi sequence to gain a semblance of control over his mind and body. After the sequence is over, he feels more steadied and in control of his thoughts.

Later, Polly walks in with a big smile on her face. She has on her crisp white taekwondo suit. Slipping off of her shoes at the door, she bows to the photo of her sensei and then, in turn, to the dojang emblem of 'The gifts of strength and honour are given to warriors to protect those that cannot protect themselves'. Polly moves gracefully and lightly over to where Chris is standing. She smiles at him and brushes her auburn hair behind her ears. When Chris does not smile back, she hesitates. Polly pauses and is concerned now. Leaning her head on one side and placing her hand on her hip, she starts to feel worried but also a little defensive too, being aware that Chris knows something, he has been acting like he is a bit suspicious of her for the last couple of days. Asking her questions. Looking at her intensely with his penetrating green eyes searching her hazel eyes for more information. He knows she is not being honest.

Polly decides to play it casually 'hey, you've already put out everything' she says sweeping her hand around the dojang to demonstrate the point. 'What do you need me for?' she blushes, the bold way she says this sounds like she is flirting which felt like a weird thing inside this moment, between her and Chris. He smirked and blushed too. Eventually, he blurts out 'Polly, do you trust me, I want you to talk to me Polly and I would like you to know you can tell me anything and that I want to help you.' Chris said this with such intense honesty that Polly felt surprised and dumbstruck by his directness. She then felt embarrassed for not trusting her friend but something in her also felt annoyed that Chris did not see her as a strong capable person that could handle things on her own. 'That's nice to hear Chris but what do I need your help with?' She turned her face away and was talking into the window front of the dojang. Her shoulders tensed up, strained with wariness. Chris sighs in exasperation. 'Okay Polly. If that's the way you want to do this.' Chris stood up erect and strides over to the nearest mat and stands facing inwards on the edge of it. He assumes the fighting stance. Polly looks over her shoulder and sees what Chris is doing. She slowly turns and walks quite deliberately and slowly towards the other end of the mat to face him. 'You want to spar here and now?' she asks tentatively. Chris nods once.

Polly pulls a hairband off her wrist and moves to tie up her long hair into a top knot. Both bow towards each other, neither one breaking eye contact. Chris moves forward immediately, sweeping down with his right hand and missing Polly by a millimetre. Polly was not expecting the battle to commence with such a direct assault, so she stood on her right foot evaluating her opponent's emotional state. This may give insight into anticipating the next move. Chris was being unpredictable which meant he was angry, so she expected a relentless attack with little defensive sparring. She pivoted into a defensive position. One arm up covering her face and the other facing down to strike but also as a shield to protect her body. Chris advanced. He jabbed right, left, left then right and his shots were hard and aimed at penetrating her defence. She was being pushed backwards off the mat with each move and eventually, both of her feet were planted on the floorboards outside of the mat. Point one to Chris. Polly vaulted forward and landed on her left leg, all the while, aiming for the back of her right heel to come down in an arc on Chris's left knee. She was deliberately holding back but Chris still winced a little with pain. He pivoted on to his left side keeping it rigid and solid in order to shoot his right foot into her side. He made contact but there was no reaction, which stunned him and his body language showed this by momentarily stopping and relaxing. She hesitated and jumped back in a delayed faux response but she knew it had been too late a reaction.

Chris smirks, narrowing his eyes and Polly turns red in the face. 'so, Polly, are you going to tell me where my hoodie is and what you did with it after the fight? Also, you might want to explain if I'm incriminated in anyway by lending it to you'.

Polly reeled back in shock but managed to keep her composure and concentration on the battle somehow. Chris punched out hitting her in her ribs. 'What fight Chris?'. Chris mockingly laughs 'you know, the one on the news last night, it was you and you were wearing my hoodie. You know it and I know it so let's cut the pretence'.

Polly went in and punched Chris in the right arm then left then right. Polly was very close now and Chris kicked out her right leg and she tumbled to the floor. He held her down with his hand and placed the weight of his body on top of her. He knew this move infuriated her leaving her feeling trapped. She went to get up and he pinned her back down and her back smashed into the floor. He started counting out loud with the aim of announcing a point. 'I. don't. know. what. you. are. talking. About.' Polly said through gritted teeth, in a laboured way and showed her frustration at being held down.

'Three! No? You don't know what I'm talking about, huh? You were wearing my hoodie; YOU fought a man three times the size of you and held him over your head AND this was down the same side road of the department store we all visited yesterday AND you are going to deny it to my face?' Chris was very frustrated with her, he slammed his fist and followed through with his elbow into her arm.

Polly was livid that Chris had used this move on her, it would have had him disqualified from any tournament. The unfairness of his action really angered her, triggering her deeply. She kicked up with her legs and with her new strength, flipped Chris over and pinned him to the floor, as easily as if he was made of air. She sprung up, touching the ceiling and spun around in the air about seven times, then landing with her fist down smashing into the wooden floor. The punch went through to the foundations of the building below. Fragments of the herring-bone wooden flooring splintered all over the place. But, more importantly, Polly and her powers were revealed.

Chris stared at her not really believing what he was seeing in front of him but knowing it was true. He had deliberately goaded her into anger to drop her guard and get her to reveal this to him but part of him thought it just couldn't be true. How could a human possess such strength he thought to himself.

'So, now you know,' Polly shouted with tears falling rapidly from her eyes. 'Now you know, you've seen it. Are you happy Chris that im....im well this thing that I can't explain and I don't know what's happening and I'm frightened I'm going to turn into a demon or something worse. I'm going to be a freak' with that irrational outburst, Polly moved with super speed and ran out of the door, she was gone from view within seconds.

Chris lay still for a moment on the floor. He seemed confused at first, but laying there in the stillness of the moment gave him a chance to process what he had just seen and a sense of calm spread over him. His face relaxed, the knot in his neck eased. His plan had worked. In all the emotion, Polly had revealed what she had been hiding and it was so much more awesome than he could have ever imagined. He knew what he had to immediately do so he got on with it. He had to protect his friend.

He moved across the remaining parts of the dojang floor and went outside. He scoured the streets and he found a local skip with some breezeblocks in it, and pulled a couple out. He put them on his shoulders and walked back to the dojang in complete contemplative silence.

When he opened the door, he could see the mess within with a fresh perspective. It was unbelievable that Polly had this much strength. He was deep in thought as he positioned the breeze blocks, so they looked like they had been hurled into the room. One of them he positioned at an angle in the hole made by Polly's fist. Yet, before he did this, he run his fingertip lovingly around the edge thinking about Polly and if she had hurt her hand.

There was no time, his pace quickened. He put away the mats and equipment as quickly as he could, turned off the lights and let himself out, locking the door behind him. He went over the street and got his favourite breakfast of cappuccino and a fresh croissant from a deli on The Green. Sitting there gazing out of the window and across the road at his father's dojang, he decided to WhatsApp Polly. He did not know what to say at first. Who does when something life changing like this happens. The message was tapped out and deleted a few times, trying to find the right words to express how he felt. He settled on telling her he was sorry for upsetting her but that he had been frightened that something was seriously wrong. He hastily added, that he was here when she was ready to talk about it, he suggested they could come up with a plan together. He felt like he needed to reassure her so included at the end that he was really excited about her new abilities and thought that maybe she should be too. He put down his phone when he saw his dad's Audi pull up outside of the dojang. Sam, Chris's Dad got out carrying more equipment in his hands. Chris looked at his leather strapped watch. It was thirty-five minutes before opening.

Chris stepped off the cafe high stool with ease, being a tall person with long legs, he did not need to do the wriggle and tentative, cliff edge hop that average-sized people do and gently jogged over to the dojang. He also managed to pick some debris out of his curls noticing these at the last minute in passing a shop window.

 The door was open and Sam stood staring at the devastation inside his studio. He looked panicked when he exclaimed 'Chris, omigod I think the vandals that smashed up Polly's mum's shop hit us too. I don't know if they've taken anything.' He said looking all around. Chris felt sorry for executing his plan at the dojang at that point, forgetting it would mean that Sam had one more thing to sort out 'Can you get on the computer please and send out a circular text and email to say the dojang is closed for lessons with immediate effect and we will be in touch soon. You'll have to be quick before people start travelling to get here.'

Chris wanted to ease some of his guilt so leapt into action while Sam called the Police. He ran to the small office and switched on the Mac computer. Years ago, he had created an emergency contingency plan for the dojang business when he was twelve years old nearly thirteen, on one quiet afternoon when it was raining and he was bored. He had found the template on the internet and started populating it with an emergency plan procedure. He had all the emails and phone numbers of parents and older teenagers stored on a spreadsheet. He wrote an email and text explaining the situation and then punched send, sending out hundreds and hundreds of messages and emails all in one go. There was something really satisfying to Chris about being this organised. Chris didn't believe in natural abilities. He believed in capability to develop habits, consistency, structure and systems. In his view, with careful planning, one can become great at anything with enough dedication, discipline and time. Chris gave a satisfied smile to himself and placed his hands behind his head.

Sam watched Chris through the doorway unseen. He stood with his arms across his muscular chest and looked at his son through the gap in the door. He shouted 'hey Chris, have you seen Polly.' Chris hesitated and knitted his thick eyebrows together in a quizzical gesture. Why would his dad ask him that he wondered? 'Ummm, no, I better text to tell her not to worry or to come to the dojang. she'll get the text along with everyone else and come straight here but there is nothing that can be done, right?'

Sam said that he agreed. He watched his son. Chris had blatantly lied to him and he thought to himself that Chris was a really good friend. He pulled the clone phone from his top pocket and looked at his son's last text to Polly. The grimace on his face said it all. His mouth was set in a tight line. He shouted out 'I'm just going to make a call to a contractor to fix this mess. I'll be outside.' He walked over what was left of the damaged floor and outside into the sunshine. He took in a deep breath and then stretched his legs, rolling his neck. An old habit he picked up in the military that he performed when he was about to do something he really did not want to do. His eyes were oddly distant and had a milky glaze over them. He punched a button and a number came up on the speed dial. It began to ring. It was picked up within seconds. 'She's running, look out for her.' The line clicked dead.

Polly was crying and running on, blind in her upset. All the events of the last few days came crashing in on her and her emotions bloomed forward. It all felt more real somehow because Chris had seen her use her strength. She could no longer question her new abilities. This was both a relief and overwhelmingly scary at the same time. She slowed down to a walk realising that she shouldn't be seen running at super speed in broad daylight because the last thing she needed was being picked up by the government and experimented on.

She was grateful that it was still early on a Sunday morning, so no one was around. Her thoughts were turned to going somewhere secluded to test out her new abilities, to see what she could do and see how far she could push herself. Thinking of where to go, she suddenly remembered what the tree in Hyde Park had told her; to go to the Willow that talked to her when she was younger. Maybe she would be able to get some answers there. When she was a child, she used to go to a large forest in St Albans, Hertfordshire just outside of London, called the Old Wood. She loved it there and would write stories about elves and living trees, and animals that could talk. This was all under the canopy of the big trees where she would spend hours writing down conversations with the wood and the trees themselves. These conversations taught her of ancient civilisations when the world was new and about humans who had magical powers and some who practised witchcraft. They told her to stay strong and believe in herself, to own her own magic. Do not pay attention to Mother and Father they would whisper. She would listen and take it all in, in the cool shade of the canopy of the trees.

This one special tree would talk to her and tell her stories. It was a huge weeping willow. It would move its branches and leaves like hands to hug her close when she was feeling cold and would wrap her up in a blanket of leaves when she was feeling sleepy. It poured love into her when she felt despair, alone. Generally, she just felt happy and content in the presence of the willow. She had thought this was a child's imagination. A game of sorts, a small child's mind trying to make sense of her world and her home life but now she was wondering if all that she had thought that was her imagination, had been real all along. Polly would get to the tree to find out some answers.

Polly ran at lightning speed to the old wood. Choosing to stay off the main roads and use only abandoned pathways along the new river loop, these footpaths are barely used. She needn't have bothered as she was travelling so fast that all people saw was a blur in their peripheral vision as she passed by and if any person happened to see anything they would have thought it was the wind moving through the bushes and trees.

Arriving at the wood, she slowed down to walk among the trees. A dog, a husky in terms of breed, bounded up to her and started barking in approval at finding a friend on his walk. He stumped his feet in appreciation as Polly patted his head and he gruffly said 'thanks, thanks'. She looked down at him, quite taken aback and said 'did you just say thanks?'. He smiled up at her and his owner walked into view. The dog barked and wagged its tail and started walking by its owner's side. The dog looked back and so did Polly. She waved goodbye. She felt awe inspired at this world within a world that was opening up before her eyes.

Polly was starting to feel like her brain was going to explode with all this new information. That was when the trees burst into greetings with their melodic voices, talking to her as she stepped by. They were excited to see her and shook their leaves to show this. They marvelled at how tall she had grown. They told her that the Willow was waiting for her and so was the witch. Polly asked who the witch was and they told her that she was a friend. A friend of the forest and all living beings. A guardian of the land. Someone to talk to and explain all to her. She walked through mud, mulch and bracken. Snagging her now filthy suit as she went on. The trees were becoming thick and knotted together with barely any room for her to pass let alone put her feet down on the forest floor. Eventually, she reached the enclosure of the willow and looked inside through to the glade. The willow was even bigger than she remembered and its overhang was so dense that she couldn't see the trunk through the fullness of the branches and leaves. She moved the branches aside and stepped through, the inner branches automatically parted, greeting her like a long-lost daughter. The environment under the willow canopy was cool, still and soothing. Dabbled light danced across the grass under Polly's feet. The willow pulled her close cradling her in its branches like arms. It wept with happiness and love and lamented that she had stayed away for too long. Polly started to cry remembering how happy she had felt all those years ago; knowing that she was loved and rejoiced in being held again with such tender loving care. She began to glow and started to emit a green light. Polly was renewed and she felt like she had returned home.

Eleanora saw the willow moving and stood up to walk towards the clearing. It was time. She held her amulet in her hand and with the other pulled aside the Willows branches and entered the space.

At first Polly did not see the witch. Her focus was still on conversing with the tree, she was engrossed. The older woman cleared her throat trying to draw Polly's attention to her presence. Polly got down from being cradled and the willow parted its branches. 'You, what are you doing here? you're the woman from the shop?' Polly said, rather confused.

'Listen, we do not have a great deal of time. There is so much I need to tell you, but it would take too long to explain. So here are the important parts. There are a group of people, collectively called The Company, that are out to find you and will kill you and me too, but before they do they will extract information from us both in the worst way possible. They want your powers and they want me to decipher an ancient text that tells them about a prophecy that will give them unlimited power over this planet and the universe. We have to stop them from getting this information at all costs. The Prophecy and your powers are connected. Do you understand? They are on their way here now.'

Polly was not expecting any of this from the older woman. She opened her mouth and closed it and opened it again and closed it again not really knowing how to reply to a statement like that. It was just too big a situation to understand the implications of straight away. She felt quite dumbfounded. 'Pollux did you hear me? You need to leave this place and go to Lady Cadmun-Hernes in Glossop, Peak District and I will meet you there. The Lady will protect you. There is a spell on the Manor she lives in and none of their equipment will work. They cannot track you there. I'll explain everything when I next see you. We will have more time. They know all about you by now because they kidnapped the team manager from the shop.' Eleanora ended her explanation by turning and walking away. Polly shook herself and asked in shock 'hey wait. Gracie, they have Gracie did you say?' Polly managed to stutter this out. 'Yes, but there is nothing we can do for her now. They took her to the Premiere Compound in Worcestershire and she is being held there. She will be killed soon.'

Polly found this all very alarming and hard to take in. All this new information was pretty overwhelming and she sat down because her legs were feeling wobbly. The Willow started to rub its leaves through her hair. 'Stop that' Eleanora said, pulling the branch away. 'She has not got time to be cuddled now, Child, you need to listen to me and get going, do you understand?' Eleanora physically shook Polly into taking action and Polly jumped up. She was still in her Taekwondo outfit that looked absolutely ruined now. She needed a change of clothes and something to eat as her stomach was growling. She knew what she had to do and she was not about to leave Gracie to her doom, that was for sure.

Polly and the Tome of Herne

Chapter 8 The Blackness in us all

Sunday afternoon

Eleanora departed, placing her hood over her head and vanished into the interior of the wood. She told Polly to head straight to the Peak District as The Company had more than likely placed Polly's house under surveillance and they had an abundance of resources at their disposal to trace and retrieve anyone at any time. There were a few details that Eleanora had chosen to omit. What she had not told Polly was that the Lady had some secrets of her own and her powers were unequalled in the world of the occult. Polly had not been entirely open either. She did not tell Eleanora that she wanted to prioritise the rescue of Gracie. She got the impression that Eleanora would have disapproved and she did not know how she would have reacted.

Polly immediately left wishing she could spend more time with the weeping willow tree. There were promises made to return as soon as she could, to hear more about her powers and the history of the world. Polly felt energised and focussed. She was on her way back to her family's house to get a change of clothes, something to eat and call Chris for help with finding Gracie. She knew he would want to even though they had not spoken since their argument.

Polly walked through her front door. The house felt different and she was different but her environment and, she expected, her parents were exactly the same, which felt quite surreal. She decided to eat first and WhatsApp Chris then get dressed and leave. She was walking through the house to the kitchen thinking about how she was going to get out of the last week of school without it being noticed when she walked straight into Mother. Mother was dressed in her Pilates outfit. Mother was wearing a bodysuit that was a beautiful shade of lilac with matching leggings and a cream loose knitted summer cardigan. Mother felt the cold more than other people and

Polly suspected that this was moreso to do with how little body fat she had due to her eating restrictions, more than anything else. 'What in the blazes…… 'shouted Mother automatically wasp-like. Mother looked Polly up and down and began commenting on Polly's dishevelled and dirty appearance with gusto and venom.

Polly noticed another new diamond bracelet clinking on Mothers arm along with all the other little trinkets and realised that this might be the reason why Mother was being quite extraordinarily vindictive today. Polly waited patiently for Mothers vitriol on her person to end and as she waited in silence, she became angrier and angrier. A glow started to build around her. She started fiddling with her chain and it gave off a set of sparks. 'Listen' Polly raised her voice and interjected 'I came home to eat and change, then I am going to stay at Chris's and will go to school from there. Is there anything to eat?' Mother immediately stopped mid-sentence and a distant gaze slid over her eyes, giving them a glassy unseeing quality. Her limbs became rigid and straight. Mother spun around and headed to the kitchen.

Following her, Polly was wondering what this was all about. Sadly, Polly really was very used to Mothers erratic switches in mood, so did not question it too much, at first.

Mother walked through the kitchen past the island unit (which was the size of an orca whale) and walked to the fridge. She opened it and pulled out a pre-made harissa chickpea salad and took out a tub of hummus with some fresh carrots. Mother began peeling and chopping the carrots into fine straws. She assembled everything on a fine bone china plate and placed it in front of Polly. Finally getting out a knife and fork then placed these either side of the plate. Polly stood in front of the food with her mouth wide open, gaping at her mother. There were a lot of what Polly would relay later to her friends, as 'Firsts' here to acknowledge and take in. What is meant by this is 'First Times'. For instance, this was the First time Mother had listened to Polly when she had asked about food or a meal. This was the

First Time she had prepared Polly food since she was a baby. This was the First Time she had made a vegetarian meal for Polly because usually she would order meat for her. This was the First Time she had done something purely for Polly and Polly alone.

After she had finished preparing the delicious food, Mother stood there looking with those unseeing eyes at Polly expectantly. Polly rather tentatively picked up her fork, not taking her eyes off of the other woman. Mother smacked her hand away and dashed to the fridge. She pulled out a zip lock bag and placed it on a chopping board. She unzipped the small plastic slider and then ran over to the white sideboard and pulled out a set of little tweezers and used these to carefully pick up a fragile looking edible purple flower and began to dot these on Polly's salad creating a beautiful display.

'Tastes like chives' mother said earnestly then stepped backwards and indicated to Polly she could eat now. Polly nervously looked at her mother standing there and realised to herself that she was waiting for a catch. After a while her stomach started to growl with hunger and she couldn't wait anymore and began to wolf down the food. It was delicious. 'What next?' said Mother looking attentively at Polly with those wide unseeing eyes. Polly considered Mother for a while. 'Well, you could clear away then help me get ready I suppose...... 'Polly said laughing as she said this, to Polly, this was the most outrageous idea she had ever uttered. Mother had never cleared away plates nor had she ever helped Polly to get ready. 'Brilliant' said Mother with a clap of her hands. 'Let's get started' then she spun around in the weird little rigid way that she had adopted today, while scooping the plate off the island and placing it in the dishwasher along with the cutlery. She then led the way upstairs. She was humming and then started singing while she was going, and it resembled a tune that Polly remembered from her childhood.

'Hush little baby don't say a word, mothers going to buy you a mockingbird and if that mockingbird doesn't sing, mothers going to buy you a diamond ring and if that diamond ring don't shine...........'

Polly started to think that something was really wrong with Mother. 'Erm, are you ok?' Polly stammered out, Mother had gone into Polly's ensuite and had turned on the shower. She placed the towel on the heated rail then came out into the bedroom and started choosing Polly's clothes. 'Get in the shower dear' she nudged Polly into the ensuite and closed the door. Polly stood there for a while still staring at Mother and wondering when this bizarre behaviour would cease but then decided to get into the shower as the warmth of the steam was very enticing.

Afterwards in the bathroom, she wrapped the towel around her and looked in the mirror, it was then she noticed she was covered in a pale green glow. It was hard to see herself properly in the mirror, being too steamy 'I wish this steam would clear', the steam immediately rescinded from the room like it was being sucked up through a vacuum or powerful extractor. Polly was taken aback but two things suddenly occurred to her, the glow must be what is giving her strength and she bit her lip as she thought this, the glow must be giving her other powers too. Unlocking the door and striding over to stand before Mother, who was still singing away her lullaby. 'Mother, do a downward dog.', she said in a whisper, feeling slightly uncomfortable. Mother stopped what she was doing, put the clothes she had in her hands on the bed and placed her hands in a namaste prayer position then assumed a downward facing dog yogic pose.

'Mother, stand up' Mother stood up. Polly stared at her for a long while and then cleared her throat and said rather quietly with a graveness to her voice, she was very unsure, but she really had to know 'tell me what you know about my adoption'.

Polly WhatsApp's Chris and asked him to come to the house for 4PM which would just about give her enough time to get dressed and pack some essentials. Like what, she did not exactly know as she had not been on a rescue mission before. She went through the house and picked up a random selection of items that just might be helpful in a rescue situation; like a hand torch even though she had one on her

109

phone and a charger, rope and small wax candles from the garden shed, while she was in there, she also grabbed the smaller bolt cutters and a Stanley knife and put this all in her black holdall along with a black jumpsuit and a North Face gilet. She got dressed in a black tight-fitting top and leggings. She put on a pair of running trainers and picked up a black beanie and slung it in the bag too.

A little while later Chris rang the doorbell and Mother went downstairs to let him in.

Polly felt dazed. After mother had recounted the story of her adoption, Polly was in shock and needed space to think. Mother had been brutally honest about everything including her own thoughts, feelings and observations. Polly felt giddy and sick so asked Mother to go to sit in her own room. She was not entirely sure how to switch Mother back to normal. Well, normal for her anyway. She didn't know how this situation had happened in the first place so she hoped Chris would have some ideas.

Chris walked in the room but he continued to look backwards and down the stairs with an odd and quizzical expression on his face. 'erm, what's up with Mother? She was trying to be, well, nice I guess downstairs.' Polly closed the door. 'I really need all your attention right now Chris. I have a lot to tell you and it's going to all sound a bit crazy' Chris's eyes widened, and a gleeful look came over his expressive face 'Crazy I can do. Come on, spit it out.' With that Polly began.

Polly told him about her birthday celebrations and that uncle jack had revealed she was adopted, she explained about the day that she got her powers and how she had run from Winchmore hill to Shoreditch in minutes 'I knew it!' Chris exclaimed smugly and rather loudly too. Polly looked at him and raised an eyebrow then continued with a 'not now' look on her face. She told him about the man who was dragged into the sewer by vines and tree roots that appeared from nowhere when she felt threatened. She went on to explain about the tree talking to her in Hyde Park and the special connection she made with the Willow tree and lastly, about what Eleanora had said about a group of people called the Company, and that they had kidnapped Gracie to get information out of her, taken her to Worcestershire and were holding her in a Premiere compound, which was one of their secret locations. That the Company were probably watching her now and if they found her, they would try to kill her. As Polly talked about this openly and it came tumbling out, Polly began to realise these things were all connected but she could not remember all the little details of what she found to be strange incidents over the last few days. Her brain kept getting foggy and felt overloaded.

When she had finished, Polly flung herself backwards onto her chaise lounge, exhausted by the effort of explaining all of this in one go. It was now 5:15 PM. There was so much more to say about what Mother had told her about her adoption but that would need to wait for now. She did, however, share that Eleanora had told her to go to Glossop to meet someone called The Lady, real name Lady Cadnum-Herne who had powers and would be able to keep her safe. Polly then went on to list all of the powers she seemed to have; super strength, speed, an ability to communicate with trees, if she focussed, she could get steam to clear from a room and rather embarrassingly she said while casting her eyes downwards, she seems to have put some kind of spell on Mother who is doing whatever Polly says.

Chris just sat there for a while staring at her, mouth agape. His eyes were shadowed with concern and his brow was deeply furrowed. Polly was scared that she had broken him in some way, so she got up and sort of poked him into focus. Chris pulled himself together and cleared his throat and said 'Wow, that's a- a- a lot to take in and I'm really sorry but I don't think the human brain was designed to take in that much information all at the same time so I need some time to process this before I can be helpful to you' Chris offered. Polly was a little relieved as she did not really have the energy to dissect all of this at the moment. Her head was spinning enough just talking about the key events from the last few days, let alone the smaller stuff that had happened.

'Right, first things first, we are going to need to figure out how to get Mother back to normal. We can't leave her here without her own free will. She might not be able to eat or drink without you telling her to do this so let's go downstairs and do a few tests to see if she is safe to leave on her own.' Chris was so very practical that she wanted to kiss him sometimes. He was a very stable influence on the group of friends because he was so very logical.

They found Mother in the morning room. She was sitting with a glass of water, some avocado and prawn sushi rolls and one Japanese mochi, her meal for the day, watching a film on Netflix. She was laughing at a comedy, usually she tried not to as she often said smiling causes wrinkles. On this occasion, she seemed to be laughing with wild abandonment and seemed so engrossed that she had not noticed them as they walked in. 'okay, she can eat, drink and entertain herself' Chris observed out loud like Mother was a particularly tricky science experiment. 'Great, let's go' Mother shot up as soon as she heard Polly and said 'what's next' again. It then hit Polly what Chris had said upstairs. She absolutely did not feel comfortable with the spell or that Mother had lost her free will. It's something she had not really understood at the time as she just thought that Mother was being more cooperative than usual but when Chris had explained that he believed she didn't have free will this made Polly feel awfully bad. She needed to understand how this had happened so she could make sure it never happened again.

'Right Polly, let's go through what had happened when you came home, that might give us an idea of where to start.' Polly explained she walked through the house and bumped into Mother and Mother was in a foul mood and started saying these really horrible things that made Polly mad and then Polly asked if there was any food. 'That's it, nothing else Polly? Show me where you were standing and physically what you were doing at that time.' Polly and Chris reconstructed the situation and Chris noticed that Polly had been fiddling with her necklace at the time. 'It's the necklace, I'd bet anything. You must use it to channel the power in some way.' Said Chris while clapping his hands together in delight. Polly smiled. Chris's excitement was making her feel joyful at the possibilities of her new powers. 'Right, concentrate on Mother while holding the necklace and ask for the spell to be broken.'

Polly took a deep breath and concentrated on the necklace in her hand, it felt cool to touch. She conjured up and held the image of the willow tree in her mind. A sense of serenity floated through her, she was still a bit scared and frightened that she couldn't remove the spell but knew she had to try. Visually, a faint light glow started to emanate from her, and wisps of wind start to swirl around her lifting at her hair and clothes. A power flows through her body and she directs some of it at Mother by lifting one of her hands in Mothers direction. 'I release you from the spell' smoky curls of light trickle from her fingers and start gliding towards Mother. The glittering dust settling on Mothers eyes. At first it enters softly and Mother is smiling while the glow settles all around her then she starts to pant like she could not get enough air into her lungs, next, a dense tar like substance seeps out of Mothers mouth while she stands there slowly choking before their eyes. Her body is lurching back and forth, and she starts convulsing. Polly abruptly breaks the connection but the black substance continues to spill out onto the floor, spewing forth in vast quantities. Mothers' knees give way and she falls unconscious to the floor. Polly is panicked and starts screaming to Chris and crying. He takes hold of her and looks deep into her eyes, telling her that losing control now will not help Mother at all.

Holding her hands, he encourages her to trust her instincts and use the magic once again to help Mother. Polly gets up and intuitively knows what she must do. She closes her eyes as she is frightened when looking at Mother. She searches for something positive and solid, a memory to fight the evil blackness. Recalling the strength of the Willow tree and the forest in her mind's eye and she begins drawing the power to herself and sending the beauty and energy of the forest into her mother to make her strong enough to withstand the blackness.

Polly stays calm, even though she is frantic inside. The thick liquid of blackness starts to dissipate and mother is slowly able to breathe normally once again. Exhausted by her ordeal, Mother lays there still for a while and slowly but surely, colour starts to spread into her ghostly white cheeks. Blinking and holding her head she looks at Polly, who has bent down to sit by her side, holding her hand. 'What, what happened? Why am I on the floor? Where is the sorceress, The Lady, where is the baby? I did everything she wanted. I want my baby now.'

Mother seems very disoriented and distressed but at least she is alive and breathing now. Polly and Chris both confer and agree that Mother might feel better after a good night's sleep, so they both take her up to bed. They are left feeling shocked by the sudden turn of events and the added complication of Mother talking about a sorceress has meant that there is another dimension to worry about. Reeling from the ordeal, Chris decides to look up magic on the dark web and Polly finishes packing her things with essentials; before, she retreats to stay in Mothers room with her tonight. Lest something else happens and she needs to be on stand-by with the magic or worse, the ominous sounding company decides to break into the house. Polly decides there and then to leave in the morning to find The Lady. They all needed protection including Mother, which meant taking her on their journey with them. She would hatch a plan to rescue Gracie once they were all somewhere safe. Polly could not decide who was the biggest threat at this present moment in time, the company or Polly and her unwieldy powers. She needed to learn how to use them and when not to use them too.

The Company Agents had reported back findings from the sweep of Eleanora's apartment. The only clues they had found were references to places called Trent Park and St Albans. Eleanora had worked for The Company as its lead specialist on the occult and paganism some months back. She had found something and after she defected, The Company had a personality profile built on Eleanora from in-depth discussions with her colleagues of the time. The company had found this pretty challenging to do as she had worked really hard to keep key details of her life secret and away from The Company. Her colleagues did not know that much about Eleanora, like where she lived or if she had a family or not or if she had a partner. She had been really careful but being that careful usually leaves behind details of omission. For example, it meant that Eleanora had deliberately infiltrated the company and had chosen to avoid revealing details about herself from the very first day, which means she had intention from the start. However, to blend in, unassumed and without raising suspicion, she did have to engage in small talk from time-to- time, which had left some important information about her preferences and lifestyles choices. On this basis, The Company could make some predictions and forecasts in behaviours. They knew that she preferred to camp and that she often spent time walking in nature and had a very keen interest in ancient trees and natural medicines. The Company had used their resident behavioural psychologist and profiler to predict what she would have been doing in Trent Park or St Albans. It was predicted that she would have the necessary skills and expertise to camp in more remote parts of the areas, so they deployed teams to sweep in a targeted way looking for her. They had been using facial recognition software for over 3 months now and she had not appeared on any of the tracking radar systems. This was their last chance to establish a trace.

The Company and Trent Park

One of the teams that were searching Trent Park discovered a small log cabin construction that had signs on the outside warning passers-by of electrical cables storage and High voltage electricity conductors. The Team called in to check and the construction was not referenced on any maps or owned by electricity companies in the area. It was therefore assumed that this was some sort of hideout used by Eleanora or for some other illegal activity by organised crime gangs. Caution was being advised on entry. The Company team on site had settled under a tree to devise a plan. They agreed to circle the hut from afar, keeping their guns trained on the entrance and the exit while they sent in a munitions deactivator unit to ram open the door then four of the agents would follow the unit inside leaving the remaining four agents to remain outside, crawling forward to offer back up should the need arise.

The eight agents were in camouflage and had a range of weapons to help them execute their plan. Before commencement, one of the Agents spotted a rune carved into a tree and there was a circle of white stones around it too. Striding forward, she stepped into the stone circle to inspect the craving and she started weaving unsteadily on her feet before dropping to the floor.   A second agent looked round and noticed his colleague laying on the floor. He stepped forward into the stone circle and immediately lost consciousness also falling to his knees. The six agents left, observed the fall of two of their team, sensing danger, formed themselves into a circle back-to-back. They held up their guns and used the telescopic camera unit to look around the woods for any assailants. They could not be sure if the agents had been shot and didn't know what had happened.

The agents decided the priority was to storm the hut. They signalled to each other, the area directly in front of them was given the all clear. One-by-one, they turned towards the hut. One of the agents pulled out the radio control for the munition's robot. It rolled forward out of the interior of the forest. it had tank-like wheels and five arms. These types of units are used to deactivate munitions and bombs at close range. The unit rolled towards the hut, breaking small trees and bracken in its path as it rumbled by. The sound of the unit, in the stillness of the forest, stuck out. It had an industrial and mechanical sound that did not align to the environment, which was calm. The forest was still, waiting, holding its breath.

The unit had a plate at the front likened to that of a snow plough and it was this implement that the agents were intending to use as a battering ram to gain access to the hut. It took the unit a matter of seconds to break down the door and then the team were inside the hut. They swept the entire confines of the place and noticed that the ceiling appeared to have a drop-down hatch. Inside the hatch there was a very small office space which included a computer, wooden desk and matching chair. There was also a wooden futon with a feather-down mattress on top, the place had a rustic feel. The team homed in on the computer and checked for a USB portal. This was a very old computer with a disk drive and inside was a disk labelled The Tome of Herne. This was ejected and a call was placed to The Company HQ and orders were given to retrieve the disk and immediately bring it back to base.

Polly and the Tome of Herne

Chapter 9 Motives

Somewhere in New York

Miles Luxemburg sat in his minimalist office facing out onto the sprawling skyline of New York City, his office block overlooked central Park. Miles rarely looked at the view and he detested the mediocrity of central park, only coveted due to it being the only expanse of greenery in the city. Miles did not like NYC, what the locals called The Big Apple. It was too heavily populated for his liking, with too many hungry people trying to get to know him for an opportunity to play in the big leagues. He found the average person quite unfathomable. With their feelings, needs and insecurities; desires to be something that they were not. He related to technology more. Mathematics, equations, algorithms and data programming. The beautiful simplicity of building an algorithm that picked up on a person's preferences and then repeatedly exposed that person to their hearts desire. The programme would bombard the individual and in a moment of weakness when the person was tired or stressed or had been rejected in some way, 'WHAM' they would buy, buy, buy to get that dopamine hit that promised a chance of a better life for a second or too. Then they would chase the dopamine high FOREVER. Sweet simplicity itself and regulators were not equipped to understand the technology nor able to prove the intention behind it. It's simple really, its instilling addiction behaviours. People are familiar with substance addiction and abuse but they tend to have no idea that social media algorithms are instilling the same effect on the human body and creating the same set of behaviours. Tech junkies created en-masse and it was making billions for the elite.

Miles smirked to himself. It always baffled him why people never thought more about the motives behind technology or more accurately, about the characters of the people that were building advancements in technology and why they would be doing it. Critical thinking tended to be completely absent from most of the population in his view. He often thought that people were highly stupid. Miles observed people like humans look at monkeys in a zoo. He understood their basic needs but did not ever feel like he was part of the same species. Sure, he knew how to behave and act but he always felt like he did not understand social queues or interactions so preferred his own company and that of his inner circle of followers; they-being, like-minded people.

Miles grew up in a boarding school in England and this was paid for by his father under an assumed name. Miles being the illegitimate Son of a high-ranking member of German nobility who was of royal family lineage pre-1919. Miles and his all-American alcoholic show-girl mother were both well looked after financially but his father had not wanted anything more to do with him. Miles had contacted his father when he was a teenager and had made his first million through tech design only to be rejected coldly once again by the emotionally austere man. The nobleman had referred to him as 'new money' and common - Miles had built up a story in his head that his father would love him if he was a self-made man of fortune, something to be proud of. Sadly, he was mistaken and this incident had driven Mile's to become more self-sufficient and alone. He did not trust anyone and relied on power to sustain him. Miles had, had the last laugh though and he had made sure of that, personally.

His office and building in New York were a statement. He did not personally get any enjoyment from it. His estate agent was told to find an office that would make his clients realise just how powerful and rich he is by walking into the building and being sat down opposite his desk.

Everything in his world was about managing perception. The perception of social media that Miles and his inner circle perpetuated is that it is a technological platform with the aim of bringing people together and that a person could find a little piece of the internet that was a reflection of their own values and inner world. The truth was darker and less obvious. It is more of an cattle milking station for humans, where people connect to a global system and get placed on a conveyor belt while being distracted with shiny new things, celebrity culture – which triggers dopamine centres in the brain, and it goes unseen that algorithms are suctioning out and data mining to use the information to exploit the people connected. The sad truth is a person is being milked day in, day out of their money, their time, their opinions, their choices, of EVERYTHING.

Miles did not personally have access to social media himself. A successful drug dealer does not take their own product. You will find that most people who created social media don't use it at all. He paid others to manage his accounts for him. He knew how dangerous it was. Miles did not watch any television too. The human brain is constantly consuming information via the senses. The subtle messaging being conveyed was deliberately contradictory so one could not achieve the instructions, therefore are left always hungrily looking for answers. For example, be skinnier but eat more fast food and be more attractive but look natural. Miles' personal favourite was the one where they were sending out adverts to inform people that they needed to understand how to use the internet to build their own businesses which meant people would sit at their screens for hours at a time and this was followed by other adverts that encouraged people to lead a healthier, active lifestyle. This was about distraction so each person pays less attention to what is going on in their own community or inner world and what is happening to them. It is no coincidence that mental health and wellbeing issues are on the rise as is loneliness which is the number one public health risk of our time. Social media is a fool's game and he owned it – like the ultimate snake oil salesman.

Miles much preferred meeting with the Inner Circle and strategizing and planning. Most of the recent wars were of the inner circles making. Division created fear and isolation. Under these circumstances people are so much more easier to control. The Inner Circles view is that the real problem is that the planet is too overpopulated so the Inner Circle continues in the background to work out the ideal population size to continue to provide essential infrastructure and at the same time, support consumerism and enable recovery of part of the natural world so that the planet did not completely fall apart. The Inner Circle needed the planet and its resources for themselves.

Miles did not really care about animals, but he wanted the planet to still be in a position to support human life. He also was researching human longevity and transhumanism to unlock his own immortality. The inner circle had already determined which parts of the population would be deleted, it was the very poor people who could not afford to buy anything so were classified as non-consumers, they were using precious resources but were not considered by the Inner Circle to be a resource in of themselves which made them redundant. The Inner circle just needed to work out now how many needed to be deleted then they were going to release a virus that has been DNA sequenced to highly impact the specific populations identified. Miles sprawled out on his cashmere lined chair and leaning back, he smiled to himself knowing that all his efforts were for the greater good.   He was looking after the planet in a way.

Miles looked down at his phone when he received the message from his executive Director of operations. He was being informed that a disk had been found at Eleanora's hideout and it was conveyed to Miles that the disk was labelled as containing a reference to an object called the Tome of Herne. The Director explained that the disk was on its way back to the base in Worcestershire, England. The aim was to crack the password and then decode the disk to see what is on it. Miles explained to the Director in a high pitched, falsely nice voice that he had precisely two hours to open the disk.

At the other end of the call, the Directors face turned white and he looked ill at ease knowing the consequences if he failed to deliver. Miles then enquired politely who was going to crack the code. Miles softly explained that he only wanted a very trusted hacker on it. thinking to himself that this could be the missing piece of the puzzle in terms of understanding human longevity and surviving a climatic planetary emergency. He wanted the knowledge to remain in his control and if this information was to fall into the wrong hands, then the Inner Circle would be at the mercy of the individual who owned the information. Miles ended the call by waving his hand at the sensor and the screen displaying the face of his director went blank.

With one flick of his hand Vivaldi's The Four Seasons started to fill the room. Miles casually pressed a button to turn the windows opaque and got up from his desk. He walked over to the back whitewashed wall. His loafers made no noise on the marble tiled floor underfoot. He pushed a button on his phone and a secret door opened up that was concealed in the wall. Miles ducked inside and the door slid back into place. It was not easy to see the opening from the outside but inside, there was a huge door with a metal frame leading down to a set of galvanised stairs. Miles descended the two flights of stairs within seconds. He was obsessive about his fitness regime and nutrition and was at all times in prime physical health at the age of twenty-nine.

 At the end of the stairwell, was a glass box room and inside was the remains of the two-thousand-year-old woman. Miles had transported the skeleton to New York to be tested and assembled. He was then going to ship the skeleton back to the United Kingdom to be placed on display in his home. The bones fascinated him. He was mesmerised with wonder as to how the being had remained alive and in good health for so long. His scientists had speculated that the woman would have still been in prime health for many more centuries, but she had been attacked and killed shortly after childbirth. Miles touched the skeleton and wondered once again what the woman had looked like. He then went over to a glass cabinet which held part of a bronze dagger in it. This was the weapon that had killed the woman. It had strange symbols on it and engravings of what looked like stags and horned beasts. It was imbibed with a solution that was not recorded in any records on earth. The team of

123

scientists were trying to isolate a compound found in the woman's DNA plus they were following a similar method to extract the solution found on the blade.

Miles stood there feeling something like excitement. It was the first time in years of searching that he felt close to the means to extend human life or unlock the secrets to the homosapien gene structure. Remembering to himself that Eleanora had discovered something in the caves where the bones had been found and was scared enough by it to flee The Company and detonate the area. With a slight shiver of exhilaration, he realised that the hunt was now on to understand more about this Tome of Herne, which meant finding Eleanora and the girl displaying superhuman strength. With each step closer to his quarry, he would be closer to securing his immortality and he would stop at nothing until he possessed the key to extended life itself.

Toni's surprise

Sunday evening

Toni was at her family house getting ready for the last ceremony of the wedding. Maami had told her that all the women of her family were meeting at their home to perform a secret rite before the concluding ceremony this evening. With everyone there, there would be lots of laughter, eating and dancing. It made sense to Toni that her mum would be hosting the event as Maami was such a big part of her community. Helping people came naturally to her because she had such a good heart and loving nature. If people from the community were sick or they needed help or legal advice, they would come to see Maami and Papa first. They were both highly respected community leaders and she knew how lucky she was to have them as her role models and her parents.

Toni was getting dressed in a cobalt blue long dress. She had on a fresh long black natural hair weave. The dress, hair and dramatic eye makeup gave off an air of mystique. As Toni started putting the final touches of make-up on her beautiful face, she started wondering where her friends had gotten to over the last couple of days. Chris and Polly were spending a great deal of time together and she had noticed that quite a few strange incidents had occurred in quick succession. Toni immediately shook off this idea as soon as she had thought it. The unexplained made Toni feel weirdly uncomfortable but it was a little bit too familiar at the same time which caused her a bit of confusion. She concentrated on her two friends. With a smile on her face, she also could not help imagining scenes of Chris and Polly falling in love; looking at each other across a breakfast of croissant and beans on toast, gazing lovingly into each other's eyes and realising they had strong feelings for each other. She giggled to herself. The thought of the two of them having taken their friendship to the next level was just too funny.

This made Toni excited but also a bit fearful. She had known for a while that there was this awkward attraction between the two of them. If things didn't work out between them how would their friendship circle survive? She would try her best to put a stop to it and find Polly a boyfriend. These thoughts were interrupted by her Aunty Ola shouting up the stairs for her to come down. Aunty Ola had a booming voice that was like a gospel choir, all silky and smooth yet powerful on the crescendo. Aunty Ola was not Maami's real blood sister, but she was treated like family nonetheless. Maami and Ola had met as young girls in one of the boarding schools in Nigeria. Ola had been recently orphaned when they first met and Maami had befriended the sad and shy girl. They were steadfast friends and had grown up together and were inseparable. They were a dynamo of a team and even had their own secret way of communicating. 'Coming Aunty' Toni shouted down the stairs. It's a good thing they live in a detached house as their whole family and lifestyle was so colourful and loud that they would have surely driven any neighbours to distraction by now. Toni thought this to herself with a wide grin on her face. Her and her brother, Edmund, had so many Aunties, Uncles, cousins and distant relatives that birthdays and festive holidays were becoming really too expensive. It was lucky that her parents run a successful legal firm in the heart of London's business district and were generous with her allowance. 'Toni, stop daydreaming girl and get down these stairs' Aunty Ola was as kind as she was fierce, and she had clearly lost patience with Toni by now.

Toni slipped on her new studded Louboutin shoes courtesy of Maami's credit account at Selfridges, did a little twirl in her floor to ceiling mirror and then walked through the door, ready to greet the family guest's downstairs.

When Toni walked through the house, she was surprised at how quiet it was. This was in considering that four or five Aunties were in residence somewhere. Usually, there was hollering and whole lot of impromptu dancing, booming voices and very loud laughter. She typically could work out which room they were all gathered in from 300 metres outside of the house. Today was different. Today was quiet and a little sombre. The house was in darkness apart from large candles everywhere and there was a hush of whispering, piping throughout the house. Toni laughed aloud. Thinking to herself they were trying to scare her. She went to flick the light switch on, but it was not working. She tried one of the lamps and that too did not work. This was starting to make a little more sense now thought Toni nodding to herself. The Aunties and Maami were probably worried about the power cut and were being quiet while they were rushing to sort out candles and the electricity outage, preparing for the gathering.

 Toni quickly started to walk through the house, easily navigating her way in the darkness from a place of familiarity with her surroundings. At the end of the ground floor atrium, she could see that a light was on behind a door as a faint glow was coming from under the door in one of the side rooms, off of the hallway. This was in the back part of the house. Toni approached this room cautiously. The glow was now quite bright and was reflecting off of her dark brown eyes. She

126

carefully placed her hand on the doorknob. Her hesitancy was borne out of a deep-rooted behaviour that had been instilled in her from when she was a small child.

It was made very clear to her and her brother, Edmund, from a young age, that the rest of the house was theirs to roam freely apart from this room. This was their parents' inner sanctum. Toni and Edmund were very respectful of this instruction as their parents were kind, loving and caring people, yet Toni remembered this one day. The door had been left open and Toni had walked in on Maami acting in a strange way administering some sort of natural medicine or fluid to an older woman with arthritic knees and hips who was wheelchair bound. The woman was shaking and delirious while she was attempting to stand up and Maami was whispering words over her head with her eyes closed. She was holding a stick with feathers in it and feverishly swaying above the older woman. Toni remembers the stillness in the room, a reverence about the situation that could not be interrupted so Toni had closed the door and did not talk about what she had seen with anyone.

A week later, the woman and her daughter were in church. What was odd was that she had been able to walk with the aid of a stick and telling everyone she had a hip replacement on the NHS. The congregation rejoiced and sang in celebration of her ability to walk. The older woman kept turning to Maami in the middle of the melee, to give the sign of thanks, silently.

Toni was sixteen years old now and not a little girl anymore. She encouraged herself to look beyond her fear and the incident all those years ago and to open the door to the room. She could hear a humming of united voices from beyond the door and she turned the doorknob, walked in.

The sight that she beheld in the room, was confusing and familiar at the same time. All five of the aunties were formed into a circle and each one was positioned at the tips of a star drawn onto the earthen and uncovered floor.

Four of them each held in their hands a candle, a piece of reddish root and a rock encased within a small glass box. The faces of her aunties were bathed in light and they were wearing cloaks with hoods covering their hair. Underneath they wore vibrant dresses with Nigerian colourful prints. They swayed side to side to the rhythm of faint drumming. The drumming was coming from the fifth Aunty who held a small instrument in her hands and she tapped on it with two fingers. A large earthen clay pot was in the centre of the star and it had a lilac-coloured mixture bubbling in it. Toni's eyes widened in fear at the strange sight. None of her aunties had uttered a word to her since she had entered the room and this was making Toni feel ill at ease. Toni had expected the rite to be a little odd as some of the customs were strange and did not make a great deal of sense to her hybrid western sensibilities at times. The customs were handed down through generations, reflecting back to a different era of heritage and culture of which she willingly took part in for the sake of her community but tonight this was at another level.

'Don't be afraid, daughter of mine, this is your birth right' said Maami soothingly as she walked into the room wearing a paler version of the cloaks her aunties wore, with the hood up. It looked like linen or some sort of course, natural fibre. Maami was wearing a mask of clay painted in red and blue and she was carrying a wooden staff with an uncut and raw diamond on the tip. The mouthpiece of the mask was an open hole and there were symbols unfamiliar to Toni on it. Maami reached the centre of the star and placed the staff in a small groove carved out in the floor. It stood erect, glinting dully in the light of the candles. As soon as this action was done, the aunties started to hum louder with panting intermittently added into the song.

The beat of the drum was getting faster and louder and the swaying from side to side corresponded with the beat. The heat in the room was rising from the earth, scattered on the floor. 'Maa, where is the bride? When will she get here? What is happening?' Toni asked in a terrified voice. Silently, the four aunties placed the candles, the root and the earth on each point of the Star and the woman with the drum sat down at the fifth point with the drum between her legs. She started closing her eyes and drumming a sorrowful tune. The other aunties approached Toni and put a cloak around her neck and pulled up the hood all the while singing in a low guttural chant. Their eyes were luminous and looked cobalt blue in the strange light of the room. Maami walked towards her daughter and held out her hand to touch her cheek. She softly spoke these words.

'With these earth gifts that you are offered from your female ancestors you must promise to use them to help, support and empower those that cannot do for themselves. You are a guardian of the earth, of the wind, of the mountain and your roots will go deep into Her, The Earth Goddess. She will share power with you to heal, to share strength and look after her children but do not cross her ma sab as she is nature and nature is beautiful, but it is also chaos and treacherous. Do you accept these gifts?' Maami softly asked.

Toni looked perplexed. 'I-I-I don't understand, what do you mean gifts…. I don't understand what is happening.' Toni went to turn around to leave back through the door and the Aunties crowded round her. 'Toni' her Maami called softly. 'Listen to me, you have been a child who has loved to dress up and buy beautiful things for yourself, go to parties and have fun. Now is your chance to grow into the young woman you are meant to be. There is a gift that we take from helping others. To look after others and be a guardian of the earth as I have and other women before me. Do you accept these gifts, child?' Toni reflected on these words. Her Maami had always guided her. Given her excellent advice and shared her perspective with compassion when Toni was behaving from a place of self or ego. Toni did not know what the gifts entailed but if her Maami had accepted it then she would do too.

Toni slipped off her shoes, looking down at her feet for a while she resolved that whatever this was, she would embrace it with all of her heart. She lifted her chin defiantly and squared her shoulders and prepared to accept the gift wholeheartedly. She was still afraid but she was also resigned.

 Maami took her hand and laid her gently on the floor, near the centre of the star symbol. Maami and the Aunties began chanting together. The shadows in the room started spinning around the walls. Bubbles of white light flew out from the staff and orbs of red light flew out of the roots and the rocks placed on the floor. Amber coloured spheres were emitting from the drum.

The bubbles, orbs and spheres in a constant stream, floated into the air circling where Toni lay down rigid and then, they started landing on her. Joining her aura, being absorbed into her being. She was lit up, her soul could be seen in the centre of her body. Toni felt warm and with each absorption, she was getting hotter and hotter. She started to feel pain in her legs, her arms and her ribs and started to scream. Maami watched with tears in her eyes knowing the searing burns of the Rite too well. She felt all that Toni felt but was helpless to do anything but weep for the suffering of her daughter. Although the gifts were voluntary it was understood that if Maami's line did not accept them, then these would be offered to others who may not use them with altruistic intent as her family line had done through the centuries. She would explain this all to Toni at a later time. Toni would understand.

The young woman writhed in agony and she began to feel frightened like the spell would never end. She pried herself up off the floor against the invisible force that was holding her down. 'Stop' Maami said 'it is nearly over, don't break the Rite, we do not know what will happen'. Toni looked at her own mother and blinked back the hurt in her eyes and screamed 'how could you do this to me...........nooooooooooooo.' In her anger and rage she became wrath embodied and ripped away from the invisible bond that held her to the floor, with the ferocity of her own power. The last remaining spectral orbs and spheres that were floating in the air, popped out of existence. The Aunties were crying and screaming in distress. Toni ran for the door and was too quick for the others to stop her. She ran out of the house and was running barefoot, to Polly.

Chapter 10 The lies we are told.

Monday at dawn

It was the early hours of Monday morning, when Toni walked through the front gate of Polly's house. There was a chill wind in the air, but Toni did not notice it nor feel it fully. She was burning with anger inside at her Maami and Aunties. Her eyes were opaque and black. How could they have treated her this way? They had led her to believe that the gathering was a part of the wedding celebrations when really, they planned to do something to her. Toni was very hurt and angry at her family, they were usually so good and kind, why would they conspire to do this to her? She hid her sadness behind confusion and anger. Toni thought to herself that she had not seen any ropes, but she knew she had been tied up and held down to the floor while weird objects were sort of thrown at her by someone in the room. What was Maami thinking and what gifts was she talking about? There was nothing in the room apart from the staff, rocks and manky old roots. She thought to herself that probably the gift was of womanhood or something metaphorical like that. It all made her feel uncomfortable and scared, she still had so many questions like would they do it again if she tried to return home? Sometimes, and this was one of those times, she felt like tradition was more important than her.

Toni's phone vibrated in her clutch bag. It was Maami again and Toni was so angry, she clicked the end call button and switched her phone off entirely. She refused to talk to her Maami right now. Toni was so fixated on her thoughts that she was not paying attention to her surroundings. There were two people dressed head to toe in black following her. They had gotten silently out of a van parked at the end of the street and followed her to the front of the house. They were now crouched down and were hidden behind the panelled fencing of the house and from view.

Toni stood outside the front door and cursed under her breath knowing she would need to turn back on her phone to call Polly to open the door. She could not very well knock on the door this early and risk waking up Mother. She called and a very alert Polly answered the phone on the first ring which threw Toni off slightly. 'What are you doing awake at this time? Listen, can I crash at yours please I'm standing outside your front door. It's a long story.' Toni said suddenly feeling overwhelmed and exhausted. A light went on in the hallway and Chris came out of the door. He didn't immediately greet Toni at first. He was dressed in camouflage combat gear, a tight technical all-weather hoodie and black trainers. He leant over Toni and looked both ways up and down the street then he took her by the shoulder and drew her in for a hug, bringing her into the hallway at the same time.

Breaking away from his arms, she started asking him lots of questions like why he was here and why he was dressed like a soldier because 'it isn't Halloween'. Chris placed his finger to his lips and pointed upstairs shaking his head. This was the universal language for signalling 'be quiet, parents asleep upstairs. Chris caught a glimpse of Toni's blackness of eyes and took a double take. Toni recoiled, fell quiet and followed him to the living area. Polly was in the room. She was focussed on looking out of the front window and she seemed to be visually sweeping the street. She was also dressed up in tight fitting black combat gear, like a ninja. Toni looked down at her dress and shoeless feet and suddenly felt out of place. However, on seeing her friend, her darkness disappeared and the blackness in her eyes faded returning the iris to warm brown.

'Erm, Hi Pol pol. Why are you guys dressed like that?' She leaned forward and hugged her friend. 'Hi T, what's up? Why are you here this late? Hey, you feel really cold' Polly said, rubbing her friend's arms vigorously to warm her up. 'I'll go and get you some clothes. Stay here.' Chris leaned forward and raised his eyebrows at Polly. 'I think I saw two people crawling alongside the front fence, but I can't be 100% sure. It's pretty dark outside.' Chris puffed out his cheeks and sighed. He rubbed his eyes hoping to slow down his need for sleep.

'Wait, what?' Toni said, suddenly alarmed and dashing to the window. Polly left the room. Toni looked round the room and noticed the signs that her friends were about to leave. There were two holdalls on the floor and some rope and duct tape, three gallons of bottled water and camping equipment. She also noticed a small suitcase with Mothers initials on it. Toni was getting upset. She had seen the items and assumed that Polly and Chris were getting ready to go on holiday without her. 'So, you guys are going on holiday and were you planning on telling me before or after you arrived?' Toni looked livid and ended with adding an accusatory 'Are you guys dating?'.

Chris started blushing and he tried to explain and quickly realised however he explained it, it would sound unreal. He opened and closed his mouth a few times and cleared his throat 'well, the thing is…. 'Polly entered the room. 'The thing is Toni, we are in trouble. We don't have time to explain it right now because it would take too long but we will as soon as we can but it's going to sound unbelievable in all fairness to you. In short, Mother is unwell and we need to get her to a specialist and we think someone is outside and they want to get in to hurt us really bad and may even try to kill us. Can you get dressed and go home where it's safe and leave through the back?' Polly said this in a very matter of fact and forthright way. Toni's eyes brimmed with tears. How could she explain that home was not very safe for her right now and those that she trusted the most wanted to hurt her.

'The thing is I need to tell you guys some stuff and it's unreal too. if there are people outside who want to hurt you then let's face it, they have already seen me coming in here which means I'm in this with the two of you' Toni let out a long-exhaled breath, blinked back her tears and then went on 'I'm going to get changed and when I get

134

back, we're going over the plan together. Oh, and there better be a sleeping bag in there for me too.' With that Toni flicked her hair and walked out of the room. Leaving Polly in complete admiration of the courageousness of her friend.

When Toni came back in, Polly and Chris went over the plan to exit the house. Polly was going to cause a distraction at the rear of the building by letting off firecrackers in the bins, tipping them over while Chris, who recently passed his driving test, 'first time' he will add whenever anyone asks, will crawl out of the front and start the car, moving it from the driveway into the street. His satellite navigation system on his phone was pre-set for Glossop and Polly would run to the car with Chris and everyone else already inside. Toni gave out a whistle. 'It's a good plan, it's a bit flawed though. Like how we are going to get Mother out of the door and into a car when she is unconscious?' Toni said this while pointing at Mother lying horizontally on the sofa. 'Well, you see....' Chris started to explain. Toni held up her hand 'I have not finished with my questions.'   She said to Chris who replied with a broad smile as he was quite amused with the conversation 'oh, do please continue' he said. She cleared her throat and carried on 'how will Polly get to the end of the street within a couple of minutes. That's impossible.' This is what Chris had been waiting for. He turned to Polly. 'I can do it' is all Polly volunteered with unshakeable confidence. Toni looked at her friend and laughed. 'Well, okay then. Let's do this thing' she said excitedly, clapping her hands together.

Chris heaved Mother onto his shoulder and started carrying her towards the door. Mother started groaning restlessly and Toni laid her hand on her forehead to see if she had a temperature. Toni felt her hand warming, but it was not from a temperature it was coming from within Toni herself.   Mother gave out a blissful sigh, she instantly relaxed and went back to sleep. Toni kept looking at her hand and shaking it - it was tingling with energy. Polly walked into the hallway and synchronised watches with Chris. They had given Polly a minute to set off the firecrackers then Chris would have two minutes to get into the car and onto the street and meet Polly at the end of the road. Chris would carry Mother and Toni was loaded up with the equipment, ready to go.

Polly nodded to indicate that she was going to start the countdown. She told them to take care and be careful before saying 'three, two, one' and she was off running to the back of the house. Chris and Toni watched with amazement at the speed of her run. Within seconds they heard the bins explode. Chris unlocked the door and headed for the black range rover on the driveway. He crouched low with Mother on his back. The car beeped and flashed with its front mirrors unfolding in response to Chris pressing the unlocking mechanism. They had not accounted for this and the plan felt like it was slipping into chaos. Chris ran forward, opened the back door, placing Mother inside and jumped in the driving seat. Toni ran to the boot and flung in the equipment. She was still holding one of the bottles when an Agent came up from behind and grabbed her arm. Toni reacted quickly and flung the agent over her shoulder and onto the ground. She swung the bottled water round and hit him, then punched the agent twice to stun and then disengaged. She ran round to the back of the car and got in besides Mother 'drive, drive, they are out the front' she frantically urged Chris.

He pulled the car out of the driveway at speed, it screeched as it turned onto the street. He accelerated to the end of the road and kept going at high speed. Polly was running alongside the vehicle then jumped and somersaulted onto the roof of the car, effortlessly. All the while, Toni was watching her in disbelief. She rubbed her eyes to check she was not imagining things. There was a bang on the roof like something heavy had landed on top of it, which indicated that Polly was above them as planned. Chris used the controls on the steering wheel to roll down the passenger window and banged on the roof three times. Polly flipped into her seat through the window and

Chris sped away, heading towards the motorway with the satnav issuing instructions via google maps.

Toni looked at her friend and said with a sly smile on her face 'it looks like you have a lot of explaining to do so you may as well get started'. They all laughed, giddy with the excitement of the execution of their plan and exhilarated to be finally on the move, onto the next part of their adventure together.

The Company Agents watched the range rover pull away. Their van was down the street and they were in no hurry to catch up with Polly and her friends for now. They casually got into the van and then called in to Central control to request access to the satellite navigation system that the range rover was using. The agent turned to his companion. 'Looks like we are on our way to Glossop. Buckle up your seat belt.'

The ride was smooth onto the motorway. It was the first time that Chris had driven on one, but he took to it with remarkable ease. He understood the theory of motorway driving and the seamless flow required; speeding up to overtake a lorry and easing up off the accelerator and every now and then topping it up to remain at a consistent speed. He was in the rhythm of motorway driving, so was not very talkative. He contributed here and there as Polly explained the events of the last few days. Toni burst out laughing occasionally waiting for the others to do so too and when they didn't, she fell back into silence knowing what she had heard was not a joke. Her friend really did have superpowers and she herself had witnessed that there were people out to kill them. Toni asked 'yeah, but why? Why do you suddenly have superpowers? What's it for? These things don't just happen for no reason' all three of the friends sat there in silence, exploring the question in their own separate ways.

Toni smoothed Mothers blanket when Polly got to the part of accidentally putting a spell on Mother and taking control of her free will. Toni felt sorry for the older woman even though she was not a very nice person. Toni knew how very awful it felt having a spell put on you unawares was. Toni realised that this is what Maami and her aunties had been trying to do. She was now too tired to ask any questions or share her own experience. She rested her head on the armrest and fell into a troubled sleep next to Mother. Polly rested her eyes and fell into a dreamless sleep too.

Chris put on the radio. They had been driving for three hours now so should arrive in another forty-five minutes or so. The Lady Cadmun-Herne was easy to find on the internet and social media. She was not a Lady at all; she was in fact a Duchess or The Duchess of Derbyshire but some of her family's lands had been sold off and she preferred to be referred to as Lady Herne of Herne Hall anyway. Her family line had held the title for a very long time and from what Chris's research had turned up, was that there had been a Herne family or Clan of renown in the area pre-roman times which was remarkable. The Cadmun-Herne family's wealth was amassed through farming, trade, steel and precious metals and minerals and then they had diversified their portfolio into investments and global property markets and loans at the turn of the century.

Lady Cadman-Herne's Grandmother had started a private boarding school on the estate. Pupils and scholars were identified by the school rather than applying. What was odd was that as much as he searched, Chris had not been able to find out how the pupils and scholars were selected. He had surmised that local surrounding schools would be approached for nominations or scholarships but this was only a guess at best. This intrigued him a lot. How were the children identified and why was it kept secret. The Lady had also started up a Charity to preserve the Peak District and Derbyshire in its natural state and support its ecosystem, she had included the school in the site and had instated herself as Protector in Chief of Derbyshire and the peak district and the British Government had acknowledged this title. The Lady regularly held fundraising events in major cities such as London, Edinburgh, Derbyshire, Dublin, New

York, Los Angeles, Paris, Munich and Switzerland. She had a son, Raphe of Herne who had been very ill and had not been seen in years.

The last leg of the journey was through luscious green and bountiful countryside and the views were breath taking. The wooded areas were dense and emerald green with sun lit tinges of amber, from the late afternoon rays. There were river dales and lime gorges set within the landscape. The whole of the counties surrounding the peak district were picturesque. Driving through the winding lanes, Chris could have sworn that he caught sight of a golden eagle flying into the trees. He had to stop himself from swerving off the road and parking to get a closer look. Polly woke up as they were slowing down and nearing the first set of gilded entrance gates to Herne Hall.

They had passed the area that hosted Kinder Scout and were now coming through to Glossop. It was still light and bright, but Chris was feeling tired having had to concentrate all of his attention for the last four hours as he was still a relatively new driver. Chris pulled up outside the three-metre-tall gate that was held by a limestone wall. He got out of the car to look for some sort of intercom device. Polly shouted to him that she was getting out of the car to help, when the gates made a creaking sound and slowly started to open. Chris thought to himself that he must have tripped a sensor but the gates opened for Polly. The stately home was still quite far away so he resigned to look out for the cameras.

A pair of ospreys flew behind the car and seemed to be following them along the lane that led up to the main building. The landscape was rugged and wild but also well-tended. There were stags, deer and wild ponies grazing in different areas quite accustomed to seeing vehicles in their territory. Great oak trees lined the lane and there were batches of wildflowers alongside more manicured and tended areas and rose gardens. It was an impressive sprawling sight to behold. Herne Hall itself was a stately home of Pembrokeshire stone and was the size of a small castle. To the right of it was a smaller less grand stately home that Chris guessed was the school. Both buildings had flags raised and family emblems carved above the huge wooden entrance ways. The coats of arms portrayed a huge stag surrounded by roses on one side and the other was a majestic looking sword.

Toni woke up with a start as the vehicle pulled up to a semi-circle of flood lights that were there to light up the battlements and statues on the outside of the grand house's exterior walls. Mother started murmuring and crinkling her brow and, in her delirium, kept repeating the word 'sorceress'. Toni had a cold sickness in her stomach that could be hunger or something else, like foreboding.

A slight woman dressed in a tweed coat and matching skirt, with serious looking leather walking boots, that were highly polished and gleaming, descended the stone steps. She strode down to where the car was parked, with the engine still running. She smiled at the group and approached the driver's side. 'Hello, I hope you had a pleasant journey. You will want to freshen up and then you will be taken to the Grand Hall for something to eat. Lady Cadmun-Herne will receive you before dinner. She is waiting.' Without another word, the woman turned on her heel and with a range of different signals, ushered some of the household workforce to attend to the luggage and help the group with their things inside. One of the hand signals had clearly communicated to help Mother, as a wheelchair was brought over to the vehicle and Mother was gently lifted into it and whisked away.

Polly jumped out of the vehicle as Chris cut the engine and put on the handbrake, he then followed Polly and did the same thing. Polly caught up with the wheelchair and stood in front of it not letting anyone pass. 'Hello dear, my name is Dr Carmichael and The Lady Herne asked me to look after your mother. She will be in the room next door to your own. Pop through to see us when you come upstairs.' said the doctor. He rather sternly took the handles of the wheelchair and navigated his way around Polly and into the building leaving Polly, Chris and Toni standing on the steps outside.

140

The agents were about twenty-five minutes behind them but closing fast. They reached the borders of Kinder Scout then the tracking equipment started going haywire and the coordinates changed, meaning that they started driving in the opposite direction. Each agent was repeating the words 'St Ives in Cornwall' and they had faint green light covering their eyes. The agent in the control room called through to the team as he noticed the change in direction but as he connected to them; a pale green light seeped from his microphone into his mouth and his eyes started to glow. 'St Ives in Cornwall' he murmured and he deleted the notes he recently made on his case file.

An hour later the trio were being escorted to the Grand Hall by a butler. Polly and Toni had been given silk pyjamas to wear with belts and shoes and Chris had been given a black evening suit with a beautiful silk shirt and Italian butter-soft leather shoes. His hair was in ringlets and Toni whistled when she saw him. 'Someone looks swish and dapper' called out Toni. Chris looked at Polly and winked. Polly got all flustered and Toni could not help but notice her blushing so she decided to leave that conversation there for now, but she would be picking this up some time soon with her friend.

They were escorted to a wide and very high-ceilinged hall. It had a number of marble statues of human size in various laying, kneeling and standing positions and each of these statues were mounted onto a solid slab of marble. There were four fireplaces in the cavernous Hall and each of which a person could stand up in. It took them a while to walk across the vastness of the space to where The Lady sat in wait on a raised platform of marble stairs due to the number of things to look at in the space. Many years ago, this was probably used as a banqueting suite and ballroom hosting royalty and nobility as it was simply magnificent to behold. The friends were in awe of their surroundings and each one of them was distracted and studying different objects and parts of the hall, when a booming and very clear voice rang out through the space.

'Now, please do step forward and introduce yourselves or I shall have no alternative but to think you quite rude. You have kept me waiting quite long enough I would say.' Polly, Toni and Chris quickly walked over to the person sitting in a high-backed chair. She was an older woman. Her hair was white and cut into a bob that emphasised her strong features. She looked quick witted and sharp. She was dressed in a Chanel boucle suit in a beautiful shade of magenta with black borders. The buttons were glass and she paired this outfit with a three-string necklace of pearls with matching earrings. Her shoes were of a similar fabric with a diamante buckle at the tip. The overall effect was one of exquisite splendour. She was groomed to perfection and dressed by her team of stylists. Physically, The Lady was very slender yet strong looking. Chris and Toni introduced themselves one at a time and The Lady nodded courteously at each of them. When Polly introduced herself, a strange look crossed The Lady's face and she seemed to lose her composure for a microsecond. She looked quite excited to see Polly and her eyes changed to become quite wide and wild looking. The wind outside responded to her shift in emotional state and started to batter the leaden panelled windows then died down when she regained her composure.

She curtly nodded. 'I am the Lady Cadmun-Herne, I am the crowned Protector of the Forest, and this is my land. While you are here with me you will be safe from all outside influences. To protect these lands, I have placed a spell on the whole site and be warned that time behaves differently here so please keep this in mind. It has bearing when you leave this place. What seems like days here will mean that months have passed in the outside world. It is a sanctuary and safe haven from the world outside. Please do ensure to make arrangements with your schools and contact loved ones so they are not alarmed or report you missing. This draws too much attention' The trio of friends made a note of this. Polly would not need to bother as Mother was with them and she doubted very much that Father would care or miss them. Chris would call his father and Toni her

Mother, to advise that they will be spending the summer at a camp in Glossop. They were sure to be helped with magic should the need arise.

The Lady continued 'You will feast on organic home-grown fruits, vegetables, fungi, nuts, legumes, herbs and seeds. We do not feast on flesh unless it is organically given through the death of an animal. You need not worry; you will not go hungry as our tables are bountiful. We do use animal by- products such as eggs, milk, honey and whatnot. You will eat and sleep well tonight then Polly you will begin your training in the morning.'

With that the Lady flicked her hand and a butler stepped out from behind a stone column hung with velvet folds. 'Please do follow me. The Lady has set a sumptuous menu for you that is quite a treat.' the Butler reassured.   They walked single file from the room and into the dining hall. Upon her exit, Polly turned to look at the Lady and was met by a face of hawkish eagerness, and the Lady seemed to be coveting Polly's presence and hiding something from her.

When she was sure that Polly had left the hall, The Lady stretched her legs out and stood up making her way languidly over to a small stone basin. She slowly and quite deliberately waved her hand three times over the clear water within it. She was searching for answers from the crystal-clear water from the lakes on her land – these had potent magical qualities. She asked if Polly had all the items needed for the spell with her and the stone bowl turned murky. She could not see. There was something blocking her vision. The Lady sighed and thought to herself that she would have to do it the old-fashioned way and break into the girl's room. She squeezed the sides of her nose and closed her eyes; she was tired and needed the power to revive her. She lifted her head and caught Radley the Butlers gaze. She nodded to him and psychically instructed him to search the rooms.

Polly and the Tome of Herne

Chapter 11 - A warrior's power

Tuesday

There was a lot of food, drink, laughter and talking long into the night. The friends enjoyed their surroundings and felt at ease to take their time to inform Toni of the strange happenings and occurrences over the last few days. The Lady had been absent from the frivolities, excusing herself due to organising an event taking place soon.

The next day Polly, Chris and Toni were feeling tired. They sat quietly in the morning room and filled up on coffee, pastries and bacon sandwiches from the buffet laid out on one of the side tables, served in the finest of silverware. The room they breakfasted in was decorated tastefully in different shades of pink and cream. It was a very light and airy space with large windows that overlooked the rose gardens. They had arrived at 10:00AM unable to get up any earlier as the queen-sized beds in their rooms were ever so comfortable. The conversation was stilted. All that could be heard was the gentle clinking of cutlery on fine china plates and bird song blowing in from the garden. Polly sat at the table looking at a map of the grounds and Toni was looking out of the window admiring the manicured garden, while Chris was helping himself to another bacon sandwich. All of a sudden, a bell rang in the grounds and about a dozen young people between the ages of eleven to eighteen years old came out of the school doors and down the steps walking onto the grassed area adjacent to the main part of the manor house.

Polly and Chris ran to the window to see what the commotion was about. An adult was with the young people; an older gentleman with grey hair who was tall and portly. He was wearing corduroy trousers and a plain rather sensible cotton shirt. A whistle screeched through the air that he had blown and the students organised themselves into two rows facing each other and at an arm's length distance between them. The teacher placed an everyday item in front of each student, such as a football, an apple and other mundane objects. A couple of people had hats or shoes. The teacher walked along the lines, nodding at the students and then took his place at the top end of the rows and blew the whistle again. Nothing happened at first, but the students' eyes were transfixed on the objects placed four feet in front of them. Some of the objects started to glow and a couple glimmered and some slowly evaporated. Some were fading and temporal looking, like they were there but also not there sitting between two dimensions. Polly was fascinated. She guessed that this was a lesson of some kind in using their powers. 'Let's go downstairs and see this up close.' Polly did not wait for an answer, she hurried out of the room eager to join and find out more about magic.

Polly ran all the way downstairs and over to the teacher, quite forgetting her super speed was on display. The students all gasped in amazement and a general murmur of excitement spread through the crowd. 'Well, well, hello Polly I assume? I'm Professor Rothchild and I'm the head teacher of the Herne House Academy.' Professor Rothchild explained beaming with pride. Polly was amazed that he knew who she was. He tapped his head 'can read thoughts and, in all truth, the lady has been watching you for some time, making sure you are kept......... safe, I would say' there was something not quite right about the way this was said. Polly doubted the safe part for some reason and it seemed so did the Professor. Her senses started tingling and it put her on high alert.

'The Lady has powers of the Earth and her ancestors founded this academy for children with powers like yours and mine, many years ago', said the Professor proudly, 'Some interesting facts for you, we have a curriculum of magic and, some lessons that meet the United Kingdom's educational statutory requirements, for appearances sake, you see. We produce a set of SAT scores for the students, but the majority will go on to be employed within the magical communities around the world or into politics. That's where we are focussing our energies at the moment' Polly shifted uneasily at this point. It sounded all very planned and strategic. She was wondering if there was an end goal in mind. 'The students are sorted into classes by their primary magical abilities, and these are aligned to the principles of the four elements; earth, fire, air and water.'

He pointed to a teenage boy and waved him forward. 'Edward, this is Polly. Please share your gifts if you will. A demonstration would be helpful' The boy straightened up with a happy smile on his face that he had been chosen. He started moving his hands in a circle. A few sparks flickered in the centre of the circle and a fiery orb burst into life. He carried on rotating his hands round the orbs edges. As he was doing this, he was pulling at the margins to make them bigger and bigger. He lifted it in the air and then threw it a long distance and it burst into flames, scorching the grass beneath where it landed. A girl then stepped forward. Holding out her arms above her, she summoned the clouds and they became heavy, swollen and dark with torrential rain which down poured, putting the fire out. Edward looked over at the girl and gave a tight smile not of thanks but of displeasure and then his languid gaze landed on Polly. He pointed at her. 'Well, Sir, what can she do?'

'I'm not sure Edward, but I believe we are about to find out' The Professor announced with a chortle.

Polly then followed the group to a much bigger part of the estate grounds nearest to the forest. There was a lake to the side, glistening in the the heat of the day, and what appeared to be some kind of assault course in the centre of a huge expanse of mown and flattened grass. Chris and Toni had arrived and asked Polly what was happening. 'I think we are about to find out a bit more about my powers,' Polly explained rather excitely.

'Right, Polly there are eight parts of this obstacle course, each one is designed to test a core component of your magic. There are magical objects that have been set up in each section and these have spells on them that will automatically trigger your powers to show. Students tend to have one or two core powers, meaning their strongest power where they can perform significant feats and their other power is usually smaller and less significant. It usually balances the primary power in some way. Take Edward here, he can conjure fire and direct it and his secondary power is the ability to conjure ice. To put out the fire if needed. These gifts are balanced and exaggerated parts of nature itself. I can't read minds per se. I read thoughts and intentions like dolphins have sonar. I pick up signals and my balancing magical skill, what we call the secondary power, is to encourage unconsciousness in others and I've performed it on myself by accident on occasion, you see?' Professor Rothchild said with a chuckle looking round at the children and the students laughed knowingly back, remembering their own accidents. 'Erm, not really, It's all new. I do have a few questions......what......' Polly fumbled on, unsure. 'Great, let's get started', Professor Rothschild said, motioning her forward. Polly sighed and stepped onto the flattened grass. Chris gave her two thumbs up and Toni kind of smiled in an unsure, but attempting to be encouraging, kind of way. Polly blew out her breath and inhaled in very deeply trying to concentrate.

Then it began, Polly walked forward into a single square patch of long grass. The atmosphere changed, it felt ionised and charged with static electricity, her hair stood up on end. There was a rippling giggle from the crowd outside the force field. She could hear them but only faintly. There was a copper rod in the centre of the ground. 'Lift your hands' she heard the students shouting in the distance. She lifted her hands and a huge stream of a lightning bolt shot out of them and connected to the rod. It was frightening, the sheer volume and power of the energy she was projecting. It was crackling and vibrating so loudly that she wanted to cover her ears and she could no longer hear any noises outside – only the crackling of the beam. It was deafening. Polly put her hands down and immediately disconnected the lightning surge. She looked over at the group gathered round. They were all standing there in silence, with terrified and confused looks across their faces. They had not seen this type of power before. The Professor looked concerned, but then he started waving her on. 'So, your primary power is lightning,' shouted Professor Rothchild with a tremor in his voice.

She stepped out of the long grass and onto the next area. The floor was covered in transparent tiles that hovered off of the ground and swayed. There was a great big fountain of water. She lifted her hands once again and fire balls as big as watermelons shot out of them this time and she threw them into the water. They hissed and evaporated in clouds of steam. She summoned the fire again and this time she held onto it to change its shape, it shot out of her hands in a stream like molten lava. She put her hands down and it stopped. 'This is unusual. The secondary power isn't usually equal to the primary.' shouted the Professor, his face scrunched up in confusion. 'Carry on Polly. The rest of the course should be quite uneventful as most people only have two significantly stronger powers.' The Professor offered encouragement but his faced belied this as he continued to look deeply concerned.

Polly stepped out onto a grassed area and there she raised her hands for the third time, this time, wind as strong as a tornado shot from her hands. The sky overhead darkened and the breeze picked up, and changed to a hurricane like gale, shooting all the way round and into other parts of the assault course. Polly was knocked off of her feet, she had not been expecting anything to happen this time because the Professor had been sure that there would only be a primary and secondary power. Without thinking, she turned towards the group standing on the side-lines. They were looking surprised, but some looked scared and terrified. She forgot to lower her hands in the confusion and knocked some of the children to the ground. Cyclones slipped from her fingers and were free-wheeling, heading towards the group and Polly did not know how to stop them. People started screaming and shouting and, in their fear, started running away. Quickly lowering her hands, she burst into tears, realising she had hurt one of the teenagers quite badly. Polly wanted to get away, so she ran in the opposite direction to the group and ran through the centre of the obstacle course. Professor Rothchild, firstly, made the cyclones disappear and then called for the healers. All the while, he watched Polly as she went through the course. He counted all the powers she displayed as she ran through each section of the course, in turn, and to his surprise, she had all eight powers in equal measure.

Professor Rothchild had summoned the school healer who immediately started using her powers to mend one of the student's broken arm. The healer could feel someone's energy behind her and turned to see Toni standing there. The healer sensed in Toni her healing powers and asked her to awaken it to help her calm the students.

Toni felt this unreal sensation, likened to a dream but instinctively knew what to do. She placed her hands on one of the students' grazed legs and summoned warmth from her inner core into the child's knee. The grazes and cuts started to bond together and heal, and Toni felt immensely happy and connected to the true essence of herself, the student and the energy of everything. Professor Rothschild was watching Toni and he could not quite believe what he was seeing. Toni had not shown any sign of magic through her aura over the years. Lady Cadmun-Herne had been watching Polly but here was Toni and she was displaying witchcraft powers. Now, he wondered what else she could do. He thought to himself that he would investigate that later. He wanted to find Polly and test out the rest of her powers with her. She would need a guardian to train and help her and he was intending for that guardian to be him. He cared for the girl.

He found Polly sometime later curled up and cradled at the bottom of a yew tree. She had been crying and her sobs could be heard in this part of the forest. It was dense and dank in here, where the trees grew closer together and the canopy was heavy with very little natural light. It was warmer and there was a lingering smell of decomposing vegetation and it was very earthy and organic; left untouched for hundreds of years. There were also more insects and more burrows than in other parts of the forest. A stream ran through the centre and the sound of the tinkling and babbling water bounced off and around the trees. Polly felt safe here. Cocooned in this environment. 'Polly, it's okay. You are in shock. I should not have pushed you and for that, I am sorry.' Polly slowly sat up and rubbed her red eyes. 'Please do not be upset and scared of your powers. They are a part of you and you will learn to use them. They are nothing to be ashamed of. In fact, I would call them wonderful gifts and you my girl will use these gifts to help others, of that I am absolutely sure of.' Polly wiped her tears away and smiled.

Professor Rothschild held out his arms. Polly hesitated then drew closer and allowed him to hug her – it felt strange to her being comforted by an adult, something she was not used to. Polly remained tense but was starting to calm down with the goodness of the Professors intentions. After a while, Polly let go and stood up. She took a deep breath, sighed and then began talking 'When I was running through the obstacle course, I could sense something like all of my powers, I think. It was strange like I had layer upon layer of different powers inside of me trying to get out. When I thought of each layer, I could sense the essence and core of the magic within.' Polly looked up, seeking out Professor Rothschild eyes for a reaction. He nodded, agreeing this sounded about right. 'Go on, ' he gently encouraged. 'I know I have fire, lightning, wind, water, speed, strength, mind powers and...' Polly fumbled to articulate it 'I think I have some sort of power to change gravity or something. I can jump and sort of fly, but it feels more like gravity releases me more than anything else' Polly ventured thoughtfully. 'Very good Polly. Yes, I think you are right. You see certain individuals are born with gifts that are exaggerated forms of nature locked in our DNA. They are a gift from the Goddess Gaia, mother of all things. A small number of people are given all eight powers to use at a time of significant peril to protect what she holds most dear, which is life and existence itself and the connecting energy of the universe. The miracle of being part of this amazing universe.' The Professor moved his hand around to indicate the forest and all things 'You seem to have all eight gifts and this is extremely rare. I think you may be one of the warriors of the Goddess that I have read about and there is recorded magical history about this. The chosen warriors are gifted immense powers when the earth needs it most in times of great crisis. A chosen one comes forth.'

Polly stepped back in shock. This was too big to contemplate, so she started with smaller questions first. 'If the chosen one is given these gifts to protect life, then what are we protecting it from?' Polly asked, quite taken aback by the deepness of this conversation and the wonder of the revelation of the existence of a Goddess. To Polly this did not seem too far beyond her thoughts on the universe and the magic within it. It was easy for her to understand. It was like she had always known but had just forgotten.

'Well, everything is in balance and perfectly designed, Polly you see and when the natural order of things is out of balance then a type of universal turmoil grows and energy becomes confused and chaotic; primal. It vibrates erratically waiting for change and evolution to move beyond this shift in energy. This time is dangerous, it can lead to evil things growing in strength and humans who have become too dark, become more powerful. Gorging on the chaos' The Professor sighed and continued on 'Hungry to harness this chaotic and unstable energy for themselves. For every one of us with powers from the Goddess, there are an equal number of evil things, demons and people who just want to watch others suffer under their cruelty and spite. They have no love for nature or the positive energy of the universe and want to destroy it. The pull of power is too alluring to the weak and selfish, I'm afraid.' The Professor looked round at Polly and she was deep in thought reflecting on all of the cruel people that she had come across in her short life.

The Professor gazed at Polly 'anyway, that's enough for now, we are still in the daylight and we should only talk of such dark things when we have to. We can learn about all of this as part of your training. What do you want to do now, Polly?' He asked. 'I want to use my gifts to help people starting with Gracie. I want to save her first.'

Professor Rothchild nodded and smiled 'very well, Polly but first I want to teach you something. How to conjure and direct your powers. When you were running through the obstacle course, I noticed that your necklace was glowing. I believe your necklace can be used as a conduit to channel your powers until your mind is more honed to using them. It will also help you to not let your emotions take over your magic. Here, let me show you.' The Professor placed one of Polly's hands on her necklace and the other hand he turned over, so the palm was facing up. 'Now, Polly, suggest to your necklace that you need a tiny flame of fire in your palm and hold that in your mind. Go on, do not be afraid of your powers. They are a part of you. They are you. Befriend them. Get to know them and cherish every part of you.' encouraged the Professor. 'Even the dark places?' Polly asked, looking petrified. 'My dearest Polly, especially the dark places' The Professor said very seriously.

Polly closed her eyes and focussed. A warmth spread from her heart down her arm and a flame appeared in her hand. The flame flickered in the dark place within the forest and reflected off of Polly's and Professor Rothchild's glassy eyes. They both gazed at the flame like it was a newborn baby, inspiring hope and dreams. 'This is only the beginning' The Professor uttered quietly and in amazement – it was a beautiful moment to behold, shared by the two of them.

A while later, Polly and Professor Rothchild entered the stately house and Polly went to find Chris and Toni in the guest bedroom suites. She had formed a plan with Professor Rothchild to rescue Gracie. One of the students could conjure portals and connect two spaces bringing them back-to-back so Polly was planning on opening a portal between the stately home and the Premiere compound where Gracie was being held. They had found her with a locator spell. The students' powers were still being explored with her but she had been able to accurately open a portal within 20 yards of an identified location, of late. Polly would slip in, rescue Gracie and then jump back into the portal with her. It was a simple plan.

They would then place a spell on Gracie to wipe her memory and return her home while also placing a protection spell on her. Professor Rothchild would arrange the memory charm and protection spell while Polly was rescuing Gracie. He had all the ingredients in his library, so he was off to prepare the mind-altering spell and the protection one too.

Polly bounded up the stairs and found Toni and Chris in Polly's room. They looked tense and worried when she entered. 'Where have you been? We have been so worried about you.' Said Toni. '...and the children?' Polly enquired. 'The kids are ok. Look, there's something about this place that just doesn't feel right, Polly,' said Toni.

 'What, above and beyond that most people here can do magic?' said Chris rolling his eyes at Toni. Toni replied 'look, I went to see Mother and she was really out of it and The Lady's staff didn't want me to stay in the room with her and... 'Polly interrupted. "We don't have time for this, guys. We need to rescue Gracie and find out what she knows. There's something bigger behind all this and we need to find out so I can keep everyone safe'. Toni did not say another word but she felt like the real danger was in the manor house.

Annika was a brilliant student. She had been at the academy for 2 years and during this time she had discovered her primary power was opening portals between spaces and her secondary power was closing openings of any type. On a very practical level this was removing doors, openings like windows, as if they had never existed but on a magical realm level, this was removing gateways that had been opened by others and left open. She could sense Portals and most of the time she sealed them without investigating where they led to. Annika instinctively knew if a portal had been opened with good intentions or with bad ones. She would see in her mind's eye that the portal would glow red if it was opened with bad intentions and a shimmering light if it was opened with good intentions. She could not explain how she knew this, but she trusted her gut instincts. At the beginning of her learning, she would be encouraged to follow a portal with her mind to the opening or exit portal at the other end. The red ones always led somewhere hellish with demons trying to get through from the other side. She would scream as soon as she saw these terrible creatures and tremble while being so close to them closing the portals. Visibly, she would be left shaking and trembling for days afterwards and nightmarish visions would cloud her mind until Professor Rothchild had noticed and started to give her a clarity potion after each session.

Over the last year and of late, The Lady would always attend portal finding and closing lessons. She would ask Annika questions about the locations of the red portals and note details on a scroll. 'To avoid them in the future my sweet child' she would murmur in a comforting way while barely looking at Annika. It made her feel strangely uncomfortable and not seen. This time she would be opening a portal for Polly to rescue someone. There was something really noble about that. There was a rumour going round the academy that Polly was one of the warriors of the Goddess, a chosen one which gave Annika hope that the creatures trying to get through could be stopped by someone like the champion of the Goddess. She would need to make the portal big enough for everyone without making it too big because this draws the attention of the dark things from the other realms. Annika shivered and trembled with her eyes closed. Polly came over to her and placed her hand reassuringly and gently on her shoulder. 'Are you ok? We will be quick and I will protect you from whatever it is that you are afraid of.' Annika smiled and jutted her chin out. She wanted to be brave too like Polly.

Chris and Toni walked over to the window where Annika and Polly were standing in the ground floor hallway. 'So, what's the plan?' said Chris. Polly explained that Annika was going to open a portal in the library that would lead them to one of the subterranean levels of the Premiere compound where Gracie was being held and that they would need to find her and bust her out of the room she was in, either, with force or by hacking into the system. It was made clear that they had not been able to fully see where Gracie was being held but they would land somewhere nearby. Polly wanted to bring her back to the Manor to talk to her about what she had seen and heard, before transporting her back home. 'Got it' Chris said 'So, we sort of know the location but don't know any of the circumstances and don't know how she's being guarded or what type of weapons they may have or anything' Chris said slightly bemused 'sounds like a walk in the park' he continued with a grin.

Polly turned to Toni. 'Could you go and find out how Mother's doing? I thought about what you said earlier and it is a little odd that in a magical place like this they haven't been able to wake her up.' Toni nodded in the affirmative and left immediately for the upper floors. She turned and shouted down 'be careful' and Polly caught her eyes and mouthed 'You too.'   Chris nodded, looking a little concerned but hiding it with a wide, rictus Grin.

The Lady had been watching all of this unfold in her magical stone basin. The reflection was showing the three friends, then the image whirled away. She was supremely happy that Polly had shown all eight powers and, she thought to herself 'how remarkably strong those powers are. The prophecy is in motion.' She decided she could not wait for the harvest full moon around the Equinox when she would be able to perform the rite and take the powers from Polly unawares. This was going to be a lot trickier than she first thought as Polly also had the necklace on and it was behaving in a way that meant that Polly could be The Chosen One, ultimate Warrior of the Goddess. It was protecting her from outside influences.

The Lady sighed. She was going to need to take the powers by force. Her fingers touched lightly on the piece of the bronze dagger by her side. She moved over to the bed and Mother was laying there

156

muttering to herself. She was in a restless sleep. Agitated, she writhed around in some sort of pain. The Lady had discovered that Mother had a very powerful spell placed on her 16 years ago to wipe her memory. It was this that Polly had accidentally corrupted when she unknowingly took away Mothers freewill.

The Lady waved a hand over Mother's forehead and a dark purple light emanated from her finger tips and dropped onto Mothers brow and seeped into her skin. Mother whimpered and cried out but suddenly stopped writhing. The Lady was holding Mother prisoner in her own mind and it was an awful place to be in. Mother had to face parts of herself that she would not accept and the more she struggled to run from her true self; the tighter the spell bound round her and lashed her with pain.   The Lady smiled venomously. She loved magic. It was so nasty to those that did not accept themselves for who they truly are.

The Lady paused and looked round at the door where there was someone about to knock.

Polly and the Tome of Herne

Chapter 12 Saving Gracie

Tuesday evening

The library was the Professor's, Timothy Rothchild, sanctuary. It was spread over two floors, one above the other. The ground floor, housed the comfortable and vast reading areas and the first floor, was where the books were shelved. The first floor was accessed via a two-person deep spiral stairwell made from glass and wood. This stairwell extended through the whole height of the Manor house, and went down to the basement area. The ground floor was opulent with four large fireplaces. Around each of these, were two-seater, red plush velvet overstuffed sofas. A huge chandelier was placed above each seated area, four in total. Over recent decades, the stately house had been upgraded and modernised. There had been underfloor heating fitted throughout and this area often had low lit fires going too. It was a very comfortable and warm part of the house and a favoured spot for avid readers. The upper level of the library had floor to ceiling shelving and rows upon rows of books from every century.

Half of the library was dedicated to magical objects as well as books. Timothy was immensely proud of the contents of the library. He and the other library custodians, over the years had amassed a large number of rare treasures and he had personally devoted a huge part of his life to restoring and expanding this collection. It held magical books and artefacts from every corner of the world. Magic has been in the universe since time began. It was a part of everything and there at the birth of the cosmos, it was part of nature and space, the wonder of all living things, from the smallest atom to the largest beings, of which humankind has not yet met. It was only humans that had forgotten the magic within ourselves.

Timothy had designed and built a hidden chamber under the ground floor of the library – in the basement. This is where he stored the dark magical books and artefacts that he had tracked down, at the Lady's request. Only the ones that he could not destroy were kept there under lock and key. Rather sadly, his own brother had been killed by a dark magical spell and he had made it his life's mission to hunt down dark magical objects and people doing evil, to destroy or remove it to somewhere safe, where no one could ever use it again. On this chosen path, he later met Eleanora and The Lady and they joined forces to protect the earth from evil, but that, as they say, is another story for another time. He had already filled up an entire basement room in the house with these relics. When he ran out of storage space, he then built another room under the library. It too was getting full. He patted the black key in his pocket and he did this whenever he was thinking about the dark magical objects that resided within there. It was reassuring to know that he was the only person with access to the hidden chambers below.

Timothy was reading through a book on the Aberithguine tribe of Wales whose magic was of particular interest to him at present. The tribespeople appeared to have learnt the ability to have an unnaturally long life. Legend has it that The Goddess herself had given them this ability for the tribe to be the first Guardians of the sacred objects and the Vessel of Life.

The Lady had asked him to research the Vessel of Life, when filled with something called 'the tears from the earth', it was supposed to reveal an ancient prophecy. It could give new life and energy to those under The Goddesses protection. This being all living things, including the planets, space, humans, animals and plants.

The book he was reading was written in an ancient language and he was struggling to decipher some of the words and translate it into English. Polly and Chris strolled in and had to cough rather loudly to prompt the Professor to look up and out of his revelry. He did glance up but not for long. He dropped his head back to the book with the intention of marking it but let himself get distracted again with one of the complex symbols. Chris was looking around the place in awe. He loved the thought of the sheer amount of knowledge and power housed in these walls. He was taken aback by the ambience of the place. It felt to him that you could stand here and absorb the wisdom from over the years just by being in this space. He closed his eyes and breathed in the smell of beeswax candles, books and the smoke from the fire crackling in the background. It was a sensory experience like no other. Both the Professor and Chris seemed in their own worlds. Polly stood for a while and then cleared her throat. When this did not elicit a response, she stamped on Chris's foot and he yelled 'what was that for?'.

The yell had the desired effect. The Professor looked up and this time he put down his quill. 'Oh, you're both still here?' he said, squinting at them through his brass rimmed circular reading glasses. Polly couldn't help rolling her eyes as she looked at him with exasperation. 'Yes, Professor, remember you said that you were going to help us open up a portal to rescue Gracie. She's being held by an organisation called the Company and we need to get her out of there. 'Ahhh, yes, let's get Annika and then we can get started. And please do call me Timothy, Polly. There is no need to be so formal' he said, with a great deal of affection. 'If you don't mind, I'd rather call you Professor, like everyone else does', said Polly and the Professor gave a twinkly smile in agreement.

Annika lightly strolled in and crossed the floor of the library and stood beside Polly. She looked quite nervous. Standing there, biting her lip and clasping and unclasping her hands. Polly gave her arm a squeeze and Annika instantly relaxed. Polly and Chris started doing some stretches while the Professor assembled a large pewter pot in front of them. He placed water and some other ingredients in to it. There were dried herbs, a stone and some other metal looking objects. All the while he was whispering words of magic over them and the potion within started to bubble and glisten. 'Annika' he said softly. She looked round at Polly for courage, gulped and stepped forward in front of the pot. This was obviously something that the Professor and Annika had done before as they both worked together in a very practised way. Annika leaned over the bubbling pot and inhaled deeply. The steam circled round her face and curled up through her nostrils, and when she opened her eyes, they glowed bright with a golden glaze.

Annika held out her arms and hands, she began circling them in front of her, getting wider and wider. Behind the bubbling pot, a white dot appeared no bigger than a coat button at first. As Annika's arms moved wider, the white dot turned into a spherical ball then grew bigger and bigger in size.

It was filled with a brilliant gas filled light. Instinctively, Polly knew they would need to walk through it and the Premiere compound would be on the other side. The Professor told them to follow the ball of light when they got to the other side. He had placed a locator spell on it to lead them to Gracie. The catch was that they had five minutes to get in, locate Gracie and then get out. Otherwise, the portal would close. Annika was only practised at holding the doorway open for five minutes, six at the very maximum.

Polly and Chris looked at each other. They were both shiny faced from the heat of the bright light in front of them. Annika seemed to be in a trance and muttering a spell. The ball of light was now an entrance hole to the portal and was just over seven feet in circumference and ready to be walked through. It was hard to see what was on the other side, so this would be a leap of faith for Polly and Chris. Chris took hold of Polly's hand, lifting it up gently to his face and kissed her knuckles absent-mindedly. Polly blushed and looked at him in confusion searching out his eyes to understand what it had meant. He looked back horrified. He had kissed her hand automatically and had not thought about what it meant. 'I meant for luck' he stammered these words out, thinking quickly to try and stop the situation becoming awkward for them both. 'Oh,' Polly said, looking hurt and confused. 'Well, I. When I. What I wanted to say was....' Chris stuttered on. 'Ok, you two. Let's concentrate on the task at hand. Let's remain focussed or you will run out of time'. The Professor said.

Chris and Polly both nodded and they both seemed to come to some sort of non-spoken agreement to explore whatever just happened later. For now, they would focus on the task ahead. They held hands, took a deep breath and braced themselves before stepping through the ball of light.

Polly held onto Chris's hand because she wanted to, but she did not need him to guide her through the shining tunnel of the portal. Here she felt at peace, in her element and at one with herself. Her powers glistened and glowed around her, and she was bathed in a warm light. When they had both entered the portal, Polly had been behind Chris but as he stood still, directionless, she had sensed where to go. Closing her eyes and using her senses to guide her. Walking in front now, Polly led the way to the other side of the glowing white tunnel and towards the exit. Chris held Polly's arm and they both dropped down out of the portal on the other side of the tunnel. They were in a smooth concrete corridor with strip lighting. It looked dull compared to the iridescence of the portal.

The architecture of the building they were in was very urban and stylised with no windows, so it was hard to tell which floor they were on or where in the building they actually were. It was dull and very dark inside. Polly had concentrated on disabling any motion sensors with her powers which also controlled the lighting so they would need to quickly adjust to the darkness. Chris having not moved away from the portal yet seemed very nervous. He was ghostly pale and crouched down to vomit. When he stood up, he looked better but gave a shrug. 'Didn't walking through the portal make your head swim and your eyes shake inside your head?' Chris asked Polly. Polly shook her head and she shrugged back. An orb appeared out of the portal and started moving away down the corridor. Chris quickly pressed the start button on his watch which had a five-minute countdown timer. 'Right, Let's go. We need to be back here in four and a half minutes and enter the portal before it closes' Chris said. The orb started moving quickly down the corridor through a set of doors and down another corridor. Chris and Polly chased after it. They were being mindful to keep looking around as they were going.

They expected some form of guard to be posted outside of where Gracie was being held. Eventually, the orb of light stopped in front of a door and glowed brightly indicating Gracie was inside. They were here and Gracie was behind that door. Chris quickly established it was a computerised sealed unit, hence, why no guard. The company clearly was completely confident in technology. Well, enough to believe that Gracie could be held unguarded anyway.

Chris pulled upon the control panel by the door entry system and started hacking into the software. It was not that long before he had found the administrator reset sequence and entered his own passcode in. He had also created a circuit loop like an override so that the reset did not trigger any type of alert to the administrator. The door automatically opened and a huge triumphant grin spread across his face. He looked at Polly and wiggled his eyebrows playfully. Polly smiled and rolled her eyes upwards, not quite understanding why men felt the need to show off at every given opportunity. She walked forward into the room and Chris went to follow her in.

The room was dark until they walked into it. There was a motion sensor that triggered the lights to come on. Everything in the building was designed to be eco-friendly and energy efficient. It was, however, a very sterile environment. Nature was not honoured in any way.

Polly opened the first set of doors of the cubicles within the room and laying on a bed in an unconscious state, was Gracie. Wearing a white boiler suit, Gracie looked different without her full face of bold makeup that she usually wore. She looked much younger, fresh faced and vulnerable. She also was thinner and malnourished. Polly went to go to her when Chris held her back by gently squeezing her upper arm. He was looking at something on the other side of the room. She followed his gaze and noticed another door with glass panels. They could see through into the next room which seemed to have lots of lab equipment and computers in.

 Chris signalled with his right hand that she should go to Gracie while he went to explore the Lab. They both silently nodded in agreement. Polly bent low and started to move forward. When she got to Gracie, she kneeled beside her and checked her pulse and tried to rouse her awake. Gracie's eyes gradually started to flicker open. They were unfocussed and she looked in a drugged state. Her skin was waxy, quite badly dehydrated and her lips were flaky and chapped. She looked pitiful and Polly wept a little.

Slowly, Gracie's eyes began to focus and she recognised Polly standing there. Gracie went to say something but all that came out was a hoarse gurgle. Polly held her hand and whispered while choking back tears, 'it's ok Gracie. We are here to take you home.' Gracie nodded and smiled weakly. When she turned her face, Polly could see that she had been beaten quite badly and her cheek was swollen and inflamed. There was swelling and purple black bruises near her eyes too. Polly was angry that somebody had inflicted such pain on another human being. She lifted Gracie to a seated position, but the frail and injured Gracie slid back down, unable to hold her own weight. Polly cradled her in her arms and lifted her up with ease. Gracie winced in pain as she held her ribs. Polly was crying as she whispered words of encouragement and turned towards the door and yelled to Chris 'we are leaving.'

At that very moment, Polly turned her head and noticed vigorous movement in the lab area. Chris was not alone.

All of a sudden, she could see Chris being lifted off the ground and his back smashing through the window panel that divided the room from the lab. He came hurtling backwards into the room, landing with a crack on the floor. Glass fragments splayed out on impact with the floor, like ice. Chris did not move. With horror, Polly watched as an enormous man stepped over the debris into the room. His eyes were red rimmed and his face was contorted with rage. He looked unnaturally pale and he had an ill look about him. Polly strategically placed Gracie down on the floor. She went over to Chris to check on him. He rolled over and groaned in doing so. His lip had been split and one side of his face was red where he had been hit but he gave a thumbs up to Polly and started moving slowly away towards Gracie. Polly stood up and lifted her face towards the man moving into the room. He growled at her and beat his chest in animalistic way to establish dominance. Polly was angry at the way Gracie had been beaten and after watching Chris being thrown through a window, she was ready to teach this creep a lesson.

'Hey, get it over with quickly we need to go' said Chris, he had managed to get up and was carrying Gracie towards the door. 'You have two minutes, ' he shouted over his shoulder. 'Good, all I need is one' shouted Polly back with a wicked grin.

So, it began, Polly bowed to her opponent. He lunged at her clumsily, aiming to smash his clenched fist into the side of her head. Polly reeled back. The force of the punch had an impact. This guy was super strong. She had underestimated her opponent and had already started to overly-rely on her super strength in battle. There was a need to re-evaluate her mindset.

He lunged again, this time she was ready and darted to the side. He stumbled forward. She uppercut him into the stomach a few times. He yelled and retreated. He swung wide, wildly with his arms. Polly used his clumsy punches against him and did a roundhouse kick to the throat. He stumbled back gurgling, holding his throat with both hands. She moved forward and landed strategic punches on him a few times and when he used his hands to cover his face, she kicked out both of his legs and he fell backwards to the ground. She rendered him unconscious with a final knockout blow. Polly got up panting, looking down at the man and bowed before running for the door and out into the corridor. Observing the rules of combat enabled Polly to remain disciplined and reduced the need to give into reckless emotions.

At super speed she streaked through the doors into the second corridor and she could see Chris holding Gracie. The Portal was getting smaller around him. Chris shouted 'hurry' behind him and he vanished as he stepped inside. The portal was closing and Polly ran and then jumped, flying through the air head first and landed inside the portal seconds before the entrance popped out of existence on that side.

Polly was walking through the portal tunnel, guiding Chris who was holding Gracie, through to the other side. The tunnel was warm and iridescent, with pink and purple hues that shimmered as it lightly touched their skin. The lights glided over the trio and Polly absorbed the magic of the place. She held onto Chris's arm, the warmth of the magic spread through her and into her two companions and started to heal their wounds. 'Was it just me or was he super strong?' Polly said furrowing her brow with concern. Chris touched his lip because it started to burn and realised with awe that it was binding back together and the swelling around his eye started to reduce and heal too. 'Yes, most definitely, but how is that possible?' Chris answered unsurely. 'Let's get back. Maybe the Professor will know.'

They stepped back into the library and were greeted by the oddest sight. Annika, Toni and The Professor were kneeling in front of the pewter pot, with their hands behind their heads. There in front of them stood a figure in a green cloak with a hood, holding an elm staff with a precious stone at the tip and it was pointed at their heads. As soon as Toni saw Polly she bristled into life and shouted 'look out The Lady is a sorceress…' and before she could utter another word the ropes around her tightened and the ends worked their way like snakes around her head, tightening around her mouth, too tight to even breathe.

Polly jumped down and went to lunge forward to stop her friend from being hurt. 'Now, now' said The Lady moving the staff away, out of Polly's reach. 'You do not want to do anything that would harm your friends',as The Lady said this, a strange light came off of the staff and towards Toni. She twisted and turned and gave out a muffled yell into the quiet of the room. Polly halted to a stop. 'What is going on? Why are my friends tied up? W-w-why are you doing this?' Polly said this in a trembling voice.

The Lady's eyes widened. 'I'm not doing anything, Polly. it's you, can't you see that?' Polly shrunk slightly. She had been told all her life that she was the problem by other people who didn't have her best interests at heart and when you hear something enough you tend to start believing it. 'You were given powers that do not belong to you. You cannot control them. You are hurting people and I think it's best for everyone if you give them to someone more worthy.'

 Polly shrunk smaller again and looked down at her feet, defeated. It was true, having these powers had caused her nothing but problems over the last week or so. She was starting to feel tired, confused and relieved that someone else would be taking them. "Someone more worthy." Polly repeated these words to herself but, oddly, they did not ring true and jarred in her mouth – she could not quite understand why.

'May I ask a question? The Professor proffered, polite even in circumstances such as these. 'who would be the person chosen to receive them if not Polly' said the Professor with his steely gaze looking at The Lady, 'well, I'm astonished you would even have to ask this. it would be me, Timothy. I would be the most obvious choice. I know how to wield great power and am not afraid to use it!' replied the Lady, quite confident in her assurance of herself.

'Yes, but it is a different type of power that you know how to wield, is it not? You know how to be strategic, how to plan and scheme, but I'm sorry my Lady but these powers are connected to the warrior spirit and the heart of the brave and of the true. The legends indicate that the warrior of the Goddess embodies the essence of truth, courage and bravery' The Lady's face was becoming red. She looked very angry now and insulted. Her white, blonde hair was turning black around the edges.

'ENOUGH' she shouted and aimed the staff at Polly. Wind was swirling in the room and whipping around, The Lady. It was a frenzied gale like her glaring eyes. She muttered a spell and a red light shot out of the end of the staff and zig zagged towards Polly. Polly closed her eyes waiting for the impact, but it did not come. All of a sudden, a golden orb of light sprung up around her and it was placed there by the necklace around Polly's neck. It was a shield charm. Polly looked down at the glittering jewellery and felt strangely connected and grateful to the object for protecting her. It felt alive and comforting around her neck.

The lady looked confused and Polly made a decision right there and then, she did not want to hurt the Lady but she was intending to harm her friends – she must be stopped. Moving rapidly, she run over to the fireplace, Polly unsheathed one of the swords that were hanging above it. She stood opposite The Lady, holding the sword above her head and assumed a fighting stance, crouching low and ready for the battle. Again, The Lady cast another spell and once more the necklace threw a protection spell around Polly. Not waiting for another attack, Polly advanced on The Lady and swung the sword up, and around, and with the momentum, cut a chunk of wood from the bottom of the staff. Polly glared at The Lady and said 'don't push me any further. You will not like me when I am angry'. Purple lights started to pour from the cut like blood flows from a wound. This was a warning shot and The Lady knew it and her eyes glowed black as she looked murderously at Polly. 'Stupid little girl, do you think you can stop me?' with that she flung her cloak up in the air, covering herself and spun round, disappearing from view, leaving a black curling mist behind in her wake.

Polly and the Tome of Herne

Chapter 13 The Need to believe.

Tuesday night

Polly ran over to the captives, making the decision to help Toni first, as she had been bound really tightly and could not breathe. She pulled at the ropes and broke it with her hands as easily as breaking apart a piece of tissue paper. Toni had tears in her eyes and the friends hugged each other close. 'Are you ok?' Polly said. 'Yeah, The Lady had put a spell on Mother and was keeping her trapped in her own body. I found this out when I went upstairs to check in on her, the lady conjured ropes out of thin air and they bound round me. I couldn't move. It was awful. Also, my Maami and aunties tried to put a spell on me too and it brought back those memories to my mind.' Polly was shocked to hear this and hugged her friend again. 'Maami had been trying to transfer healing powers to me, I think, but they didn't tell me and just started to perform magic on me without my permission or any forewarning'. This came out as a tumble of words and Toni was in shock. Polly hugged her friend more tightly 'I'm sorry this happened, I had no idea'. With this small gesture of kindness, Toni's eyes started to glisten with gold shimmers.

After a while Polly asked Toni gently 'Do you think you could help me untie the others?'. Toni nodded in agreement. She slowly got up and headed towards Annika who was nearest to her. Polly walked to the Professor and untied him. She looked around the room at the group. Nearly everyone was moving rigidly or tentatively, quite a few were injured and holding their wounded limbs. Chris was holding Gracie and the two of them looked healed and well, apart from the weight that Gracie had clearly lost. The Professor had been tied very tightly and had rope burns, the same could be said for Annika and for Toni too. 'Hey, my mum makes a special tea made from Rooibos root, lemon balm and chamomile, to help the body soothe cuts and bruises, and lighten the soul. Shall I get on and make it for us?' Toni offered. The Professor nodded. 'What a great idea. Please use the ingredients on the table and trust your instincts. You have the energy

171

of a healer'. With that Toni walked off and took Annika with her to make the special brew.

'What happened? Why did the Lady do this?' Chris said, shocked, as he walked over with Gracie to where Polly and The Professor stood. The Professor was crestfallen. He took off his glasses and rubbed his eyes and the bridge of his nose, releasing another sigh as he did so. He looked really weary and sad.

A few minutes past and the Professor eventually came out of his deep thoughts and uttered to no one in particular 'first things first'. He pulled out a large leather-bound book from a stack on the table and flicked through the pages. He held up one of his hands to the sky and called on the goddess to protect the manor from anyone intent on harming it or its inhabitants, he did this by using one of the spells from the book he was holding. A clear liquid shot out of his hand and then flopped onto the floor in front of him and vaporised with a hiss of steam. 'I'm a bit too weak to do this properly. Polly, do you mind joining hands so I can amplify my powers?' Polly looked over at The Professor and reached out her hand to join up with his immediately and without hesitation. Together they recited the spell and this time a huge bubble of liquid floated above them and expanded as it floated upwards and settled around the whole of the stately Manor.

'Right, the next thing we must do is to get Gracie home. This is not her fight. We will cleanse her memory of these traumatic events and send her home through a portal and then put a protection spell on her. This will all be too much for her to understand and it will break her if we don't help her soon.' The Professor rolled up both of his sleeves and began casting the spell. She was in a trance. Chris stepped forward and held out the palm of his hand to halt the process. 'Professor, I know that we need to get Gracie home but' Chris was worried about voicing the next part of what he was about to say 'the thing is, she is the only person who has spent any time with the people that are after Polly so we do need to know what she knows.' Chris said this in a low and gentle voice, not wanting to alarm anyone.

'No, Chris, she's been through enough as it is, lah' Toni said this through clenched teeth, displaying her anger at the very thought of it. Polly stepped forward and then said, assertively 'no, he is right. We need to know what they are planning and why that man had super strength.' Polly looked at the Professor and he hesitated before reluctantly nodding his agreement.

'But only for a short while and please choose your questions carefully'. He beckoned to Chris, who started asking Gracie questions, she stirred before answering them in a distant voice. 'Be careful you are talking directly to Gracie's subconscious thoughts so do not say anything that will influence her or lead her. She will believe anything that you say right now. It will become her truth throughout her life'. With that the questioning began.

An hour later Gracie was transported back home through one of Annika's portals. Gracie's mind had been wiped but what she had revealed had left them all stunned into silence. They were all now drinking the special tea that Toni had lovingly made, and their spirits were lifting with each mouthful of the warm and light liquid.

Gracie had shared that she had been held prisoner for the last two months or more. She did not know exactly as she had lost count of the days. Her captors had repeatedly asked her questions and tortured her, not accepting that she did not know anything. As the minutes and hours passed in her cell, Gracie had taken to listening into the guards' conversations when they thought she was unconscious or asleep. What she had discovered was that they had found the bones of a woman who was really ancient when she died, and she descended from the line of warriors of the Goddess and that a book called the Tome of Herne had been found with her skeleton. They were trying to decipher the book with coding as it was written in an ancient long forgotten language.

The skeleton of the bones of the woman had revealed that she had, had a child just before she had died. This was an important fact to the agents. The Company, as it was called by all the Agents, is led by a group of very rich billionaires and they had been carrying out tests on the skeleton and had isolated a unique part of the bones or something like that and it had not been registered before. They were injecting it into people they kidnapped from the streets and, mostly the homeless, to not raise suspicions. The man that had attacked Chris and Polly was the latest of the new group of test subjects but there had been others. Gracie had also explained that she had heard that the earth was near to collapse and years ago someone had found a prophecy that when partly decoded seemed to imply there was a way to save the planet or at least the chosen ones would be saved but it was all unclear, some of this information she had not understood too well. The agents had said the code had not been fully deciphered yet. Gracie had explained that the Agents talked about magic and powers like they existed and this overwhelmed Gracie at times.

What Gracie had not mentioned because she had not been directly asked, was that there was another woman being held prisoner in the cubicle next to hers. She was a well-spoken older lady who did not seem to want to talk to Gracie or she was too defeated to. There was a young man there too. He sounded like a street hood from London.

They were all drinking their tea in silence and each one of them was lost in their own thoughts, each feeling despondent. Gracie had revealed an uncomfortable truth that the world of humans was entering its twilight and the earth could not sustain humanity in the way that it had done. Humans had over-farmed, over-polluted, given little to no respect to the laws of nature and destroyed the balance and harmony of life itself. The planet was fragile and in disarray and un-balanced. It would trigger a catastrophic event in the form of a drought that would last for years wiping humanity from the face of the earth. Polly looked at her friends. Her heart was heavy, but she wanted nothing more than to offer them courage and reassurance. She looked at the Celtic talisman around her neck. The strength of it had protected her and if it really was a gift from the Goddess then it meant the Goddess herself wanted the earth and humanity to find a way through all this turmoil.

Although, this was an inconceivably big problem that could not be solved alone, sitting around doing nothing was not helping anyone. She kissed the talisman and it glittered and twinkled at her. She stood up and cleared her throat and as she did so, a bang erupted over the roof that shook the mansion walls and rumbled around the building.   Polly lost her footing and careened to the side, only managing to steady herself by leaning on a bookcase to break her fall. Another huge impact and another against the roof of the mansion. The group rushed over to the windows and could see a few of the older students and The Lady forming a circle outside. They were summoning huge boulders from the bones of the earth and the boulders were being hurled at the centre and the roof of the mansion.

The protection spell was holding thus far, and the stones were reduced to rubble on impact. However, the magic would not be able to remain intact for long given the magnitude of the assault against it. Ceiling dust and debris were falling to the floor, everywhere. The Professor jumped away from the window and summoned one of the books from a distant part of the library. It was very old, crumbling in places and had to be managed very carefully. 'Aha!' he shouted with delight, as he found one of the pages he was looking for and with a piece of ragged chalk, he drew a pentagram onto the floor and then placed a candle, a rock, a glass, a feather and a metal cup at each point. He settled into the middle and then placed his hands directly on the floor. He slipped into a trance like state and lights started to float up all around him. His eyes were closed and he was muttering. Snippets of words could be heard 'bind the stone to the bone, remain in the ground'.......eventually, the group ran back over to the window to see what effect the spell was having. The students helping The

Lady were broken away from the circle and shrieking at one another in their frustration that the earth was yielding no more boulders. They looked annoyed. The Professor got up and smiled 'well, that should hold them for a little while but we need a plan to get out of here undetected and fast'.

Polly looked around her and her gaze lingered on the spiral staircase that was leading downwards, through the floor. 'Professor, where do these stairs go and are there any tunnels under the building at all?'. The Professor hesitated before he replied as he alone knew that the tunnels would take them through the rooms of the dark magical artefacts, that he had hidden from view and magically binded there out of reach. Before he could answer, Chris had jumped on the library computer and brought up the plans for the mansion. 'Hey, it looks like there is a tunnel and catacombs underneath the house accessed through the old hunting room quarters of the basement,' Chris told them all. He gave a thumbs up to Polly and the Professor looked quite alarmed in the background.

'Great, let's get prepared to go. Toni can you and Annika get Mother please. Professor, you and I should find weapons and spells that might be useful if we have to fight our way out of here. And Chris, can you print the plans to bring with us?'. Polly assumed the role of leader very easily and each time that any doubt crept in, she held the amulet and breathed in its guiding strength – it was like the amulet was living. It protected her when she needed it; almost intuitively.

Chris maximised the view on the plans then hit the print button. He was watching the inkjet print on the paper. It would take a while as the plans were very intricate and detailed. He had highlighted the section of the plans that they needed to follow in yellow highlighter. He looked around the room making sure everyone else was busy before he pulled a memory stick from his trouser pocket. He had not told Polly that he had taken it from the lab. He clicked it into the drive and then started up the firewall before downloading the contents. On the screen were encrypted folders. he broke the coding easily with his advanced skills and the information downloaded in English. There was a huge array of folders. One was called 'The Prophecy', another 'The Tome of Herne' another was called the 'Lab Test results. He was interested in all of them but decided to click on the Tome of Herne file and began to read the content, he became quickly engrossed and oblivious to what was going on around him.

After about thirty minutes, the group were assembled by one of the large fireplaces ready to embark on the journey underground through the tunnels and out to freedom. The tunnel they were going to follow, led to an opening on the outskirts of the forest beyond the land owned by the Lady, out from under her reach. They were a motley crew of six; Polly, Professor, Toni, Annika, Mother and Chris but only five of them stood by the fireplace at that very moment. Chris was still on the computer. They all looked tired and grey from their exertions, they had been working as a team to pull together supplies for their journey. They had camping equipment, non-perishable food, selected small axes and mallets and swords, weapons, each of their own preferences, a compass and Toni had insisted on bringing herbs with her.

Toni had been helping Polly and during that time had the chance to explain how fulfilling she had found healing others and she wanted to learn as much as she could about being a wiccan healer and using the essence of life to heal others.

Polly called out to Chris. He didn't respond, he was absorbed in what he was looking at on the screen. Polly walked over to Chris, 'we need to go. We are running out of time here'. He snapped to attention with a panicked look on his face and pulled the memory stick out of the drive. He had also loaded the content as a back up to his phone.

Years ago, he had created a code for deciphering any language. It was now being used to decode the Tome of Herne. 'Listen, Polly, I didn't get a chance to tell you earlier, but I found a memory stick in that lab and I've been looking at it, it's worse than we could have ever

177

imagined. Worse than what Gracie had overheard. I think the company is lying to their own agents. The planet is dying at an accelerated rate. A billionaire club called the inner Circle, use the Company to carry out their illicit plans. They are building an underground city of bunkers for the few to survive the coming apocalypse. They are not trying to find out what the prophecy means to save the planet or humanity, they want to know the secrets so they can be the chosen few who live for thousands of years until the world heals itself and is reborn ready to host the next species but instead of there being a new species, the Inner Circle plan on shaping the new world into their own image and will wipe out the rest of the humanity to create a paradise and preserve it for the chosen few. Chris held his head in his hands completely overwhelmed by the information he had just taken in.

Polly looked at him and held her amulet, she knew deep down and within the depth of her core that she was somehow meant to know all of this and had been chosen to be the champion who would guard the earth and all living things against this from happening. In the distance of her memory, she could feel the power of the warriors before her, her ancestors and she could sense the power growing within her. She felt a calmness of spirit and of purpose. She placed her hand on Chris's cheek and lifted up his face gently. 'The Goddess lives in us all and we are going to find a way to stop this together. come on, get up and let us go wherever the tunnel may take us.'

Chris looked into Polly's eyes and she looked back at him. He could see in them she held an unwavering belief in herself and in her ability to do what needed to be done. He drew on that strength and certainty and dimmed the growing shadow in his mind. 'Polly, I'm here for you and we are in this together.' Chris laid his hand over Polly's 'hey, don't forget me you guys.' Toni bounded over to lay her hand over Chris's and placed her other hand under Polly's and cupped both of their hands together, this gesture captured the essence of the moment perfectly. Toni's eyes glowed golden and so did Polly's and Chris's. Their connection was unbreakable and the amulet around Polly's neck magnified the power of the trio. The Professor watched this. He could see the energy moving between the three. He might be mistaken but he thought he was seeing Polly sharing her powers with her friends. He wondered what would happen and what had been transferred to the other two. Only time would tell.

Polly broke away and pulled on her school rucksack and beckoned to the others to follow her. Chris was just getting the plans from the printer. Polly held the sword in her right hand and the amulet in her left. It was still on a chain around her neck, but she felt the greatest comfort when she held it out and in front of her.

Chris had charged his phone while the files were downloading. A full battery was displayed on the screen. He did not know what was going to happen in the tunnels or what was on the other side, but he knew he was with his friends. His dad had been a soldier and an officer for over twenty-five years. His dad, Sam, had also served in very hostile places like Rwanda, Afghanistan, Bosnia and had been an advisor more recently to the Ukraine. Sam also had led black ops missions in secret. He knew how to survive in the most hostile of places and environments. Without any further hesitation, Chris decided to WhatsApp him and ask him to meet them somewhere near where the tunnel opens out. Sending him the coordinates, Chris realises that he hasn't got time to wait for a response. If his suspicions are right, there won't be any phone coverage in the tunnel and catacombs under the mansion.

Chris joins the group assembled at the top of the stairwell on the ground floor. Polly smiles at them each in turn giving them courage, she then leads the way and starts descending the winding stairwell, downwards. She is followed by the Professor, Annika, Toni, who is supporting Mother, and bringing up the rear is, Chris. Polly's amulet is casting a golden glow, a few feet in front of them. The attack on the mansion had knocked the power out, this left everything in darkness.

The Professor explained about the backup generator along the corridor at the entrance to the catacombs, this can be switched on and used to light up the tunnels. As they descend, the group are holding on to each other as they move forward in the darkness. The amulets glow cast a warm and golden glow before them, but it is projecting in front and there is an eerie dense blackness closing in behind and to the sides of them.

A trickling shiver keeps snaking down Chris's spine with each step they take downwards. He felt the need to keep compulsively peering into the inky black darkness behind him even though he could not see anything. Eventually, they hit even ground and step off of the stairwell and start walking along a corridor. It's not too far off now from the entrance to the catacombs. The Professor takes a deep breath and dwells on his conundrum. He knows that they must go through the room of dark magical artefacts before they reach the entrance to the tunnels. It is dangerous to take them through the room but equally as dangerous to remain in the manor house. There is no other way out apart from through the front doorway of the great house. 'Polly' he shouts out 'be ready and please project a protection spell around us as we walk through this next part of the basement.' Polly cannot see the Professor, but she senses the alarm and urgency in his voice, yet, that is not the only reason she feels a chill in her bones and a sickness bubbling in her stomach. She feels the danger looming ahead. To her it feels like a vibration coming towards her that is making her nerves stand on edge. She senses evil and it is causing her perception to spiral into chaos, like a large gong being beaten and the peculiar, deafening sonorous sound and vibration is affecting her being – her steps are becoming less steady as she moves forward. The Professor takes out an iron key and before he knows what is happening, the key pulls itself into the keyhole and turns itself to open the door.

They enter the room and silence descends amongst the group. Underneath their feet is the sound of crunching. The Professor regularly lays salt on the floor all around to cleanse the place. Even though there is no light in the room, the objects glitter and glisten with black, blue and purple hues and this casts a ghostly light before them. Black candles with blue flames light up as they pass by and screeching winds hurl and rebound around the place. It is ice cold in here and it is a chill that enters the bones and makes the inner ear feel painful. A battered trunk begins to move backwards and forwards like someone is locked inside and trying to get out. Polly runs over to it and before she can reach down to open it, the Professor grabs her hand to stop her and the loud noises of a whimpering child can be heard coming from inside. 'No, you must not. This place is full of dark magic. Demons and witches and things of evil are trying to manipulate you to let them out. Go back to sleep, foul demon', the Professor says and the child's sobs turn into humourless laughter that sends an ill feeling through your ears and into your brain. The group separate to move through the room as quickly as is possible.

'What is this place?' Toni gasps in terrified horror as a glass bubbled with frothy blood and it starts to spill over the brim, dripping on the floor beside her. 'These are objects that will try to cause harm to people and make them do wicked things. Do not touch any of them,' said the Professor, adamantly. Polly could hear whispering from the evil in the room and held the image of the willow in her mind and her amulet as protection for herself and the group.

Annika looked round at the Professor as he issued the warning to the group, but she had already touched a locket that had nicked her finger and the blood had dropped onto the object's face. It had been imbibed and absorbed by the brilliant silver piece of jewellery. It was becoming engorged by the blood. She hastily put it back down and moved away, but also did not mention the incident to the others. Polly, as the lead, picked up the pace, keen to get the group through the room and into the catacombs. Small black creatures climbed out of the lockets face and as they scuttled away towards the corner shadows, they were becoming bigger.

As the group moved faster through the room and neared the entrance to the catacombs the Professor guided Polly to the side where the generator is stored. Polly started to hear a scratching sound coming from behind them but does not pay enough attention to it. The Professor opens the lid on a huge battered looking metal box and inside is the generator. He leans in and starts it up. Polly assembles the team checking their backpacks and equipment, tightening the rope in between them and gives each one of them some encouraging words of comfort and hope. She ignores all their grumblings and protests as this is borne out of fear.

Polly walks over to Chris and bends over to shorten the straps on his rucksack, her head whips around to the darkness behind, to peer inside the blackness. All she can hear is the dreadful clicking and scratching, but this time it is closer and coming from multiple points all around. She turns to Chris and leans forward into him. He looks intensely at her, staring into her eyes without saying a word. She gazes up at him and then leans closer to place her mouth near his ear. 'There's something I need to tell you and I don't know how to say this without you feeling alarmed,' she whispers. 'It's ok, I think I already know', Chris murmurs back. His pupils dilating and his features softening. Polly reels back and says 'you knew that there were black creatures with insect like bodies and fangs, the size of cows and you wait until now to tell me? What the hell?'. Chris startles and yells, whipping his head round now, squinting and peering off into the distant darkness. He looks petrified. Polly grabs his flailing arms from swinging about in a panic and pins them to his sides, 'wait, what were you talking about when I told you not to panic?' Polly says quietly, curiosity getting the better of her even in the present circumstances. 'The, erm, same thing you was talking about. Creatures, right?' With that explanation Chris uses his hands to make a creature crawling motion and nods at her with a thumbs up sign thrown in for good measure. 'Huh' Polly replies, very unsure by the whole interaction but she leaves it there knowing she hasn't got time to think about it anymore.

'Chris, we need to get everyone into the catacombs then it's a straight path to the outskirts of the forest and out of this place.' Polly states and Chris replies with more details 'It will take us one hour and twenty-five minutes to cover the distance, but we need to go now and keep everyone at a jogging pace. This might mean we can get through within an hour'. Polly then decides 'I will take care of my Mother and carry her on my shoulders.' said Polly. 'What are they, Polly and why are you so afraid?' asks Chris. Polly tore her eyes away from the pitch blackness behind them and straightened up and walked to the front to lead the others 'they are hell, Chris beasts of hell come to devour us all'.

Polly spent about a minute explaining the situation, that they had to run at pace as they were being followed. She put Mother across the back of her shoulders and entered the tunnel, setting the pace at a normal human run. She didn't tell the others but the clicking and scratching noises were getting closer and was coming from the ceiling as well as the ground and all around them. This could only mean one thing, that the creatures were crawling above them too. She kept calling to the others to shout their names out and where they were in the line.

After a long while running, they passed the halfway point and kept together. Annika had dropped back behind Chris and he had started pulling her along to the side of him. The lights were dim and at ground floor level. They made the place feel more subterranean as the light projected from the ground onto the dirt, rock and dust of the environment. It had a strange otherworldly feel and it smelt of dank earth and mildew. The group were exhausted.

On they went, for the second leg of their journey through the tunnel, as they were nearing the exit, natural light started cracking through the fissures and Annika started shrieking in a high pitched, agitated voice. 'Something bit me, something bit...oh my god it's burning me alive.' Polly put her mother down and placed mothers' hand in Toni's 'take my mother out of here, now'. Toni understood, but she did not

183

like the way she was being spoken to but now wasn't the right time. Toni started leading mother towards the opening 'hey, be careful' Toni said before turning back to the task at hand.

Polly moved back and along the group. She encouraged each one of them to keep moving forward and out of the tunnel. She was hot, sweaty and tired but also on high alert which was confusing her senses. She moved back and towards Annika who was hollering in pain and looked down at her leg. It was dripping with a yellow goo and making bubbling sounds, eating away at her skin and she looked like she had third degree burns. Something had spat acid on her. 'Get her outside to Toni. she can heal this, I'm sure.' Chris hesitated. He heard something behind him and stood by Polly looking out into the darkness at the sea of writhing and oily black figures, climbing forward and over each other. They were covering the surface of the tunnel walls. It was a horrifying sight. The creatures were getting closer. 'Chris, I said move, now' Polly commanded.

Polly, in one move, unsheathed her sword and held her amulet above her chest and shouted to all around 'illuminate this darkness and shed fire upon our plight.' The whole of the tunnel instantly lit up with the most astonishingly bright and dazzling light. The scene before them was too grotesque for words. The heaving sea of bodies were too many to count, and the oily blackness of the creatures hid multiple limbs and huge fangs from view. It was a heaving mass of slithering creatures and hideous to behold.

 The creatures stopped as they noticed they were being observed and they quelled before the light. One huge creature jumped down onto the path. It looked like a humanoid male with an arachnoid body. It opened its mouth and its eight eyes blinked at the light in sequence. It had a smile stretched over its face revealing sharp fangs. It readied itself to rear up on to its hind quarters, to spring forward. Polly, without hesitation, intuitively, crossed the sword and the amulet together and a fiery flame shot out of the combined weapon. 'You shall not move forward from here creatures of darkness' she bellowed with fury and repeated the phrase again and again each time louder and stronger than before. It was focussing her intent.

The fire raged forth and the ferocious flames caught light to every part of the tunnel including the creatures within. Chris hugged Annika and he covered his ears to prevent him from hearing the screaming of the creatures, as they were being slowly burnt alive. Although that wasn't the worse thing about the experience, he will never forget the sound until his dying day, yet, most of all and being the hardest to forget, was the expression on Polly's face while she cleansed the tunnel of its inhabitants.

Chris, Polly and Annika stood together quietly for a short while and then collectively but without a single word, turned around and ran on until the end and climbed out of the tunnel exit. They gulped in the clean and fresh air. Coughing and spluttering as they emerged and pulled themselves up and over the steep ridge that led out onto a green and lush valley. The others were out of the tunnel, laying on the grass and panting, trying to breathe in the air. Some distance away, stood a cloaked woman whose hair and cape were flapping in the breeze and as Polly sank to her knees on the grass verge, the woman turned to her with a twinkle in her eyes. 'Tell me Pollux, what kept you?' and she said this with a teasing laugh. It was Eleanora, splendid in her shining disposition, who had come to guide them the rest of the way.

Polly and the Tome of Herne

Chapter 14 Protection from what we know.

Wednesday morning

Upon seeing Eleanora, Polly slumps to her knees and the ground. Relinquishing the heavy burden of leadership to the woman she trusts. Polly lays on the floor and lets out a sigh. She needed someone to take care of her friends. She cannot believe that it had only been six days since her world changed in an instant, well six days to them but time in the mansion was not the same as time out here in the real world. Her brain was struggling to keep up with the magnitude of the changes she had experienced during this period. Her heart was heavy, her mind a mess of fog and in distress. Being gifted with powers was lonely she was slowly coming to realise. One had to be the leader and it was not always an easy role to play.

Should she even call herself a leader? Was that egotistical too? She felt that the others had resented her in the tunnel, driving them on, pushing them beyond their limits, to get them to safety, while the beasts of hell had been behind them. This need to lead them to safety had made her feel disconnected from her own fear at the time. Here in the light of day she was frightened once again. Eleanora walked over to where Polly was. She saw the distance between the girl and the group and bent down to her level. 'You can't be seen to fall apart like this, you know, for their sake, get up', she delicately whispered. 'You are the Chosen One and they need to believe in you, so whatever you are feeling right now, don't show it. Push it aside and be who they need you to be, you have it in you anyway, it just takes practise and I am going to teach you' Polly nodded and blinked back tears.

She wanted to fall apart, to sit there with the group and share her fears, and be comforted by them as equals, but something in her got up for her friends. It started to rain. Polly stood up and surveyed them all. She looked at Eleanora with a burning intensity, rain dropped and saturated Polly's eyelashes, mingling with her tears and she turned around and started striding down the hillock. Eleanora thought to herself 'the way of the warrior is strong in this one.' Eleanora started striding down the hill behind Polly and the others looked around. The group saw Polly and Eleanora together and got up and started walking after them both. The wind blew and whipped around them all and on a patch of high rush weed, he was hidden from view, Sam watched and waited.

Sam had turned up at his son's given coordinates. Using a small set of field-issued binoculars from his tour of Afghanistan, he silently watched his son and his friends from a distance. Not knowing that much about this older woman who Polly had called Eleanora or what she was up to, Sam was worried about the safety of the three of them, but this would change soon as he intended to contact the company for a report. He kept looking for bars on his cell phone but there was no coverage. Polly looked and moved differently in Sam's eyes. She had been a very shy kid when he and Chris had met her on the first day of training in the dojang. She had grown in confidence somehow. He made a decision to track and follow the group to observe Eleanora and find out what she was doing with Chris and his friends.

Polly walked further down the hill to where Toni was kneeling over and administering to Mother. Toni was gently rubbing some herbs she had found in the forest onto mothers' forehead and Mother seemed to become more alert and less confused than she had been for a long while.

Chris walked over and supported Annika to sit down. Annika was crying silently in pain. Toni immediately stopped what she was doing and moved over to sit beside her. Annika's right leg was completely covered in a yellow goop-like substance and it was translucent. Toni could see the surface of the skin beneath had burn marks and large blisters. Eleanora and the Professor had conjured up an ointment to heal the burns and regrow the skin. Toni tore up a clean t-shirt that she had in her backpack and slathered the ointment onto it before placing it on the burns. Eventually, the task was completed and Annika, exhausted, fell to sleep. The others had piled their coats and spare clothing onto her to keep her warm.

Polly built a fire from the dead bracken and tree branches scattered on the forest floor. She had created a perimeter barrier with a protection spell. These were precautions for the time being but she did not want to stay too long. Giving the group just enough time to rest and recharge, then she wanted to move them away from the borders of the Lady's estate and to somewhere safe.

Eleanora sat down next to Polly, who was sitting on a tree trunk that was lying horizontally on the ground. It looked like it had been uprooted in a storm rather than been felled. Polly sighed and her eyes were itchy with tiredness. She needed to sleep but she also knew that she needed to rouse the group soon and start moving them on, which was not going to be popular- everyone was exhausted. 'Pollux, what happened to you in there? Why did you leave? The Professor sent me a coded message to meet you here and he said that he had grave news'.

 Polly looked at the spritely older woman. She didn't know how Eleanora and the Lady knew each other or their connection but she sensed that the news of The Lady's deceit and treachery would not be taken very well by Eleanora. Afterall, it was Eleanora who had suggested that Polly come to Glossop for The Lady's protection and to learn how to use her powers. 'There is something I need to tell you and I don't think it's going to be easy for you to hear'.

Polly, quite earnestly, started at the beginning, from when they had entered the manor house. She explained that mother had appeared to be getting sicker under the Lady's care and that Toni discovered that Mother was under the enchantment of the Lady. Polly continued to tell Eleanora what had happened and that the lady had betrayed Polly and her friends as she wanted Polly's powers for herself because she didn't think Polly deserved them. That the Professor had helped them escape and there had been a lot of dark magical objects hidden in the manor house. The expression changed on Eleanora's face with each new revelation and word. She was shocked and Polly could tell that she was genuinely upset. The Professor then joined them to sit on the trunk. He took Eleanora's hand and nodded in confirmation that the Lady had indeed attempted to take Polly's powers away and use them for herself.

Eleanora looked troubled and words had been forming in her mind while she had been listening. 'This cannot be possible. She is my sister and we were both chosen by the goddess when we were small children to find and protect the chosen one. It has been our lifelong ambition to find the One who will bring about the prophecy and protect all living beings from the apocalypse. She has been faithful to that cause all of her life. I do not know why you are saying these things, but my sister would never betray the cause and the goddess or me for that matter.'

Eleanora wrenched her hand away from the Professor 'and you Timothy, how can you believe this knowing what the three of us have been through together? We have devoted our lives to the Goddess and the Prophecy. To stop evil from taking hold of the world. It's not true, it can't be'. Eleanora said all of this to the Professor in a voice thick and heavy with emotion and disappointment, with her head bowed down , she walked into the interior of the forest and vanished from view.

The Professor sat there for a while not knowing what to say, he appeared shrunken. 'Professor, it will be okay. It was a lot for her to hear.' Polly then stopped talking as she could tell the Professor also was trying to process why the Lady had betrayed them. She got up and moved to sit on the other side of the fire with Toni, Mother, Chris and Annika. The Professor stared down at the hand left empty by Eleanora's swift departure. Something troubled him. Eleanora was right about one thing, none of this made sense. The Lady and Eleanora had been chosen by the goddess and been trained by the

High Priestesses in an ancient form of magic devoted to the teachings of The Oneness. It was a magic based on wisdom, kindness, balance and the life force of everything and everything being connected.

He himself had noticed a change in the Lady in the past year. She had become secretive, giving instructions to the students to bore deeper into the underworld and engage more with the creatures of darkness beyond our realm. She had also taken to worshipping by herself and using blood magic to sustain her powers. At first the Professor had thought it was the stress of the coming of the prophecy and the strength and power needed to stop the destruction of everything. He tried to talk to her, to reason with her and she would not listen nor would she share her plans. He was hurt at first as they had been friends for decades, but he became worried about her and what she had become capable of. This was why he had carefully watched Polly and her friends when they entered the manor house and instantly took their side without hesitation when the lady revealed her plans but still something did not feel right about The Lady's change of character and heart. Once they were somewhere safe, he would recall all of the events that had passed to see if there was something that he had missed. He would share with Eleanora his thoughts on the subject.

After a couple of hours, Eleanora walked back into the clearing. The only tell-tale sign she had been upset was a puffiness around her eyes. The sky overhead was darkening with deep blue, storm clouds and a rumbling of thunder could be heard in the distance. The wind started picking up and getting stronger. The clearing and forest are creaking and whistling in the wildness of the weather. Eleanora appears quite comfortable in the chaos of the environment and raw power of it all. Her clear blue eyes are more piercing and her silver hair whipping around in the wind and rain that started when she walked slowly into the clearing.

'Polly, we need to get the group somewhere warm and safe. A storm is coming.' With a nod from Polly, Eleanora raises her hands to the sky and her cloak slides away from her arms, clinging to her shoulders and starts twirling behind her, lifted by the gusts of winds all around. She raises her face and shouts a command into the night sky. Her Celtic silver ring, in the shape of a white Hart, glows and pulsates, this being the centre of her magic. The others look on, enthralled. The Pagan Witch revealed to them at long last. There is a crack of lightning of fable-proportions and a rolling of thunder overhead that is enough to awaken the Goddess. The scene is lit up with ethereal light. First white, from the flashes of the lightning, then black, which is the total absence of light, and then silence, as the group disappear from the side of the hillock leaving the fire to hiss as the rain becomes torrential and puts it out.

'It cannot be possible', Sam jumps up and rushes over to the side of the hillock. He tentatively touches the ground where they had all been sitting and uses his foot to test the robustness of it. Then, using a stick and prods the ground to check for unseen openings. Baffled, and bewildered, he cannot quite believe what he had just witnessed with his own eyes. The group had just vanished in front of him. Had he just seen the older woman perform a magical spell?

The rain was lashing down now. Sam had his hood up, but it was seeping into his anorak through each opening and trickling down his entire body. He darted for the darkness of the forest and stood under the canopy of trees until he heard the rumbling of thunder and lightning; he no longer felt safe under them. It could just be his imagination, but the trees seemed to be leaning over him in quite a menacing fashion, crowding in to peer at him. He was looking up at the reaching branches, when his phone started to ring. He fumbled around in one of his inside pockets for it and it was a missed called from an unknown number. He realised that one of the group must have put a damper on the area so that there was no phone coverage while they were here. The weird thing was that he had not seen them use any equipment to do this with. He put his phone back in his pocket and headed back to his car. He was genuinely worried now for his son. What had Chris gotten himself into?

Most of the group closed their eyes when the lightning rippled and zigzagged across the sky. It struck the hillock just as the group disappeared. The sensation of being transported from the hillock to wherever Eleanora had moved them to was strange. It felt like passing through bubbles that were connected and each bubble had its own environment and climate. There was a freezing one, then a hot climate bubble, then a bubble with loud bird calls and then a humid jungle climate before landing on a hillside where it was raining and cloudy but there was no thunderstorm overhead.

The final destination was different from the hillock and Glossop in everyway. The air is crisper and baltic and the scenery more expansive, isolated and wild - free. Eleanora clapped her hands again and the strange golden gas-like substance that had covered them all started to rescind backwards and into her hands. Toni stood up swaying and then bent over to be sick. Chris got up too to see if everyone was transported here and doing ok. His head spun and he collapsed back down. Polly got up and she seemed unaffected. Eleanora gazed over at Polly and announced 'impressive, usually people are sick or unsteady during their first transportation experience, you are made of strong stuff little one. Now, help everyone up to the castle while I set up the chamber and we can get started on your lessons.' With that, Eleanora strode forward and spoke to the Professor 'you will be needed too, Professor. We need to start Polly's training immediately. There is no more time to lose the company is closing in on the Tome of Herne'. With that Eleanora started striding up the hill towards a huge castle made of sandstone.

The castle was vast and set over different levels with twelve turrets and towers. It glowed golden in the setting sunlight. Eleanora paused her ascent. She was suddenly drawn to a tree. She held her hand on its trunk then turned around and shouted to Chris 'there was a man at the hillock looking for you. He was dressed like a soldier. Who is he?' Chris gave a theatrical shrug. 'You had better come with us too' Eleanora said and then turned around 'you can explain why he was looking for you later, with or without the aid of truth serum, it's all predetermination or fate as you nonies, I mean non-magical people call it '. Chris stared after her and gulped with fear.

Eleanora's castle is hidden from the world in the hills of Scotland. It has the same protection spells on it that most other magical families and communities who wish to live their life away from non-magical folks, place around their lands. Eleanora's lands are a haven for all magical humans and creatures. Her and her sister opened up the lands many years ago when there was a spate of murders of magical folks. These had been perpetrated by non-magical humans who took exception to people who are different and also, dark wizards and witches. The castle sits on a thousand acres of arable and bountiful land. There are brooks and forests and streams all left wild. Energy for the castle is drawn from the sun, sea and the earth like most magical dwellings.

Magical creatures and non-magical creatures alike enjoy the land in its raw and untamed natural form. The inside of the castle is rustic and charming and surprisingly cosy for such a gigantic structure.

While Mother takes some rest in the suites of the castle above and Annika and Toni are in the healers' quarters, Polly, Chris, the Professor and Eleanora are in the chambers below the castle.

One of the lower chambers has been set up as a gymnasium and arena to enable combat and fighting training. There is a sparring ring in the middle lit up by huge beacons. A plethora of sparring apparatus and weapons of all kinds are on display on every wall and surface. There are also some curious objects in the gym too, such as, hovering metal balls with twelve holes in them that shoot magical spells at fighters and a set of wooden pillars hovering in mid-air separated by three feet that spin in opposite directions to each other.

These are used for boxing and flight training. There are staffs with different colour crystals and special stones in them. Shorter glass objects that look like wands. Polly is looking at the equipment with a studied interest.

Eleanora steps forward and calls Polly to do the same. Eleanora without another word rains down a firebolt on Polly. She jumps to her right, but Eleanora's spell hits her legs. Polly gets up and rubs them looking at Eleanora. 'Have you gone mad?' Polly says, quite irritated at the sudden onslaught. 'Why did you not block it with a shield charm?' Eleanora sniffs with disapproval, pulling Polly forward to the centre of the ring. 'I don't know how,' Polly answered. 'Well, then this is where we will start. Use your magic instinctively. Your whole being including your magic will automatically do the thing it needs to do to protect you. It is in your blood, trust it and Trust yourself above all else' Eleanora smiled encouragingly 'you two, go to the study and find out what you can about what the company is up to'. Chris and the Professor jumped straight up and Chris went through a side room into one of the libraries within the castle. The Professor hesitated sensing that Eleanora wanted to heed an instruction, 'Professor, please find out who that man was. Sometimes we must protect the children from themselves'. The Professor bows and leaves the room, closing the doors behind him.

 With that Eleanora crouches down and touches the hilt of her sword, she summons her power and very lightly jumps up and twirls round as gently as if she is being lifted by air currents. She twirls, kicks and punches like she is dancing but with every closure of a move she uses her magic to either issue forth fire or throw up a protective shield or summon a spray of water. It is a beautiful dance of power that complements the elements that she is calling forth. Polly is mesmerised and aching to join. 'Come my child, now you're training truly begins'. With that a light shoots out of one of the holes in the metal ball that is hovering above the ground and a very faint transparent shield bubbles up in front of Polly. She stands there and looks at it for a while then smiles. She is very glad in her heart that she has Eleanora to guide her.

Chris walks into the library and is astonished at the sheer number of books there are and shelves that hold them. The shelves appear infinite as there is no ceiling, just sky above. He cannot see where the shelves and books end. He walks backwards out of the room to check what the room looks like from the outside hallway. It's normal sized and he steps back inside. The two dimensions do not fit together at all. 'Come on now, stop messing about' says the Professor 'it's an infinity charm to fit bigger spaces into smaller dimensions, you have a fairy tale about it, the genie and the lamp' Chris steps forward, mouth agape for a few seconds 'was that a real story then not just a fairy tale?' Chris asks and sits down in a brown leather chair in front of a computer. 'Yes, most of the fairy tales of the non-magical world are based upon humans interacting with magical folks. Nonie's used to believe in magic and each village or settlement would worship the gods and goddesses and believe in the healing powers of nature. The witches and wizards were natural leaders, farmers and healers. This way of living started to die out during the industrial revolution and the invention of monetary systems and banks. You see, you cannot really worship money and power and nature at the same time. There is hope though. There is a growing community of people that are choosing natural remedies over pharmaceuticals and plant based natural meals over processed unnatural food, but we need to do more to restore the balance of nature, of magic itself and of the pure energies of the universe. It will come that I am sure of' The Professor said with a twinkle of hope in his eyes.

Chris stared ahead for a while and wrinkled his forehead. It was a lot to take in and he was struggling with it. His world view was that technology could help solve humanity's problems. He himself wanted to use it to solve global warming and work out mathematical equations that could support a thriving human race that is in balance with the ecosystems of the planet. It sounded like he was being asked to believe in the full restoration of an ecological system world order that would mean returning the human race to the dark ages and this is something that he could not support. He understood the need to restore balance but there were elements of our current way of living that will need to be preserved. Less mindless consumerism, more connection and community and understanding of responsibility towards nature and the planet we live on. Chris sighed heavily. At times it just seemed all too impossible and required a lot of people to start behaving in a different way and doing this together in collaboration.

Chris clicked the memory stick into the drive and started to review the folders within and pick up where he left off. He clicks onto the Tome of Herne file and puts in the password he discovered 'Innercircle' then starts to read through the deciphered text. He is pretty sure that this is the first time that the ancient text has been translated fully in thousands of years. There are no notes on the file that indicate that the inner circle or their cronies, The Company, had managed to decipher the text. He is reading and in doing so, starts to take notes on his phone. An old learning habit from school. The ancient text explains the prophecy in a bit more detail but there are still some gaps. But what is explained is that there are seven magical objects that are used in a spell and it is read out from the Tome of Herne to give longevity and powers to serve the Goddess as guardians of the earth. These objects are written down as; two feathers given to the chosen, the coin of Malvern, Vessel of life, The ring of Vusalia, the bone of the elder and the Crown of the White Hart. To bind them and use them, the tears of the earth were also needed. Chris leant back in his chair and breathed out.

He then started to search for the named objects. The Professor came over and handed Chris a grated cheese and cucumber sandwich. 'The cheese is made from the goats on our land, it is given freely by the animals. It tastes all the better for it. Now, eat up'. Chris picks up the sandwich and chows down gleefully, only just now realising that his stomach had been rumbling for some time. They ate in silence for a while. Then the Professor asks Chris gently ' who was the man Chris that was watching us? We need the details so that we can keep Polly and the rest of you safe'.

Chris looks up with an odd expression on his face. 'It was my dad, Sam, I WhatsApp messaged him our location as I thought that we would need back up when we got out of the tunnel. He is a very skilled soldier and has completed many tours of duty. He has also been hired as security detail and what he has never told me, but I have my suspicions, that he has completed black operations as a special agent and has also been hired as a mercenary. He is highly skilled in taekwondo....... he...he also fell to pieces when my mum died. He is overprotective of me b-because of it. He is scared to go through that much pain again you know, losing someone that he unconditionally loves....' Chris eyes widen, he feels alarmed at the revelations escaping from his mouth. These are involuntary. He cannot seem to stop talking so he clamps his mouth shut with his hands.

The Professor takes off his glasses and cleans the lens on his handkerchief and uses them to point towards the sandwich. 'Truth serum' the Professor explains with a mischievous grin. He gets up and pats Chris on the back lovingly 'should wear off in an hour or two, don't go swimming though. One of the side effects is being able to breathe underwater. People have been at unfathomable depths when the stuff wears off'. The Professor walks back to his desk and resumes his work quite in a matter of fact manner. He holds his temple on the side of his head and telepathically shares the information with Eleanora. Eleanora responds in kind with 'sounds like exactly the type of man that would be recruited by the Inner Circle and the Company no doubt'. The Professor sends his agreement.

Polly is getting tired from combat drills and needs a break from training. Eleanora gives her the sign for five minutes. She strolls through the gym and into the library. She is hot and sweaty from working out and tired from concentrating on this new form of combat. She is elated too as she has already started to see progress with each new spell and sequence she tries. 'Hey there' she says to Chris, flipping up her hand for a high five. Her clothes are sticking to her and she looks dishevelled in a cute way. Chris spins round 'oh no' he thinks out loud 'not you' he mumbles on. 'I can't stop talking' he says through clenched teeth '....and your eyes and rosy cheeks are just too pretty for words'. Polly covers her mouth with her fingers and starts to giggle self consciously, her whole face lit up with happiness. Chris is about to say something and clamps his hands over his mouth. He pushes back his chair and runs out of the door without uttering another word. Polly watches him go and gives the Professor a quizzical look. 'The cheese gave him a bit of tummy upset, it's very strong' said the Professor, barely able to contain a snort of laughter.

Polly and the Tome of Herne

Chapter 15 Things ain't always what they seem.

Tuesday afternoon

Sam called the Company as soon as he got back to his car using the Company's sole-purpose-use satellite phone. The usual protocol for engagement with the Company is dialling into the central switch board to give coordinates of current location and confirmation of identity, and security clearance, before being connected to the relevant team. He was patched through to Kane's team. He mentioned a possible person of interest called, Eleanora. Sam's other phone - the burner phone that contained a cloned sim of his son's phone - started to ping. His son was using the notes app. Sam started reading the notes as they were being written by Chris.

Sam made contact with an agent and immediately relayed the story of his son and his involvement with a person called Eleanora. He explained that they had vanished from a hillock just outside of Glossop and that he was concerned for his son, he even told the agent that Chris was now writing a bunch of gibberish about something called the Tome of Herne and the seven sacred objects to extend life and longevity. 'He is actually asking himself, is this the Chalice of Life for heck's sake' said Sam with a level of scepticism. Unbeknown to Sam, the Agent had placed him on loudspeaker. Kane could not believe what he was hearing and how lucky he was that Sam had dialled in. He did not want to spook the man as he was clearly worried about his son but at the same time, he needed him to stay connected so they could send a squad to retrieve him and the data. 'I'll take the call in my office. Patch it through' Kane gave his instructions and walked through to his office while closing the door behind him.

'Hey, Sam, can I call you Sam? What can we do to help you and your son? Sam relayed the recent events once again and explained the content of his son's notes. Kane asked Sam to send him the notes and gave him his number. Kane agreed to send a team and told Sam that they would put a tracer immediately on the case to identify the location of Chris through his phone. Sam should feel relieved, yet he felt more alone and troubled than ever. He was now wondering why Kane was willing to send a whole squad to help. He had thought that they would just give him the coordinates of his son's last location, but he followed the instructions anyway. He was just being paranoid he reasoned to himself.

Kane saw the notes downloading on his phone and saw all the words he needed to see to confirm to himself that they had hit the jackpot. 'Able, go and retrieve the asset. Here is his last location. Samson, review these notes. I want an executive summary within the hour. He gave one of the new agents his phone. The agent immediately sat down at the nearest desk, plugged it in and started working on it.

Kane strode across the gridded walkway and placed his hands either side of him on the metal bar that was at waist height, on the gangway bridge. He looked out onto the warehouse floor below, there was a lot of hustle and bustle on the ground. Teams doing drills in one corner, bioweapons and hazardous materials being loaded into trucks and there were a team of scientists testing the new version of the compound on rough sleepers and vagrants. The company agents didn't even have to kidnap these people. They were so desperate that they were easily persuaded to come with them once they had a decent meal and were given a bit of money.

Kane's usually grimacing face was set in a different formation, he was smiling to himself. People walked past and flinched or did a double take, jumping back at the very least. It created an uneasiness in them, as they did not know what this new expression on Kane's face meant for them, it was so rare to see. Kane was content in the knowledge that if he is able to produce the information that leads to the longevity potion then he was sure Mr Luxemburg would give him a place in the bunker underground. Sure, it was called a bunker, but it looked more like a city. It had water wells, rivers, contraptions to reflect natural light underground and polyphonic technology and it was nearly built. All he needed to do was figure out how to steal some of the compound when it's finally ready. He was going to make sure he would live for a very long time and ensure that his line was part of the new world order.

He strolls down the stairs and walks over to the far-right hand side corner where the glass fronted labs were built. The scientists in the laboratory were wearing goggles and sealed white boiler suits and were busy with their experiments. There were gaps in the protein chains of genomes they had isolated. There had been a decision taken a week or so ago now to use some of the other DNA found at the sites to complete the DNA sequencing. They were reviewing the new test subjects now and Kane wanted to understand the outcome.

 The scientists had injected people with the latest compound a couple of hours ago and were now ready to wake them from their medically induced coma. A few agents filed into the glass screened off section of the lab. There was an airlock between this section and the lab floor. The scientists switched on the huge screen and Miles Luxemburg instantly came into view. Miles was dressed in his usual pared down shirt and jeans and he had given an order that he wanted to see the results of each experiment as it was happening in real time. He would repeat the words 'real time' slowly like he was talking to a three-year-old. This was not popular with the scientists and he never listened to their feedback. He had a tendency to just talk over people and make people feel ill at ease.

Kane and the other agents usually attended the demonstrations and experiments for entertainment value as something always seemed to go wrong.

A couple of the healthcare porters wheeled in the test subjects. Two of them were placed in the centre of the room in front of the screen. Miles yawned loudly and tapped his fingers in a rhythm on his desk. This could be heard through the screen and usually signalled that he was losing patience. The scientists stepped forward and used stimulants to wake up the subjects. They administered the medicine and then stepped back through the airlock chamber leaving the two porters in the room to shake the test subjects awake. The female was about twenty-two, short and scrawny. She looked like she may have had an issue with drugs as there were scars up the inside of her arms. The girl was slowly rousing, she looked disoriented and confused in the first few seconds of consciousness. She started to squint at the room as if the light was really hurting her eyes, then screeching started and holding her eyes. One of the scientists leaned forward and spoke softly into the microphone and suggested dimming the lights in the lab. One of the porters turned down the lights. The screeching instantly stopped.

The female laid still for a while in silence and then slowly used her fingers to pull down the cover. Kane was watching her intently. He pressed his face closer to the glass. There was something odd about her hands, they looked disfigured and were more like claws. Her fingernails had grown long, sharp and pointy. She lifted her head and sniffed the air. With precision and speed, she jumped out of the bed like a wild animal, onto her feet and started moving towards the porter that was in the centre of the room. She moved her head from side to side assessing him like a bird of prey and was staring straight at him hungrily. Her eyes were fully black. Her forehead seemed more pronounced like a neanderthal, sloped forward, lower and over her eyes. When she blinked her eyelids moved from the outside inwards.

The porter started visibly shaking, yelling for help and the other porter took one look at the female and he bolted for the door that led out into the larger part of the lab. He knew a predator when he saw one. This one was in the middle of hunting his colleague. She crouched low and sprung up onto the back of the porter and knocked him over with the force of her lunge, her legs were powerful. She then lifted up, opened her mouth and four-inch fangs sprang forward and she bit down forcefully into the man. slurping and guzzling could be heard. Surprisingly, after a few minutes, the porter was still alive and managed to get up. He staggered forward, falling face first into the doors between this space and the wider lab beyond. With his last breath he looked through the glass panels of the entrance way and saw hundreds of beds lined up with more test subjects in them. He slid down and the female along with the male, who was now awake, both sprung at him, hungry to devour more of his blood.

Miles barely stifled another yawn. The scientists shuffled backwards and forwards on their feet, unsure how their performance was going to be measured considering the latest results. 'Well, firstly, I would like to congratulate you all for your efforts, 10/10 for creating a new species.' Miles clapped and the others started to follow 'Do we think these subjects are more invincible and less insane or more psychotic than the last batch?' Miles enquired like he was talking about a new recipe for baking cookies. 'Definitely stronger with superhuman strength but driven by a need to feed on humans. Intellectually they are...' Miles interrupted the lead scientist 'gentlemen, remember our core objective here is to create a serum that provides immortality until fatally injured. It is not to create a species of blood sucking demons. If it was then we would have achieved this by now. I would have applauded you, given you your £5 million each and then released you. But sadly, you have not achieved the desired outcome and our vision statement. Maybe it wasn't such a good idea to use the DNA from the bones that were in the cave with the human skeleton to hybridise the compound. Let's scrap this approach and revisit the basics and create the compound wholly from the omega female skeleton and destroy the test subjects. Keep the serum though as it might be valuable as in profitable somehow' Miles leaned forward and went to switch off. 'Miles, I was wondering' Kane stepped forward, just as Mile's hand hovered over the switch 'could I keep some of the subjects to see if they can be trained?' Miles looked at Kane solemnly and his face broke into a grin 'you army boys wanting to weaponise science. You are an inspiration. Go ahead and see what you can do' with that Miles switched the live link off.

The lead scientist turned to Kane and without hesitation told him he hoped he knew what he was doing. He went on to explain that the creatures had already killed a few of the guards and they should all be destroyed along with this batch of the serum. Kane looked him square in the eyes and asked the doctor if he had suddenly developed a conscience because he sure didn't seem to mind conducting experiments on the more vulnerable members of society. The scientist stepped back, flabbergasted that a soldier had spoken to him in this way and about ethics. 'How dare you, we are trying to save humanity' said the older lead scientist in a superior tone. 'That's not a good enough reason Doc to experiment on these people and you know it.' With that he disregarded the older man 'You two' Kane leaned forward sweeping aside the scientist and ushered two of the younger agents forward 'I want to save twenty breeding pairs and destroy the rest'. 'Yes sir' they both said in unison and pulled their automatic machine guns out, starting to move into the lab pushing the scientists out of the way as they went by.

Kane crossed the ground floor and started walking back up the stairs from which he came. He paused at the top step, the looks on his team members' faces made him hesitate but only for a couple of seconds. He firmly put both of his feet on the ground and said 'well?'. All the team had this shocked expression on their faces. As if they were looking at the last cup of Christ itself.. One of the researchers walked over with a two-page summary freshly printed. He had a keen look on his face and flourished the paper as he handed it to Kane. 'We got something Sir. It's a list to make a potion or something, It's the ingredients that together produce longevity. We are pretty sure of it'. Kane grabbed the paper quickly. 'What are the items and where do we find them?' Kane said hungrily, he wanted the information and to get started on the search.

The researcher responded by telling Kane about the list written by Chris and explained that they needed some things that they had never heard of. These items did not come up on the internet either.

They would need a paganist expert. The items included; the two feathers given to the chosen, the coin of Malvern, Vessel of life, The ring of Vusalia, the bone of the elder and the Crown of the White Hart. To bind them and use them, the tears of the earth were also needed. 'What do we do then?' Said Kane angrily. 'Eleanora stole the Tome of Herne Sir from the burial site when she fled but we still have the scans of the book on file. I'm pretty sure there was a reference in there to the Vessel of Life and there is a hand drawn map on a piece of preserved hide which in all probability is the location of the Vessel' he said sounding terribly English in his plummy British accent 'but we will need the Tome of Herne and Eleanora to actually create the potion.' The researcher pushed his glasses back up his nose as he was sweating with nervous excitement. Kane smiled broadly, he would recover at least one of the artefacts. This would give him some leverage to barter his way into the underground bunker city and this old dame was not going to get in his way. 'Send for the Lady. we need a locator spell on Eleanora and that goddamn book of Herne ' Kane announced. 'Tome of Herne, Tome, Sir and yes, right on it, Sir'.

Sam's story

Meanwhile somewhere in Glossop, Sam sat in his car thinking about his son and flicking through Chris's notes. He had worked with the organisation known on the streets as The Company for the last few years on various projects. One of his old army buddies had put him in touch with The Company. Blaine, his friend, had told him that the company was formed of ex-military and that the big bosses were civilians known as the Inner Circle. Sam had not really given it much thought back then as he had needed the money but what were a group of corporate civilians doing with this much military know-how in the United Kingdom? He wondered if British intelligence was tracking them. He heard a creak outside and furtively looked around and through the car windows. He was being paranoid. He rubbed the stubble on his chin, which sounded like a wire brush, and then his eyes. He had not slept much, his eyes were stinging. He started trying to recall the last mission he was on with The Company. It was over a year ago. A standard track and retrieve job near here, in Glossop. Well, that was what he had been told but it turned out to be a lot stranger than that. Sam could not quite recall the full detail of the job or his memories. It took a lot of concentration and the images of that evening, when they did come to mind, were fragmented and disjointed.

Sam felt confused so he got out of the car and started to walk back up to the hillock where Chris and his friends had disappeared. It did not take him long due to his maintenance of his military fitness level. He sat down on the hillside, boots striking out in front of him. The Hillock seemed to still have some type of magical barrier on it, a residue from the powerful spell performed. Sam could see it as a shimmering mist. The memory charm that had been put on Sam the night he was last in Glossop was being disrupted by it. Sam started to have vivid memories of that night, one year ago.

Firstly, he remembered landing in a helicopter near this hillside with two other agents and a woman with long black hair and violet eyes that glowed purple in the dark. She had barely there pupils even when she was standing in dull light and her skin was a translucent white. She was very beautiful; tall, shapely and other worldly looking but there was something off about her. Sam could not quite describe it but once he stopped looking at her directly, he could see her shape change into a black robed figure made of smoke. It was just outside of the peripheral of his vision and when he darted his eyes back to her, she would return to being a beautiful woman again. He did ask one of the other agents what he thought of her. The other agent had paused for a long time and looked concerned but then opted for a casual 'creepy but hot, am I right?' He said this with a jocular nudge and a fake grin but then looked round at the woman again with concern on his face and did the sign of the cross which he ended with kissing his St Christopher pendant.

That was all the confirmation that Sam had needed to stay the hell away from the Witch. She was called Nualla Glamdring. The agents never heard her utter a word, but her voice was in their head from time to time. Her voice had a gallic or slight Dutch accent to it. Nualla had conveyed to the team that sensor, tracking equipment and compasses were not going to work in the vicinity of the manor house and that the agents should follow her and be on high alert throughout the mission. It was important to get in, retrieve and get back out without detection. No parameter alarms or killing anyone as this would raise the alarm system immediately. Stealth was the goal. She explained that she would not be travelling back with them and would remain behind this time, but a portal would be opened and the agents would take the object retrieved from the manor house back to the Premiere holding.

The woman then stood still and in front of their eyes, transformed into a ten-year-old blonde-haired girl with two braids. She had on a pair of pink pyjamas and was carrying a mug of hot chocolate. The three agents reeled backwards in shock and the other two lifted their weapons. The little girl smiled and wagged her finger and shook her head no, playfully. In the agents' heads, there was a screeching sound that hurt the inside membrane of their ears and skull. All three agents fell to the floor and covered their ears in pain. Nualla threw back her head and laughed and giggled like she was playing a prank on friends. When the screeching stopped the agents got back on their feet and wearily looked at the girl in front of them. The little girl turned around and started to make circular motions with her arms. A large portal started opening. It was made of a crackling electric light with violet and blue hues running through it. The little girl stepped in and beckoned to the team to follow.

Sam's memory was hazy after that point. He remembered walking into a huge library with sofas, fireplaces and chandeliers. There was an older woman with silver grey bobbed hair. She was dressed immaculately. Nualla had made the agents wait in one of the recessed areas by a fireplace at the far side of the huge space, while she went over to the woman on the pretence of asking for some more hot chocolate. The lady had gotten up to oblige and Nualla had hit her with a curse in the back of the head. She fell like a dead weight. The agents came running over and bound the older woman before lifting her up ready to depart. Nualla then shape-shifted into the form of the older woman. The only tell-tale signs that it was her was that a few stray black hairs still tinged her face. Nualla then produced a portal but before she let them leave, she placed her hand on the prone form of the older woman and probed her mind. Nualla closed her eyes and looked deep in concentration. Every now and then Sam could hear the words in his mind 'where is the goddesses warrior. Give me Pollux'.

Sam jolted out of his remembrance trance and whispered 'Polly' to the blowing wind. He now remembered so very clearly that the three agents had taken the older woman back to the compound and deposited her in a white walled and glass fronted cell. Another sorceress had placed a memory charm on the three agents including Sam but for some inexplicable reason to him, since that night he had wanted to protect Chris and keep tabs on Polly. He could not explain it, but he just knew they were in danger. Having the full memory restored, he now knew why he had wanted to protect his son and his childhood friend. Sam was unsure whether he would remember all of this when he left the area, so he recorded a video message to himself with the details on it and saved it in his files on his phone under the folder name 'read me!'. He had been ashamed of himself for cloning Chris's phone and spying on him, but he reasoned that he had been afraid but in retrospect, it was still unforgivable. What Sam didn't know was that Nualla had placed a spell on Sam to keep track of Polly and provide her with updates.

Sam then called Chris. It was the middle of the night, but he did not care. He had to convince Chris to tell him where he was and let him know that he planned to come for Polly to keep her safe. The call went to voicemail. Sam clicked off preferring to record messages over the voice note function. He started his message with a greeting but didn't get a chance to say anything further as the roots of the trees underneath him had been edging upwards and forward towards him and upon reaching him, had started to bind themselves around him pulling him into the dark and warm earth. Sam was too shocked to react at first. His mind could not comprehend what it was seeing. He only started to struggle and shout as the roots were pulling him feet first into a hole under a huge oak tree. He gave out one long yell before his head was underground. Foliage and moss slowly creeped forward to cover the hole and the grass rearranged itself where Sam had been sitting so no imprint was left to indicate that Sam had been there at all.

Polly and the Tome of Herne

Chapter 16   Becoming

A lot changes in a month

Polly woke up in her very comfortable antique four poster bed. The castle was warm and cosy yet splendidly opulent at the same time. The drapes were pulled over, but she could see the warm late summer sun peeking through the gaps. She could smell the rose garden outside which always managed to surprise her, being that that her suite was at the top most part of the castle. She had slept very well and had not had any dreams. The blankness of the night's sleep had served her well as she had needed deep REM sleep to recover from the last few days of training. She stretched languidly and tensed up realising how sore her muscles were from exertion. She slipped off the bed and walked in her dressing gown to the wardrobe. When she opened it, she immediately felt disappointed. All her outfits were black and very sensible clothes like combat trousers, active wear and technical clothing. Polly touched the sleek fabrics and longed for something girly and flattering to wear like a frivolous blouse or sequin slouchy top. Of late all of her time was being taken up by combat, magic and conjuring training. She had not had time to ease off and enjoy herself with her friends for a long while. Toni had been spending most of her days with the Wiccans and healers too.

After Toni had talked to her Maami over the phone about the events of that night, she had learnt from her mother that she comes from a long line of tribal white witches or healers and that her mother was performing a ceremony with her Aunties to release her powers. Toni had cried telling her Maami how frightened she had been that night. Maami had cried explaining to her daughter how hard it had been keeping this secret from her and that she had never found the right words to explain it to her so thought it best just to show her. Maami begged her daughter for forgiveness for getting it so very wrong and

Toni had given this gladly and straightaway. The love for her Maami and her Maami's love had been consistent throughout her life. Maami had asked Toni to come home that day, but Toni had told her she needed to stay to support her friends and also to hone her healing skills by herself for a while. 'Beloved daughter of mine, I will be here always and when you are ready'. Both women silently touched their hearts and touched their phones with the same hand, both not knowing the other was doing the same thing.

Toni was sad when she got off the phone to Maami that day and was quite morose when retelling the story to Polly. Polly went over to her to hug her and silently wait. 'Everything has changed' Toni said and 'yet, staying the same at the same time which is reassuring but confusing' Polly replied, revealing how she felt. 'We both have magical abilities and the world that we are in now is awesome and terrifying at the same time. I'm just glad I have you by my side' with that Polly wrapped her arms around Toni so tightly and Toni hugged her even harder back. Both of the young women were finding their way through this phase of change in their lives and this brought them closer together.

Polly sighed when she remembered that day over a month ago now. She had felt so close and in harmony with her friend and since then had not seen much of Toni or Chris. Chris had been spending most of his time with the Professor decoding the ancient texts with his extensive computer programming skills and learning more about magical history and potions brewing. Chris had also developed a slight mistrust towards Eleanora. This had started shortly after his father had been brought to the castle in the early hours of one morning, unconscious and covered in dirt. Eleanora had literally floated Sam to a room to clean him up away from prying eyes. One of the servants had told Chris of his father's presence and his condition, Chris had wanted to see him straightaway.

What he found shocked him. He had literally walked in on Eleanora using spells on Sam and when Chris had demanded that she stop and also asked exactly how it just so happened that his father was in the castle, Eleanora had responded by telling him in a rather matter of fact way, that she had instructed the trees to bring him here by dragging him through underground tunnels under roots and trees to a portal point, where he was then teleported here. Eleanora accused Sam of spying on them in Glossop and finally ended the torrent with the allegation that he was part of The Company. Chris looked at Eleanora murderously and had vehemently denied his father was capable of any wrongdoing without magical interference. Eleanora had spat out a retort that in her opinion all non-magicals' were very capable of lies, deceit and corruption. When Polly, Toni and the Professor had arrived, Eleanora and Chris had finished trading insults and accusations but there was an unpleasant and unspoken agreement that they did not see eye to eye on the subject of Chris's father. The Professor had explained that the spell had, had an adverse effect for some reason and offered to help Chris move his father to his suite on the first floor. Sam recovery would take time but it was going well but Eleanora's and Chris's relationship was still in tatters.

Chris had angrily told the Professor that he was a bit ticked off that 'people' (Chris used his hands to emphasise the quotation marks in this speech while staring directly at Eleanora) were able to casually use magic on others without permission and control another person's free will. Chris had asked if there was some sort of code of conduct for the magical world like there is for the rest of humanity. Polly thought that Chris was referring to the incident with the truth serum and Eleanora's use of magic on his dad but this equally could be applied to Polly and the spell she had used on Mother too.

This had really made Polly think about the appropriate use of magic and that it really should be used as a last resort rather than something that is used on a day-to-day basis. Polly was thinking about the room of dark magical artefacts that the group had found and made her question some of the magical laws and spells that she had recently learnt about. The Professor had taken these concerns very seriously and had arranged a set of sessions for everyone about the Global Magical Parliament, the appropriate use of magic constitution and the set of abiding laws. He went to great lengths to explain about the Magical Enforcement task force. He then left them all with a few books on ethics and Principles of magical application. It was a strange time for the group. They were coming to terms with a lot of new changes within their social circles and were quite overwhelmed by the fact that there was a very real magical world operating behind a shroud of secrecy within the world they had grown up in and had been familiar with. All these significant changes meant a loss in terms of the view of the world that they had to let go of to adjust to this new one.

There was a lot of confusion and grief as well as excitement. Another significant factor was that Integration of magic into general society was non-existent. The rest of humanity was kept in the dark about the magical community so magic was kept shrouded in secrecy due to the persecution of magical beings throughout history. This meant it was difficult to identify and enforce any misuse of magic or mistreatment or its misapplication. Magic and the rules surrounding its use, appeared to be reliant on the ability to self-regulate and be governed by one's own ethics and principles. The only time that the magical taskforce was assembled was when there was a prolific misuse of magic or a dark wizard or witch was breaking the rules of secrecy. This had created a bit of tension and strain within the group. Polly was sure that they would work this through together but for now it was quite a difficult time.

To top it all, Mother had woken up fully recovered from the spells she had been put under and had regained her free-will of which she wished to exercise immediately and in true Mother style. Quite disorientated at first, she had stayed in her room and then when she was feeling a bit better, started to explore the castle and grounds. She had asked for a fresh set of clothes from Louis Vuitton because 'whoever owns this castle is not short of a pretty penny darling, now really'. She then started ordering the castle staff around and demanding obscure detox juices 'just like those ones on Goop' and asking for a masseuse to be in her room by a certain time each morning. She would get fully glammed up and sit by the pool reading fashion magazines and ordering the most expensive champagne. Mother had also quickly realised that the castle held an account with most stores and was ordering from Selfridges, Harrods, Fenwick's, Liberty, Fortnum and Mason etc, and was charging to the Castle's accounts with these stores. Rather embarrassingly she was treating the castle and its staff, like a luxury resort. The only thing that she completely was blind to was magic, spells and potions were all around her and she seemed completely oblivious. Her brain appeared to block it out for some reason.

Polly was worried that Eleanora would be told of her mother's antics soon and that Eleanora would want to turn her into something more manageable like a toad. Although Polly was not a huge fan of both her Mother and Father and did not understand or agree with their values and principles, she still wished them no harm. In fact, she still held onto the belief that one day they would develop empathy and remorse for their actions towards her and others. Holding onto this hope and belief was the only real connection Polly had with them, however misguided this belief was, she found it difficult to move beyond it, this being her only family. Or at least the only family that she knew of currently.

Polly was in the gymnasium going through the moves of a combat routine when Eleanora walked in carrying her staff in her hand. The older woman was quiet, silently watching Polly train. Polly's aim and moves were off centre. She was clumsy and kept forgetting the routine. Eleanora continued to silently observe while Polly huffed and puffed, directing all of her frustrations at herself and driving her upset within. Polly had been confident and self-assured yesterday but today she seemed to have the weight of the world on her shoulders. Eventually and inevitably, Polly fell while doing a high kick and landed with a crack on her back. She lay there silently with tears rolling down her cheeks. Eleanora leaned on her staff and continued to watch in silence. Polly got up, red faced and crying. She stumbled forward and started hitting out at the dummy made of wood. Her knuckles were bleeding and her frustration could be heard in her high-volume yells.

The years of pent-up anger and pain at how unfair her life had been leaking out of her. She kicked out at the frustration of not being able to make her friends happy even though they were now part of something beautiful and bigger than they or anyone could have dreamt possible. She rammed her full body at the dummy repeatedly and then she let out a primal scream and slumped forward in a prayer position, she stopped. She sat there in silence for a few minutes. Eleanora stood still and then straightened up. Polly looked over at her and with an accusatory tone whispered, 'what do you want from me?'. Eleanora stood still and smiled. Polly continued. 'I've had enough, I can't do this. I don't know what I am doing. I can't seem to make anyone happy. I'm changing nothing. I'm here training when there is a group of people out there trying to make a potion that will make them invincible. They seem to be preparing for an apocalypse or trying to start one and I'm this chosen one and I don't even know what to do or how to do it or what even that means. I think you have picked the wrong person. There's been a mistake. The Lady was right. I shouldn't be here....' Polly waited and expectantly looked at Eleanora.

Eleanora said nothing and looked back at Polly with serenity. A few more minutes passed between them and Polly became frustrated. She wanted answers, she got up and started walking towards the door to the upper floors. She heard from behind her Eleanora's voice ring out into the room 'whether you believe you can do this or do not believe you can, you are right'.

Polly paused, her hand on the door. She stopped and turned around. 'I do not know what to believe about myself' Polly rushed on 'I'm a girl who hasn't had anyone believe me. I've been told I'm no good at anything so how do I just suddenly start believing in myself? You are asking for a miracle'. Eleanora watched Polly carefully. The girl looked mortally afraid, yet she still stood there waiting for answers. Eleanora cleared her throat 'you hold the answers. You are nature, you are the trees, you are the earth, and they are you. You are one, you are life and death, the cosmos is in you. Empty your cup of all that has been poured into you by people who don't understand the oneness of everything, trivial pettiness of the materialistic world. Let it go and let us begin' Eleanora said this in a very self-assured way like she could see the answers and wanted to point Polly in the right direction.

Polly felt entranced by these words, she coveted them in the space where she felt unsure and they grew brighter, almost on the cusp of letting go of everything she had held on to before, but something held her back. 'What about Chris and Toni?' Polly said this like a frightened small child not wanting to look after herself. 'They will grow with you and accept you for who you must become to be the ultimate Warrior, or they will not. You all cannot hold onto old versions of each other because it is comfortable. Staying small is suffocating. Growing is uncomfortable but rewarding in of itself. In time you will all learn this. I wish for you to be together when you do but if not, then you need to know that is okay too'. Polly sat down and crossed her legs before Eleanora. She leaned forward and placed her forehead on Eleanora's staff. 'I am ready to begin'. Polly did not know if she had said this or if it was Eleanora but her whole-self opened to the need for knowledge and to understand the way of the warrior.

Eleanora took Polly's chin in her hand and lifted it. 'I think you are ready for the initiation'. Eleanora had been seeing portents for a number of days. Things like an egg with a treble yolk and a swallow flying backwards. A bat that followed her on her evening walk and a moth that danced for hours in her candlelight. These were all signs for renewal and beginnings. Polly was very tired and did not have the energy to argue 'I'm not ready'. She murmured. 'No one is ever ready for these things' Eleanora replied 'dig deep and do the best you can'. She said this while patting Polly on the back knowing that the girl would have to make sacrifices in the long term.

Eleanora went over to a table and conjured a simple pewter pot and a selection of small glass jars. A fire appeared under the pot and Eleanora closed her eyes and started busily putting the ingredients into the pot while singing an old Celtic song to herself. The song she sang was of the decline of the temple of Ravenplace and of the one thousand Priestesses who were killed by an army of the Pendragon king of the United Kingdom centuries ago. It was a tragic tale of loss and sorrow, but it ended on the promise of the return of the high priestess and the shield maidens of old. The pagans worshipped women as they were embodiment of life itself and this had been lost in the mists of time but soon to be restored.

'Right, this potion contains mushrooms and herbs that are very potent. You will experience an altered state of consciousness. There is nothing to worry about. Just relax into it'. She gave the brown sludge to Polly and encouraged her to drink it down in one go. Polly sniffed at it and pulled a face. She did drink it but gagged a few times. It tasted vile. Polly put the wooden cup down on the table and Eleanora took Polly by the hand and walked her over to the stairs and up into the main hall of the castle where the entrance was. They both walked out over the grass towards the forest.

Polly felt a warm sensation first of all then her mind started to shift and she could see everything very clearly in hyperfocus and all her others senses were heightened too. She could hear the buzzing of the individual bees and see the intricate detail of every blade of grass and felt each particle of light from the sun touch against each cell of her skin. The sun energised her through its ray and she gulped in the air through her nose. All was in blissful harmony; everything was about the energy of the universe. She imagined that this must have been what it felt like for the first homo-sapiens when the world was new to them and everything was in balance with nature. Its harmonious beauty was breath taking and she wished that all humans could feel this, to be at one with everything. To feel so close and connected.

They stood before a tree. It was a huge beautiful and rather grand old Oak tree. It had a hole underneath it. Eleanora positioned Polly in front of it and suggested she crawled within. Eleanora then sat herself down on a protruding tree knot and got out the Tome of Herne to read through. She shouted to Polly 'you will only have half an hour to prove yourself so quit messing about and get on with it'. Polly started, she bent down and looked into the hole, it was dank and dark. There were whispers coming from within. She could not make out the words, but she knew the voices were encouraging her forward. She got down and crawled inside. It was a long dark tunnel, just room enough for her to crawl through. After five minutes she came across a dead dormouse. She moved it to the side and over it she said how sorry she was that the dormouse's life had ended while the animal was still young and offered up a prayer.

Polly continued, the tunnel was very long and descended downwards. With each movement forward it seemed to be getting hotter and hotter. Up ahead in the tunnel she saw a strange sight. There was a large stoat with a baby stoat beside it. The mother Stoat had an egg, it was a bluebird egg and there was a bluebird in the tunnel pecking at the stoat to give her back her egg. The baby Stoat was hungrily watching the egg and it looked malnourished and very weak. The Bluebird was really distressed, it wanted its egg back. All the animals seemed oblivious to Polly's approach. She watched the scene not knowing how to help at first and realised that the dead dormouse was back the way she had come in. She hesitated as time was getting short, but she decided she had to make time to go to get the dormouse. She went back through the tunnel from where she came. After a while, she returned with the dead dormouse. She exchanged it for the egg and gave the egg back to Mother Bluebird who promptly flew away. The two stouts took the dormouse and ran away without a backward glance. Polly was a bit baffled but continued down the tunnel. She realised that time was running out, so she started bear crawling at speed and galloping through the tunnel. As she did so she thought to herself that it had been over thirty minutes, berating herself for spending so much time with the woodland animals. Would she now have enough time to prove herself as a warrior to the goddess?

Suddenly, the tunnel opened up into a vast, lush and densely green watering hole covered in giant lilies of all colours. There were succulent hydrophytes mixed with foliage all the way around the water and a flock of flamingos were pecking at its surface. On the banks were peacocks with stunning plumage and the air was humid and very hot - the water hole was vibrant and exotic in stark contrast to the tunnel in all of its splendour and great wealth of abundance.

A little way in the distance, there was a fountain with beautifully hewn statues of female warriors all in battle dress. Each one had a weapon made of precious metals and stones laying under foot. Polly made her way through the water and looked at the statues each in turn and decided that this must be the start of the test. To choose a weapon of great honour. After careful consideration, she chose to retrieve a sword made of gold and silver with diamonds studded into the hilt. She hoped this would impress and that she was still allowed to fight even though she was very late. She waded through the water, it was at waist height, past the statues and then saw a glimpse of something glittering in the water ahead. She bent down and pulled from a rock a sword that was covered in silt and sludge. It had a leather-bound hilt and was much more slender and less ostentatious than the other sword she had chosen. Polly felt an instant connection to it. Its vibration was in tune with her own. She gave it a wipe and tied the sword to her belt but thought that the other sword was showier and more impressive so moved on carrying the two swords with her.

In the water ahead of her was a woman, slender yet, gigantically tall with long honey coloured hair and luminous blue eyes. She had on her head a crown made of a stag's skull or at least what looked like its forehead. Woven into it were thick binds of green foliage and cream-coloured flowers. It was very beautiful and accentuated her dramatically striking face. She was wearing a silk tunic that barely covered her nakedness. She looked around at Polly as she climbed out of the water. Polly didn't know what to say and was pretty embarrassed by the beauty of the woman so kept her eyes averted. The woman had an ethereal glow around her, almost a golden haze.

'My name is Vusula High Priestess and Bringer of Destiny' she paused, then swooped down to look closer at the small human in her midst 'and you must be Polly' said the ethereal being 'I have been expecting you'.

'Yes, I am. I am here to be tested,' Polly responded unsurely. Polly had forgotten herself for a moment so she pulled herself up to her full height to feel more confident. The priestess gazed at her for a long while and then sat down on the bank edge, gently moving her feet backwards and forward in the water. 'You would have me set you a task to prove your skill with a sword or show me how brave you are. Is that what you want? Is that what being a warrior means to you?'

Polly looked at her curiously. 'I thought it was some type of test of strength,' Polly explained, sounding even more unsure than before and looking around her for an opponent. 'So, you value brute strength and sacrifice above all else? Very well. Go and chop down that weeping willow in the old wood in St Albans and tell me how many rings there are inside'. The High Priestess studied the girl closely. Polly froze and felt very alarmed. This was something that she could

223

not possibly do. It was unthinkable to her to chop down a tree that she had bonded with and the very thought of it made her nauseous, just thinking about it made her eyes sting with tears. But others would be able to do this. "It's a tree" Polly told herself but in her heart she knew it was not just a tree.

She stood there feeling defeated, shoulders rolling forward. She had come all of this way wanting to prove she was worthy of the mantle of the Goddesses warrior, The Chosen one. She knew that she still needed training and to learn how to utilise her skills to optimal effect, but she did think she was a pretty decent person and always tried her best to do good. 'I am sorry, I cannot do this for you. It would break my heart. You need someone that can serve and do what is needed, what is right'. Polly said quite honestly. The high priestess nodded in agreement at this statement and she repeated 'yes, what is right is very important even if it hurts at the time'. Polly with a heaviness in her heart started turning round with the intention of wading her way back through the water. The priestess watched her with a warm smile playing on her beautiful face 'Before you go, would you like me to tell you how well you did in the tests?'. The Priestess calmly said, 'it's a shame, you came all this way to be tested, so I would expect you would want to know'.

Polly stopped, eyes filled with a sudden understanding 'There were tests, as in plural, more than one? She stammered out. The Priestess nodded emphatically 'These were tests of the heart, of knowing yourself and of courage. All these are strengths that a warrior must possess or least have the capacity to develop.' She paused then went on. 'You passed the first test. Most people would have continued past the quarrelling woodland creatures not wanting to lose any time. At best, some warriors have taken a shine to the bluebird and taken the egg back from the stoat leaving her baby to die of starvation. Whereas, you saw they were all equally as important and you made the time to give them all that they needed. You even said a prayer for the dormouse. It was most touching and reflected your true spirit very well. It was a credit to you and your loving nature.' Polly stood there stunned; she had not thought that was a test. She had acted instinctively.

'The second test you partly passed but also failed somewhat. You initially chose a sword to impress others, but you did also take the sword of Hestia with you which you knew was right for you, but you couldn't be sure it would impress others. You trusted yourself only partly so there is more for you to do around building self-assurance. Now the third test took courage, to deny a High Priestess of what she has asked of you. I was impressed. You did not hesitate. You listened to your heart, and it said no and you followed it knowing that you may fail the test and not be able to be The Goddesses Warrior. Something you highly desire and prize. It took great courage and shows you have a strong moral compass even when faced with pressure to make a difficult decision.'

The High Priestess paused and looked down upon Polly's flushed face. The priestess put her hand on Polly's shoulder and continued 'I am very sure you are The Chosen One, youngling but you do need a bit more training and a lot more self-belief to lead the planet through the storm that is coming. This will come in time that I am sure of.' she said gravely and then smiled down on Polly with gentle encouragement and grace 'Hold yourself in compassion while you learn these skills and follow this difficult path fully. Do not hold fear in your heart as it will blacken your soul. Do you understand?' Polly nodded 'I will now give you the scroll that explains the prophecy and then send you on your way. Fare thee well Chosen One' with that the High Priestess lent forward and kissed Polly on the forehead, which transferred the skull and flower crown, a flash of light shot through the air and Polly was transported back to the Great Oak tree. She collapsed to the ground still clutching the scroll in one hand and the sword of Hestia in the other. Eleanora ran over to her and let out a shout of triumph. 'You did it, you did it, well done my girl'. Polly rolled over onto her back and let out an almighty sigh of relief. She was exhausted but at least now she knew for sure that she is indeed is The Chosen One.

The strangest thing happened at that moment, a lone grey wolf walked out of the clearing and padded over to Polly. It stood close by for a while with its amber eyes fixed on Polly and its tongue lolling to the side, panting like it had been travelling for a long time. It wearily walked over and then sat beside Polly laying across her neck like the wolf was protecting one of her own cubs. Polly nuzzled into the She-wolf's fur and fell instantly into a restful and long sought after sleep. Eleanora stood over the two forms and sighed. She sat down and lit a small clay pipe, resisting destiny was unwise so she would watch over them until they were ready to rise again.

Chapter 17 - Reckless ambitions

Eleanora sat in watch for a long while. The girl was exhausted. Polly awoke and laid still for a while with her eyes closed listening to the rhythm of her own breath and absorbing all the sounds of the world around her. The she wolf had gone hunting, the whole experience of the tunnel, water hole and fountain was like entering a dreamworld, very vibrant with overwhelming scents and sounds that overloaded and scrambled the senses. It was like she had been transported back to a primordial time where myths and legends walked the earth. She was trying hard to orientate herself back to reality, which was taking a while to adjust to. Polly let go of the scroll and touched her hand to her forehead, she felt the crown on her head. The flower petals got caught by the breeze and started to come apart. Eventually, all that was left was the skull of the White Hart, but Polly did not realise it at the time.

Eleanora saw a cloud formation in the distance and touched her silver ring to be given sight through the power of glimming. When she opened her eyes, she looked concerned. 'Come on now Polly, let's get up and go back to the castle. I need to know what happened to you in there and we need to read through the scrolls.' Polly groaned and reluctantly got to her feet. As they walked out of the woods and onto the grass glades the trees sang, and the birds tweeted their pleasure at Polly being named as the chosen one, their champion. Polly's doubt was still lingering about her new status but somehow it was dulled by the High Priestesses' endorsement of her as The Chosen One. Up until this point she had not believed it herself. It was slowly dawning on her that she had gone through the motions of training to fill the time while in the back of head, she now realised, that she had been waiting for the real champion to turn up. Maybe that was why she was so quickly and so willingly prepared to hand over her powers to The Lady, she really hadn't thought that they had belonged to her and that there had been some kind of mistake.

227

Polly was lost in her thoughts of realisation and awakening. She turned round to smile at Eleanora and stopped dead in her tracks. 'It was you who put a spell on the potion in the salon that day when I gained my powers' Polly gasped and called out to Eleanora 'it was you that gave me my powers'. Polly stood there very still waiting for Eleanora's response. Eleanora carried on walking. She did not turn around and she did not offer an explanation. Polly called out to Eleanora, but she just carried on walking. Polly started running and was standing in front of Eleanora in a split second, covering the distance easily with her powers. 'I deserve an explanation,' Polly said assertively.

Eleanora tried to walk around but Polly blocked her way. 'You won't understand' Eleanora said at last and then broke away and carried on walking. 'Try me' Polly replied, walking alongside her. Eleanora sighed 'the potion didn't give you your powers Polly, the potion awakens the essence of the person within. Eleanora explained 'people who possess powers, well, those powers remain dormant like a recessive gene until needed or triggered by something, like their environment. Humans once used to swing through trees and we had tails. We still have the capability to do and have all of those things, but our environment has changed as do our genetics. All humans have powers. They just need to be triggered. Do you see?' Polly thought about this and nodded, then a strange look passed over her face 'and my parents. I mean my real parents?' Eleanora stopped now and looked very sad. Her blue eyes were much bigger and shiny with long forgotten and unshed tears. Eleanora turned to face Polly and put her hand to her cheek 'please, another time. I do not have the strength at the moment and I understand you need to know, nay you deserve to know as it your story but just not now. We are at war Polly and the enemy is at the gates. If the company gets hold of the Vessel of Life, then they are one step closer to immortality and triggering their powers and with that the apocalypse. We must stop them at all costs. Polly looked crestfallen but only for a second, she wanted to know but rallied her strength and tried to focus. She was the Chosen One and she would need to start acting like it. They needed to read the scrolls and get the Vessel of Life before The Company did. 'Right, I'm ready.' Polly said. 'Of course, you are my dear. You always have been'.

Both Polly and Eleanora walked into the library of the Castle. Toni was on one of the squishy overstuffed sofas reading a book on herbology with her legs up. She looked really comfortable and was practising memorising healing balms and potions when they both walked in 'wow, you look like you've just done ten rounds with a number 19 bus' said Toni while she laughed. Polly stuck out her tongue behind Eleanora's back and waggled it. 'Learn anymore spells Merlin?' Polly threw back teasingly. Toni snorted out a laugh and they both started giggling. 'I haven't had time, I've been entertaining the new arrival and he is rather dishy, I must say' continued Toni with a flirty giggle.

 Eleanora's eyes widened at this comment and she said rather sternly 'who has arrived? No one has been invited to the Castle.'. A very tall young black man in his late teens appeared in the doorway. He was muscular and lean; he currently wore a clean-shaven look and stood tall with confidence. there was the impression left that he was not afraid to take up space. His arms folded across his wide chest, not in a defensive way but in a casual at ease kind of way. He had on a plain black leather eye patch over his right eye, which gave his face and demeanour an edge. 'Afternoon Eleanora' he smoothly said, inviting himself into the conversation. 'Balan, how did you get here? Not that I'm not pleased to see you but we thought you had been taken. You were supposed to be here months ago' Eleanora said, recovering from the surprise while, moving quickly towards him. 'What happened?' she continued and gestured to his eye. 'I did that story about Polly and then another about uncovering and speculating over the motives of The Company and they came to get me this time. They took me to one of their secret locations and roughed me up and threatened me. Eleanora looked concerned 'its ok, they didn't ask me any questions about the magical world. It was more about teaching this young black man his place in the world.' he thumped his chest 'They didn't connect me to anything else' Balan said this very casually, but one could tell there was an underlying hurt in his voice and his pride was bruised. There was also a hint at something else like he had been treated differently because he was black which Eleanora would ask about when they were next alone. She sensed he did not want to talk about it now. 'Well, as long as you are ok Balan that's the main thing. How did you get away? 'They needed to stitch me up after a beating and I feigned being asleep in the medical area and then managed to dress up as an orderly with the help of a bit of a disillusionment glamour. I managed to get myself out of the compound and headed directly here' Balan said. Eleanora nodded and beckoned Balan to follow her out of the door without a backwards glance to Polly and Toni.

Polly and Toni stood there quite stunned by Eleanora's abrupt exit and rudeness. They both caught themselves peering after her and then looked awkwardly at each other realising that they had not spent that much time alone together in a very long while. The conversation stalled. There was an awkward silence.

Polly had so much to say she did not know where to begin. She wanted to share with her friend all that was going on in her inner world – she was going through some fundamental changes, like she had thought she was going mad then discovered she had powers and that a high priestess had assessed her character, not her strength or powers, and had determined she was this Chosen One of legend. It was all really weird and stupid because she did not feel any different. She was also having these strange moments with Chris that she kind of liked but terrified her at the same time but all that came out was 'hey, what's new with you? Toni stood there rubbing the outside of her upper arm which she did when she was feeling self-conscious. Toni felt angst. She wanted to divulge that she just couldn't get past the upset caused by the way Maami had treated her. She had verbally forgiven her Maami but couldn't figure out how to practically do it. She had discovered these new powers too and she was scared of them. She could not believe that she had healed Annika with the powers of her mind and her touch. Instinctively she knew how to stimulate the immune system of others to fight infections or raise the heat in the body when needed or heal someone by using their energy field. It was beautiful but terrifying to have these powers. She wanted to experiment further with atoms but worried that she would cause harm. There was also the worry that Polly was becoming distant and isolating herself to become this more serious and sombre character just to be The Chosen One but instead of sharing all of this she let out a 'you know doing my healing' lifting up her hands and wiggling her fingers comically. Polly smiled sadly. She wanted to talk seriously with her friend, but she thought to herself that Toni was in a jovial mood. 'Well, ok then I guess I better let you get back to it. I've got to read these scrolls' she lifted her hand indicating the scrolls in and made her way over to the tables in the library. Both girls turned away from each other and sighed. Going back to being alone with their deep thoughts and worries, they also kept looking and touching the identical golden bands on their wrists that Toni had given to Polly on her birthday. It seemed like a very long time ago.

Polly sat at one of the bigger tables and unfurled her scroll. Toni kept looking over at her friend at first, she had not ever been in a room with Polly without having a connection. A feeling of loneliness crept over her coupled with sadness. She pushed down the feelings refusing to acknowledge them which was making her more anxious. Her breathing became short and she started to feel suffocated. Toni shouted out 'I'm going to go to see if I can help Balan, ok? Polly barely looked up from the scroll and waved her hand as a gesture of goodbye. Toni felt stung and bit down on her lip hard as she turned away and left the room. She walked blindly along the corridor, stumbling in the fog of her emotions and she heard Balan laughing in one of the rooms. Toni knocked on the door and did not wait for a response before she burst in.

Both Balan and The Professor stood together uproariously laughing about a spell that the Professor did when he was much younger to try and impress a girl. '......then the whole thing tipped up and covered me in manure' The Professor reached the punchline part of his tale and then both men burst out laughing again. 'It's not all bad' said the Professor, very red faced 'it turned out she married the farmer' Professor said with a wink. Toni joined the two men, their laughter felt alien to her and she waited until the mirth died down before she asked Balan if he wanted her to look at his eye. Balan looked over at her and saw the worry on her face. He put his head to the side to look at her face again before he said 'sure, that would be great. Where do you want me?' He said rather suggestively but Toni didn't pick up on this as she was lost in her own thoughts. The Professor stood there for a while then excused himself feeling like a spare wheel. 'Oh, if you could lie down on that sofa then that would be great' Toni said a little distractedly. Balan stretched out on the sofa and took a small cushion and put it behind his head to alleviate it. 'So, you a healer?' Toni nodded. She pulled out a small book she had been carrying and ran through the spell once again 'how many times have you done this before then?' Balan enquired looking quite concerned. 'Hmmm? oh take off your eye patch' Toni instructed.

Balan did not want her to see the empty socket where his eye had been. It made him feel grotesque 'Where are you from?' Balan was asking questions, trying to strike up a conversation to cover his own unease and try to understand this noncommunicative girl. Toni placed her finger to his lips and then placed the finger to her own to show him that he needed to be silent. Then she held one hand over his eye and the other on her heart, then closed her eyes. Toni felt instantly calm. She knew she would draw on the power soon. Getting a hit.   The internal seal that was holding back her emotions, slid back. Her powers rushed through her body, they were strengthened by her unstable emotional state. She discharged all of her feelings-charged powers into him and recounted the spell. This was a dangerous form of magic but without a mentor, Toni did not know this. The air around them both, became super-charged and Toni's hair floated upwards and started to stream behind her like she was floating in water. Balan grabbed his eye socket and hollered in pain, like a speeded up timelapse, the sinew and muscle was being layered and rebuilt. When Toni lifted her hand away from Balan's eye, she was panting with the effort of the magical spell and of all the emotions she had been able to discharge. She reeled back. Balan immediately sat up and touched his eye which was fully intact. He could not believe it. He had never experienced such a powerful spell. He grabbed Toni's hand and thanked her. 'You must be a powerful and experienced witch. How many times have you done that spell?' Toni smiled broadly and let slip before exiting the room 'oh that would be the first time'. She left Balan to digest this information with a very shocked look on his face.

Polly jumped out of her chair and pushed it backwards which meant it shot across the room behind her, smashing into the wall. She had just read through the parts of the prophecy that she understood. The seven objects were familiar to her somehow, but she could not quite understand how. All she knew was that she must stop The Company from getting any of the items. They would be used to start a chain of natural disasters that, in the wrong hands, would start to cleanse the planet of all life and cover it in ash to start the world over anew. Like a genesis.

She had just finished reading the paragraphs about the 300 consecutive years of natural disasters starting with 100 years of drought and famine and so on. The spell to start it all could also grant immortal life and trigger powers in the individual who melted all of the objects into the Vessel and added the tears of the earth and 'drank of its bounty'.

Polly would not let this world be destroyed and the billions of creatures and people on the planet. Not on her watch. Absolutely not! There was something else written too that filled her with a sense of renewed hope. At one time, there were twin planets of earth. What we call Mars had been a planet similar to earth millions and millions of years ago but it was knocked off course and started gravitating further from the sun - making it a desert and unable to sustain life. The scrolls referred to a spell to realign it and restore it back to its original place in the solar system. This would mean that it would have the same ecosystem as earth. For now, she decided to keep this bit of information to herself. She folded the paper and then put it into her necklace for safe keeping. There may be a way to save humanity after all.

Eleanora had given one of her foot soldiers the instruction to escort Mother on a two-week trip to the French riviera. Mother had been happy as she had been given a limitless credit card and she had run up a disgustingly large amount of transactions before the end of that day. Father had also been calling, begging her to return home. He was being investigated by the HMRC for tax evasion and he wanted her help to pin it on Polly. Eleanora had not discussed her mother's removal from the castle with Polly. She had taken the decision as the woman was a distraction from the really important work they were doing.

Miles and The Company

Miles Luxemburg was dressed in his trademark casual look of shirt and jeans. His trainers were immaculate white and did not make a sound as he stepped off his private jet and placed them on the tarmac of his private runway. He found the United Kingdom a bore. He smirked to himself and muttered 'Kingdom' under his breath. 'What a joke!'. He thought to himself that the UK's economy wasn't doing so well and their GDP was less than 10% of the Inner Circles wealth and their government was having to borrow finance from the Inner Circle and the Saudis at extortionate rates to remain afloat. He practically owned the place. When the British people complained about anything like the standard of living or the health service, the UK government would slap a Bulldog photo on the side of a party bus and hoodwink the population into thinking that the UK was still relevant, still respected on the world stage. Maybe he would buy the place and run it as a corporation dressed up like a democracy, like China. He recorded the idea in his Thought Journal on his phone and walked across to the control centre of his private airport.

He looked down and saw a white piece of thread on his black shirt. Alarmed, he turned to one of his personal assistants, he pointed at it 'am I having to put up with this, seriously?' the PA peered closely at the t-shirt and straining his eyes, he looked to see what was causing the distress. He could not see anything but leaned forward while pulling a clothes brush out of his pocket, brushing the unseen yet offensive particle away. 'Sorry, sir,' said the PA in a simpering voice. He was paid a ludicrous salary, but he was starting to think it really was not worth it. Yesterday, Miles had found a cat's hair probably left by a visitor to his White Art room and demanded the whole floor be bleached down and repainted that same day.

Miles and his executive team reached the main control building. They filed into the main board room that was built to Mile's specifications. The Company team leaders were present including Kane. They were already seated and casually flicking through dossiers and situation reports on their agents' movements and intelligence reporting. The Lady dressed in a powder blue Chanel suit and designer kitten heels in the same colour, came into the room and sat down opposite Miles. She had recently used a location spell and given the coordinates of Eleanora's fortress castle, known as the Temple, to the team in the next room who were planning the attack. Outside of the window of the control tower was a very large army transportation plane. There were forty dark figures boarding the plane outside. The Lady kept sipping from her water. She was admiring her recently done signature French polish.

Miles cleared his throat ready to address the room and everyone fell silent instantly. 'Ladies, gentlemen, Agents, witches and wizards.' The Lady rolled her eyes, she did absolutely despise Miles' attempts to be magically inclusive. He always got the appropriate greeting and address wrong in some way, preferring to use definitions from Dungeons and Dragons than understanding magical culture. 'Nualla, could you kindly show up to this meeting as your real self-please? That would be very much appreciated' With that The Lady transmogrified into Nualla, the dark witch herself.

All present flinched and let out a collective gasp and a whisper run through the room. They were all staring at the dark haired ethereal looking witch. A couple of them kept looking away and looking back at her quickly, with pale faces and gulping nervously. They were seeing the shadow creature she really was out of the peripheral of their vision. Nualla opened her arms and raised her eyebrows to indicate 'here I am, revealed in all of my glory.' Miles chuckled 'come on, simmer down now. The entertainment is over.' Miles' EA flipped up the screen and there was the agenda for the meeting. 'Right, welcome and introductions are over. Let's get on to the update. We have located the castle and there are forty of those demons being boarded on the plane over there to be released soon. They have been enchanted to hunt and retrieve any person within the castle thanks to the excellent work of Kane.' Kane nodded and saluted. He moved a matchstick from the right side of his mouth over to the left and back again slowly and grinned. An old army habit.

'We have also meticulously read through the notes of one of their little group and have managed to find the location of the vessel of life from overlaying the notes against the copies of the Tome of Herne. We think it is located deep underground within an ancient pagan temple site. We are excavating the area and will have the entrance opened back up over the next day or so. Kane, we need you to take a crack team of agents to go in and retrieve the Vessel. The archaeologists are expecting the Vessel will be guarded and there will be traps so please go in prepared for all and anything. We need that, Vessel. There will be other scrolls within the chamber that will tell us more about the prophecy so get in there and bring up everything.' Kane nodded his assent once again.

'Are there any questions?' one of the scientists immediately raised his hand. Miles looked over at the scientist and peered down his nose at him, not recognising the man even though he had met him several times before. 'Please introduce yourself to the group, tell us about one of your hobbies and then let's hear your question,' Miles said - he had recently been on a course that was about effective creative collaboration and the first principle was developing a culture of trust in your work environment.

'My name is Dr Liam Goldenheimer and I am one of the lead scientists working on developing the compound from the burial site. I, erm, like fly fishing in the summer months' he said rather bemusedly, his bushy eyebrows were set at a harsh angle, betraying the concern he felt inside 'You cannot release those creatures. They are uncontrollable and full of bloodlust. They are deranged. They will not retrieve, they cannot control themselves, they will slaughter everyone in their path'.

Miles blinked a few times and shifted in his seat uncomfortably. He did not often hear the words 'cannot' or 'no'. He was a bit baffled at first. 'Thank you, Doctor Goldhammer. Your contribution has been valuable. A demonstration might be in order to show you our new and delightful little soldiers are under our control.' Two of the executive assistants ushered everyone to the large window of the control tower. They were all encouraged to look down to the plane that was being boarded by the demons. The agents close by were ordered to pause and halt the demons from getting onto the plane and await further instructions. Miles was given an espresso in his favourite Buddhist cup and also a remote control. He sipped the frothy, warm liquid before picking up the remote control. He looked out of the window eagerly and pressed the button. One of the agents started screaming and holding his neck. Within five seconds a device was detonated and his head exploded. The demons stood there, eyes gleaming with blood lust, but they did not move forward. However, they were stamping their feet and beating their chests, bellowing out their frustration. The agents on the ground were training their guns on them. A couple of agents were looking down at their fallen team member and visibly feeling their own necks.

Miles nodded to his EA who instructed the ground agents to continue loading the demons. The mechanical blinds over the windows were slowly closing, accompanied by a whirring sound. The executive team were all eyeing Miles with peculiar looks on their faces. Some with astonishment at his callousness, others with fear for themselves. Kane, however, continued staring through the window at the demons, deep in thought. He touched his neck absentmindedly and knew at this point that he and all of the other agents had been implanted with a detonation device. The inner circle wanted to remain in control in the bunkers. He was grateful that Miles had made an error and shown this to him now. He would need to find a way of removing the devices from the troops in secret before he could take control of the bunker at the end of the world as we know it.

Polly and the Tome of Herne

Chapter 18   The master and the apprentice no more

October

It was a beautiful day in early October. The air smelt sweet in the gardens of the castle. The river that flowed around its walls, was faster than usual due to the odd rainy days and ducks and geese were pecking and nibbling at the scarce patches of weeds that had held on through the Summer months to Autumn. Polly was up early to train in the open fields, preferring to be in nature then the gym in the basement nowadays. Her hair was pulled back into a high ponytail and her outfit was all black. high-tech performance wear being her preference these days. She moved with force and gentle grace. Gone was the uncertainty and jerky motions that were linked to shaky confidence. Polly seemed more solid in her practice and sure of each move, of herself. The sword of Hestia could not be bested in battle, yet she had taken to carrying a small set of throwing knives concealed within her trouser legs, with a row down each side. The assault course constantly changed formation magically and the silver orbs hovered in the air shooting at her while she ran through and under or over the equipment, frequently stopping to crouch down to observe the landscape she was fighting in. The ease at which she somersaulted, tumbled and twirled was impressive. Even Eleanora's insults and constant advice of improvement no longer affected the Chosen One's resolve. She absorbed the advice and not the mood from the older woman. There was still a lot to learn but somehow, she had faith in herself and the journey she was on. Her self-esteem was coming from within and not through any external validation. She no longer cared for taming the storm. She was the storm.

Toni watched her from the side lines of the course. She hugged herself like there was a winter chill wind when it was actually a mild, light and beautiful day. When she was alone, the young woman realised to herself that she was also becoming something more than once she was, an accomplished healer and witch. There was something that she had not shared with the others. It was a secret. Since that day with Balan, she had started to hold and repress her emotions, to stop them from being processed and then pulled at them when she needed to perform a magical spell. This was to ensure that the spell became so powerful it was nearly beyond her control. Toni thought that this behaviour was helping her put off exploring all her hurt feelings from being betrayed by her Maami and feeling lost without Polly, her friend. Toni would not admit to herself that she was becoming addicted to the power because it was making her feel less small. Jittery and fidgety, she started looking around for someone to help with her magic. She needed to discharge the powerful emotions soon and quickly or otherwise she would feel overwhelmed with sadness and grief.

Eleanora was watching Polly, but she had also felt the need to watch the little healer, Toni, these days. She was becoming powerful, yet Eleanora was watching her for another reason, that she was becoming darker too. The power was consuming her and she could see it growing day-by-day. Eleanora had tried to raise this with Polly, but she had the blindness of a devoted and loyal friend. All there was left to do was wait for the healer witch to hit her version of rock bottom then it will reveal if she would reach towards the darkness or the light; she would watch her just in case she chose the wrong path. Eleanora nodded grimly to herself. A decision had been made. She looked over at Polly. The Chosen one was the priority. Both Eleanora and the Lady had known this for a long while and needed to keep her safe until she was ready to meet her destiny and do what needed to be done. There were things that Eleanora and The Lady had chosen to keep hidden. One of them being that the Tome of Herne was created by the Sect that worshipped the Horned God who was the embodiment of the Hunt; and male energy and fertility. The Horned God's energy was significantly present in earth today – male led destruction and dominance was the cause of this misbalance with nature and The Goddess had called forward her chosen one to address this imbalance to save the planet. The Chosen one in her feminine energy will be required to complete and restore the balance – this was her destiny.

Eleanora looked at Polly for a long while and gazed sadly on her face. Holding her silver ring, she and kept searching for her sister, The Lady, with their bond and psychic connection but all that she was seeing was a blankness across the astral planes. They were twins, her and The Lady, and had never been separated like this before both physically and spiritually. Eleanora was quite at a loss to understand why her sister had acted in this way. All she knew was that it must have been the right thing to do to protect the Chosen One. Her faith in her sister is unshakable.

Eleanora called to Polly 'come in, we need to talk to Sam to see what he knows' she hesitated 'he is finally awake and he is much more alert'. Polly cartwheeled and threw six small daggers at the wooden post and then twirled in the air to tumble down on top of it to retrieve them. She crouched down low and was nimble and light as air. Polly looked down while retrieving her knives, as she did not want anyone to see the apprehension on her face. Talking to Sam about his apparent treachery would be difficult for her. He is the father of one of her best friends but a father figure to her also. The Chosen One was torn between duty and caring for her friends. It was a heavy weight to bear at times, the responsibility was making her feel alone. She looked up with a smile. 'Ok, I'm ready' she said forcing herself to shrug off the weight of the crown.

The bedroom Sam was allocated was light and airy. It was a room with accents of calming turquoise and deep blues. The furniture was soft, rounded and comfortable. Sam was sitting up in bed when Polly walked in the room. Chris smiled and then bristled when he saw Eleanora walking in behind her. 'Hello Sam' Polly said brightly 'how are you feeling?' Sam nodded, not quite looking Polly in the eye. There was a tension in the room, Polly poured some water from the jug into a glass and then handed this to Sam to take. All four of them stared at the glass held out by Polly for a long while. Chris was physically biting back the urge to shout to his Dad not to drink it lest it had a potion in it. Eleanora watched Chris and wondered if Polly had slipped in a truth serum. Polly looked down at Sam and Sam looked at the water. Eventually, Polly opened up and said, 'Sam, you have known me for years' she smiled warmly 'would I do something like that to you?'.

Sam looked around the room bewildered and blurted out 'do I know you, Polly? I don't know what YOU people are capable of. I've been working with The Company for years and they are trying to learn more about the apocalypse so that they can stop it. You guys are trying to stop the company and the inner circle for some reason from doing this. You' he pointed at Eleanora 'walked up a hillside in the middle of the night and clapped your hands, the whole group disappeared including my son then you used magic to kidnap me and I've been asleep for months. You've got this fool tricked into believing you are the good guys Sam pointed at Chris 'but not me' and he leaned back panting. He was shaking his head and closing his eyes like he did not want to think about this anymore. 'Dad' Chris said quietly while stroking his father's arm. 'I think you've got it wrong, but you are still very weak and need to rest so I'll come back tomorrow with all of my notes, and we can go through this together, ok? Sam nodded and stroking his son's face. He closed his eyes and fell back to sleep.

They walked out of the room silently and closed the door behind them. Polly turned to Chris and held his hand. He looked grateful. Eleanora put her hand on Chris' shoulder. 'I have a calming balm that may help your father recover faster. He has had a nasty shock and whoever performed dark magic on him before made sure that if the memory spell ever was removed then he would die. We only just managed to save him on time. ' Eleanora said gently, she then straightened up and swiftly added 'you need to talk sense into the man and we do need to know the circumstances of that dark magical spell, like who did it and what for'. Chris looked worried but smiled and nodded. Eleanora led him away.

Polly followed them downstairs to the library but instead of going in carried on down the hallway to get something to eat. The kitchen was situated on the ground floor. It was the size of a great hall with hundreds of units and islands, ovens, and fridges. It had its own freezer unit off to the side. It was built to host and cater for hundreds of guests at a time. Eleanora and the Lady often held elaborate balls and fundraisers for magical and non-magical people alike, their guests flying in from across the world. The kitchen had very large windows all around apart from the side that hosted the more industrial parts of the kitchen. The sound of a huge plane flying overhead quite low drew Polly's attention for a few seconds and she gazed up at the ceiling wondering who was flying this close to the castle.

Polly walked over to an island unit and helped herself to an apple, before walking over to sit on a stall in front of a window. She looked out over the vast fields at the front of the castle and peered through the window to try to catch a glimpse of the plane she had just heard. It was gone.

There was no one in the kitchen and she enjoyed the freedom of silence while she munched her way through the piece of fruit. The grass flicked lazily in the breeze and the last of the autumnal flowers reached towards the waning October sun. Polly was remembering a time when she had a picnic with Chris and Toni on a day like this four years ago when the girls had been about twelve or thirteen years old. It all seemed so long ago now. The carefree ways they used to spend their days were so distant and hard to remember with any real clarity now. Her mind had to let go of some of her earlier memories to make space to take in the knowledge of this strange and different world within the world she had known when she was a child. The small number of people close to her all those years ago, seemed so all consuming at the time and now there was this yawning chasm of isolation from each other while they each were learning more about themselves. Transitioning to adulthood felt painful and she longed for the last summers of childhood when everything didn't feel so complex.

Polly suddenly looked up and narrowed her eyes to better see into the long-grassed areas of the field. Her instincts were suddenly on high alert and she had come to recognise this as a sign that something was coming that was dangerous. It was part of her powers that she fully had learned to trust without question. She jumped up on the worktop in one bound and looked closer into the fields some distance away. There was something moving forward through the long grass, something large and there were at least eight or nine of them that she could see. Her vision was enhanced now. Polly gauged that she had about 20 minutes until the invaders reached the castle. Acting fast was necessary. She ran towards the library and covered the ground in seconds. She called the team to assemble immediately. There was something in her voice that made everyone stop what they were doing and immediately gather round. As they stood there, they were all white faced and peaky with anticipation apart from Eleanora who seemed to have been expecting something to happen for the last few days.

'There are about ten or twenty creatures coming towards the castle as we speak'. Chris and Toni looked at each other horrified by the announcement and the Professor removed his glasses and started cleaning them, doing this only when he felt worried or agitated. 'My instincts are telling me they are not on their way to hand us invites to a party, so we need a plan'. Polly cleared her throat 'Chris, I want you to go upstairs and bring your father, Annika and the staff into the basement. Lock them in and guard the door. 'Balan and Professor, could you go to protect the back of the castle the creatures will separate to find a way in' both Balan and the Professor nodded. 'Toni, we will be the frontline of our defence with Eleanora. Is that ok with you?' Toni nodded and went with Eleanora, Balan and The

Professor to get some weapons from the chamber where they were stored.

Chris headed upstairs to start moving his dad, Annika and the staff to the basement. He had decided to tell them that there was a severe weather warning that storms would be hitting the region within the hour. Toni came back quickly with two swords and gave the sword of Hestia to Polly.

Polly held the sword in front of her and shouted a rousing, 'Are we ready to rumble?' which was what they used to say to each other at the tournaments. Toni leaned forward and hugged her friend. 'I'm glad I get to fight alongside you and whatever it is we fight it together, just how it's always been' Toni said. 'Just how it's always been' Polly repeated and hugged her friend back, any awkwardness between them melting away. Eleanora walked back into the room with a big silver axe on her shoulder and waited in silence until the two women had finished. 'Sorry, but I think we are running out of time'. The two friends smiled and broke apart and Eleanora rolled her eyes upwards to indicate that their timing was a little bit off on this occasion.

In front of the castle, Polly, Toni and Eleanora each leaned forward readying themselves with their weapons and waiting for the onslaught from their unknown assailants. Nestled on the inside of Eleanora's robes was the Tome of Herne. Presently, she had taken to carrying it with her wherever she was. Lots of people were looking for it and it needed to be concealed at all costs as it contained hidden information about the prophecy but also it was a weapon in of itself.

The creatures were now moving at pace, the sunlight bothered them and their skin was becoming hard and scaly to deflect it. Their eyes were now shaded with the support of a protruding forehead that sloped over and conjoined with the top of their noses. They ran forward hunched over almost on all fours. Fangs had grown in, leaving their mouths to gape open. The incisures were like sabres on each side of their mouth. The agent handlers were terrified of the creatures they were assigned to look after and started to refer to them as The Horde. Any Agent that was left alone with them would take in a couple of guns and always keep an eye on them. Some agents had fallen asleep and The Horde had pounced on them as a pack and had eaten them alive. Twice this had happened and some of the Agents were refusing to work with them and they 'disappeared'. A couple of days later personal items were found in The Hordes pens so the Agents had quit complaining and instead started finding ways to protect themselves from The Inner Circle as well as The Horde.

A spell had been placed on the Horde recently that seemed to be making them more subdued, malleable, less animalistic but the Agents did not trust them at all. They had taken to always watching the Agents, particularly interested when it came to security detail. One of the creatures seemed to be acting like the leader of the pack. On the plane ride over to the castle, One of the Horde was dribbling and licking their lips with menace at one of the Agents. The Leader hit the creature over the head and it stopped its behaviour with a whimper and a snarl. When the plane had landed The leader led the horde out in single file and he seemed to understand what they had to do when he had been shown the way to the castle. The Horde was then released, picking up the scent of the castle's inhabitants. They had been ordered to seek out and retrieve but the Agents were doubtful of the second part.

Eleanora touched the Tome of Herne and cast a protection spell around the front of the castle. The Tome boosted her powers. Eleanora, Toni and Polly were within the parameter of it. The Horde reached the meadows in front of the castle and within the eyeline of the three women. They started howling at each other and snarling. The Leader stepped forward into the clearing fully erect and the others crouched low before him. He signalled to them to retrieve and Polly, Toni and Eleanora braced themselves for the onslaught to begin.

The Horde, unbound, were a heaving mass of talons, fangs and taut muscle. They chaotically moved forward intent on their prey, unblinkingly. They were three feet away and were heading towards Polly, when one of them sprung forward and hit the protection spell. it blistered against the skin. The creature reeled back in pain and let out a savage howl, driven mad with rage it sprang forward again smashing itself hard against the protection spell but still it held intact.

Another creature joined the first and then another and another there were thirty of them in total. Polly watched the scene, transfixed by the protection spell and waiting for the spell to be breached. She kept moving, keeping her muscles warm for the fight. The relentlessness of the attack was slowly weakening the spell and each time a creature hit the translucent wall, they became more savage with rage and anger. Their teeth were bared and they were panting with the effort but they worked as a pack to weaken the barrier by slamming themselves against it, Polly had never seen such wanton destruction before. She was concerned for her friends as the creatures were strong and very powerful. Unbridled savagery in their eyes.

inevitably, small holes started to appear and the horde started growling with satisfaction, knowing that their time had come. One of them had gotten an arm through the wall of protection and started swiping at Eleanora who bit through the arm with her axe with all of her might. The howl from the creature was deafening and made the horde even more full of hate and rage. They started clambering together and slashing out at the spell and great big holes started to appear. Toni and Polly stepped forward and started hacking at the creatures with swords aloft. The protection spell evaporated and Eleanora was left panting with the effort of trying to keep it in place for so long.

Polly pushed Eleanora in her weakened state backwards and out of the way while Toni and Polly lunged forward, started fighting the creatures taking on ten at a time. The women were overwhelmed with the sheer numbers of the assailants. The Chosen One was besting the creatures but Toni was receiving blow after blow. Just as she was being overrun, she took a deep breath, closed her eyes and slowed down time. All around her everything and every being was affected by the spell, their motion coming to a complete stop.

Toni prodded within and touched on her suppressed rage and anger. A deep darkness crept up within her and latched onto her pain. Toni jerked forward to escape it and a dark purple and black energy beam with the strength of a black hole, shot out of her in all directions and gripped each creature with a dark force ripping it apart, into atoms. Toni was lifted ten feet off the ground, like a limp conduit held up by the dark light.

The leader watched this happen from afar and stopped to watch the powerful display. All the creatures were destroyed in seconds. The beam rescinded back into Toni like ink being sucked up and she fell to the ground. Polly ran over to check on her friend. She held Toni's head in her lap and started weeping.

Eleanora stood over the scene. Her usually rosy face was drained of colour and she was pale and shaking, but she was looking mostly at Toni with deep concern etched on her face. 'What was that? Is it hurting her?' whispered Polly. 'I think it's her powers, she is struggling to control them and they are taking control of her', Eleanora said transfixed by Toni's eyes which were completely black. 'Do something for her, don't just stand there do something' Polly begged. 'I can't' Eleanora said apologetically 'only she can find her way back if she chooses to that is. She has lived a charmed life and has not been tested. This may be too much of a struggle for her'

'I'm sorry' Polly said to Toni, rocking her gently back and forth 'I'm sorry I didn't see your pain, please come back to me' Polly kissed her friend on the cheeks. Eleanora tried to pull Polly up. 'Leave me alone. Leave us alone. Look at all of us. Me, Toni, Chris and Sam. Look what we have become because of you'. Eleanora stood back not wanting to risk saying something that would make the situation any worse. 'I'm done listening to you. While I've been busy becoming The Chosen One my friends have been hurting and in pain' Polly whispered.

Balan and the Professor arrived startled into action by seeing Toni lifeless on the floor and Polly angry and in floods of tears. 'Come, let's get them both inside' said the Professor staring into the distance at the figure of the leader who was silently walking away.

The leader continued to watch from a careful distance and then decided to hide in the forest for a while after seeing the witch collapse to the floor, he waited. Then three of the creatures appeared. One of them was carrying a limp body over their shoulder. The leader lifted the human's head up by the hair. He then signalled to the group to start moving back to the plane. The agents were waiting and it did not take long for the leader to explain what had happened near the castle to the Agents. There was a stunned silence. It was not expressed but they knew that a witch that powerful would need to be managed. The Agents loaded the plane and left the area as soon as they could. A report was conveyed back to base about what had taken place and of a witch with extreme powers of magnitude that was accompanying Eleanora and the group. Base fed back that they had decided to open a file under the folder name 'Approach with extreme caution'. Toni was officially a subject of interest even though little was known about her at present.

Kane and his troop landed the helicopter at the site where the Vessel of life was believed to be hidden in a chamber underground. There was a team of diggers and equipment including machinery, around a big hole that was the entrance point for the excavation of the site. It was getting dark now and the sunlight was slowly fading. The excavation team were switching on their head torches and going underground to continue their work long into the night. Kane and his team unloaded their weapons from the helicopter transport and proceeded together as a unit down within the hole.

They marched past the digging teams in single file and ignored greetings from members of the groups in the tunnel. All the agents' eyes were on the blackness at into which they descended. The Unit arrived at a hole which was about six foot wide, each agent had to hold onto a rope ladder and lower themself down onto a ledge below. This part of the tunnel was poorly lit. The only thing that could be seen was the head torches of the troop as they walked along the ledge over to another tunnel that appeared to have been dug out only recently and by hand.

Kane lowered his face into the hole to have a closer look at the main part of the site. There were cables of electricity and the hole led out into another much larger excavated site and this was lit up with fibre optic lighting. Below people in white suits were suctioning mounds of earth away from a huge wooden doorway that had intricate carvings all over it of animals, humans and gods. Kane lowered himself down tentatively, his huge biceps fully flexed and he walked towards the doorway slowly. He put a matchstick in his mouth and moved it side to side while he analysed the markings on the door. He ran his hands over the carvings and felt the swell and bending of the power within trying to get out. He let out a bellowing laugh that sent echoes bouncing round the chamber and muttered 'there is destiny in the air boys, I feel it and it feels me. Pure destiny'. The troops were in a line behind their boss and they all grinned to each other 'affirmative Sir, affirmative'.

Polly and the Tome of Herne

Chapter 19 - The Stand

Polly and Toni were helped by the Professor and Balan inside. Toni was laid on one of the softer sofas in the library with a cushion positioned behind her head. She was still alive but very weak. Unconsciousness still held her, enabling her body and mind to start repairing itself. Balan went down to the basement area to open the doors. He discovered that the door had been forced open. Chris and Annika were badly wounded and Sam was nowhere to be seen. Balan came running upstairs and shouted for help. The Professor went down with his wand in his hand to start administering to their wounds.

Eleanora was feeling a strange vibration from the earth. A turmoil was stirring that made the hairs on the back of her neck stand up. Something was very wrong, like that feeling that someone was walking close behind and when you look round no one is there. There was a vibrational pull towards The High Priestesses Temple; she could feel the energies of the universe pulling to this central point. Something old was stirring. She placed her hand on the Tome of Herne. it crackled beneath her hand. The book was responding to the magic in the air. Eleanora reminded herself that evil could do nothing without the book.

Polly was sitting to the side of Toni and stroking her hair as she whispered words of encouragement to her friend. Eleanora walked over to her. 'Can you feel it?' Polly asked Eleanora without looking up at the older woman's face 'can you feel something is about to happen too?' Eleanora nodded, reluctantly. 'When were you going to tell me that Sam has been taken?' Polly asked quietly. Eleanora paused before saying 'It's a trap, they want you to bring the Tome. I decided not.......' 'To tell me,' Polly interrupted, getting up from the sofa and finishing the sentence. Polly faced Eleanora and looked at her for a very long time. There was disappointment and grief etched on her face. 'I am going to get Sam and you are going to give me the Tome. I was chosen. I passed the tests, me and a warrior leads with their heart'. Polly said defiantly, clenching her fists with resolve.

She leaned forward and with a slightness of her hand, lifted the Tome from the inside of Eleanora's cloak. Without another word, Polly knelt on one knee and pulled the Sword of Hestia from her belt. She put it in front of her and leaned on it for courage, placing her forehead on the hilt. There she entered into a warrior's meditation asking the goddess for focus, clarity, and the power to stop The Company from entering the temple to retrieve the Vessel. Eleanora watched the girl in awe, astounded by her natural ability to take command. It was like she was seeing Polly for the first time. Eleanora silently backed out of the room.

After a short while, Polly opened the door. She looked the same but she had a faint iridescent glow around her being. Her eyes were clear with inner strength. 'Listen up' she said. Eleanora, The Professor and Balan stood still 'They have Sam. They are waiting for us to come to get him. It is a trap and they want the Tome or otherwise they can't enter the doors of the temple. They do not know that I am the Chosen One which will play to our advantage. There is something else. The Goddess and the ancestors have given me some information that will help us so here is what we are going to do'. The Professor went to say something but then looked at the resolve on Polly's face and Eleanora nudged him and shook her head 'no'. With that the group formed a plan under Polly's leadership and if they all worked together, they just might succeed.

Polly gave back the Tome to Eleanora and she used it to open a portal to enable them to arrive in front of the carved doors of the old temple underground. The smell of the excavated site was that of dank earth and mildew. It smelt like mushrooms in a damp forest, where rotting foliage filled the air on a wet and dark autumn day. The place was old and full of stories from long ago. It was a hallowed and sacred ground to Eleanora. Polly was quietly absorbed in the reverence of the space. You could feel the magic seeping out of the ground and all around. It was energising to Polly and Eleanora. They both felt lightheaded and euphoric in the quietness of the space. There was a humming coming from the rocks and there was a connectedness of everything within the space like it was magnetised; a field flowed through each pebble, stone, rock, earth and air, the moss was very vibrant and soft to touch.

Long ago the High Priestess, Gwendolyn, had claimed the site as sacred and had started an excavation to build a temple into the ragged rocks underground. The High Priestess had visions of the place before she discovered It. It was as if sho was being called here to a place of significant power as it was situated above a juncture under the earth where energy and magic flowed together on an axis. It served as a conduit to the Goddesses power itself.

Polly and Eleanora jumped down from the opening of the portal and Eleanora worked hard to seal it shut quickly so that they would not be spotted or seen. They both ran over to a set of clustered rocks and hid from view while they caught their breath. Eleanora peered over the rocks to survey the cave they were in. They were facing out onto the cave and the tunnel that had been dugout to give the Company access. Above them was a hole where a rope ladder hung down. Sam was laying by the entrance doors to the temple. He was distracted and had not seen them. He had a sharp piece of flint in his hands and was busily trying to cut through the zip ties behind his back. This was proving difficult; he was gagged with just enough space to breathe and had been half propped up against the Temple doors.

Polly silently held Eleanora's arm and then indicated with her other hand that she would be going up the rocks. She gave Eleanora the thumbs up and started to climb. Eleanora watched her climbing at speed for a while and turned round to observe Sam and the entrance to the Temple. She could just make out the carvings in the dim light. There were animals, warriors and Goddesses etched into the wood.

The doors were beautiful and intricately carved with runes on them that read 'full are the hearts of the daughters that enter here, love and power go hand in hand and people with ill intention will not enter'. Eleanora leaned back to peer up at Polly. She was no longer within eyesight. Eleanora heard footsteps behind her, so she quickly ducked back behind the cluster of rocks and waited. Sam peered into the darkness and started trying to shout and scream. The Lady stepped out from the shadows. She had on a loose-fitting pair of khaki pants and shirt with high tan coloured leather riding boots, used for playing polo. In her ears were a pair of very large diamond solitaire earrings and on her slender wrists large diamond bracelets. Her hair was in an immaculate bob. As she walked forward, she held her nose and her mouth as if something foul smelling was in the air. The creature could not stand to be near the purity of the temple.

As she came closer, Sam started trying to get her attention and was practically jumping up and down on the spot. The Lady stopped and lent over to retch. A black liquid spewing from her mouth. As she stood up straight, she wiped her mouth with her sleeve and the bright red lipstick on her lips was smeared onto the side of her face. Sam continued to try to get her attention. A large man and two soldiers started walking quietly behind her. Sam tried to alert her to their presence by yelling even louder. She turned around quite sharply when she realised, they were a foot away. 'Hey, nice outfit and those earrings must be worth a small fortune,' Kane said, holding out his hand and touching one of the diamonds. The Lady touched her bracelets and twisted them slightly, so they glittered in the dim light. One of the agents went over to Sam and hoisted him back up to lean against the doors and then hit him in the head with the butt of his gun to keep him quiet. A trickle of blood flowed from the side of Sam's head and he looked dazed.

'Sir, when are they getting here? The agents are getting nervous up top?'. 'Not that long now, my darling sister is already here, aren't you Eleanora?'. Kane grabbed his gun from his side belt and aimed it in the direction that The Lady was speaking. Eleanora stood up and moved away from rocks she had been hiding behind. Her eyes were like glowing sapphires and she stood straight backed with her hands on her hips and her legs solidly in a stance. 'You are not my sister, shadow creature. She would never wear such an impractical outfit like that in a situation like this and frankly she would rather die than wear cocktail diamonds with day wear. You look cheap and inappropriate. My sister has class', Eleanora shouted out.

The Lady's eyes grew dark and turned black, glinting with fury and malice. The Lady's silhouette dissolved and Nualla's feminine form sprung into view, like an octopus undulating and emerging from within a small bottle. Nualla was more than two feet taller than The Lady. She shook out her mane of glossy black hair and ran her hands down the side of her shapely body and stretched, exaggeratedly. 'Well, I had to do something, the old bag's wardrobe is really dull and boring just like you' she spate out a retort at Eleanora and then vanished and reappeared holding her glass wand to Eleanora's throat and pulling back her head with her hand. Eleanora had whipped out her own and had it pointed under Nualla's chin in a split second. A standoff.

'Ladies, ladies, let's all take a second. Eleanora has come here for Sam and she now knows we have The Lady too. Eleanora has the Tome that we need to open the doors with. Eleanora you're here on your own to negotiate, right?' Kane said with a grin. Pulling Nualla and Eleanora apart. The dark witch was so enraged that she threw a spell behind her and it missed Eleanora by an inch and ricocheted off of a rock and rebounded onto one of the Agents, cutting him down the middle into two and killing him instantly, dead. Nualla looked around barely interested and shrugged at Kane, when he threw a glare at her.

'Who said she is here on her own?' said a voice from somewhere in the rock formation above the entrance to the temple and the voice echoed, bouncing round the deep cavernous chamber. Then, there

257

followed a loud whistling sound accompanied by a sonic 'boom' as dust flew up in the air and emerging from the mote cloud stood Polly. Lifting her head and without hesitation she took out one of the Agents as she passed, on her way to lunge at Nualla, grabbing her wand and snapping it with her fingers into pieces as easily as if it were parched twigs. Polly began punching her repeatedly and in quick succession, until she collapsed unconscious on the floor. She grabbed hold of the other Agent by the leg and threw him in the air up against the rock face above the doors. Her eyes then fell on Kane "hopefully the big hulk won't try anything but I'm ready if he does". She cracked her knuckles and assumed a fighting stance.

Kane was no fool. He stumbled backwards, scrambling desperately out of her way and did the wisest thing he could have and put his hand to his earpiece and shouted 'I need back up, Ten strong and NOW'. All of a sudden those ten agents came hurtling down the rope ladder through the hole that the Professor and Kane had been asked to destroy. On the backs of two of the troops were Polly's two companions. Phase two of the plan had not been successful. Polly and Eleanora exchanged looks and knew they had to change the plan and fast.

The Agents came filing into the cavern and dumped the Professor and Balan on the ground, guns training on them both. One of the agents went over and grabbed Sam, dragging him roughly through the dirt, to put him alongside the other hostages. Kane put his gun to Balan's temple and shouted 'hand over the Tome and agree to do the spell to open the doors or I'll murder them one by one' Kane lifted his arm to take his shot. 'Don't do it Eleanora, our lives are nothing compared to the dissolution of every living thing in this world'. Kane went to press the trigger and Balan closed his eyes and drew in breath. 'No, Eleanora, the Tome, now'. Polly shouted the instruction and an agent stepped forward and took the Tome away from Polly and dragged Eleanora roughly to stand before the doors.

As this was happening, a commotion could be heard upstairs. Miles descended the rope ladder and behind him were twelve of his private guards. They could be distinguished from the agents by their desert camouflage combat gear. They jumped down the rocks and helped Miles down, before lining up to stand directly opposite Kane, his Agents and the hostages. Polly and Eleanora stood in front of the doors.

Kane's face was full of shock; he had not expected to see Miles and was visibly shaken. He was wondering if Miles knew he was going to double cross him and take the vessel for himself. That's when he looked round and saw the young plummy voiced limey standing by Miles.

'Well, hi there Eleanora. It's great to see you again and with my book. And who is this delightful young lady with you?' Miles said casually, like he had bumped into Polly in a social setting. 'Let me and my friends go and you will not get hurt. I promise' Polly said with earnest intensity. Kane laughed loudly 'listen to this one, coming on to us like a UEC fighter at a super Saturday rumble.' he said and spat at the ground in front of Polly.

'Come on now Kane, simmer down. Let's not talk to our guests like that. Eleanora is going to do something wonderful for us and we will be forever grateful to her' Miles spoke softly.

'Don't do it Eleanora' The Professor said pleadingly.

Eleanora looked at Polly hoping The Chosen one had a plan and the girl nodded and mouthed 'do it'. Eleanora opened the book and began reading the spell. Her words were loud, in the tension of the underground cave and were spiralling towards the doors. A glittering haze descended from the cave ceiling and started falling and clinging onto every surface of the wooden doors of the temple. While the agents were watching, the Professor got loose from the grip of one of them and ran forward to knock the book out of Eleanora's hands. A shot rang out, piercing through the chamber, Kane's gun was drawn and the Professor, clutching his side, fell to the ground.

'Timothy' screamed Eleanora. Kane walked forward and pushed the Professor out of the way with his foot, he picked up the Tome and shoved it aggressively in Eleanora's hands 'keep reading, Witch' he snarled. Balan ran over to the Professor and held his hand over the gunshot wound, blood was pumping through his fingers. He ripped off his T-shirt to hold it to stem the flow. Polly and Eleanora went to run to the Professor but Kane placed his gun and trained it on Balan's head so all could see. 'I said continue, Witch'. Eleanora turned round and through her tears, continued to read the spell. The particles glittered and shimmered and the doors began to part, slowly.

There was a silence in the cave as the groan and hiss of thousands-year-old air mingled with the present-day oxygen in the chamber. There was a pulling sensation towards the temple then a release as the doors clanged open. Miles whistled 'wow, stunning' he said, like he was a day tourist. 'Kane go in and get the Vessel, take the girl with you as she seems to know more than she's letting on and take a hostage, so she doesn't think of misbehaving. Kane signalled to his agents to come with him and as they fell into formation, they picked up Sam and indicated to Polly to come with them too, by flicking their guns to the side to indicate the way.

The group entered the Temple. They walked through the ancient hallway that was covered with paintings of the forest and in homage to the forest's inhabitants, antlers, skulls, and claws were a key feature of the decorations too. With each step in, a beacon flared into light; each torch was affixed to the wall. There was a whispering in the air and through the ancient building, the flagstones were covered in a thick layer of dust and dirt. Polly grabbed one of the flaming beacons and held it in front of her to light the way in the darkness that expanded ahead. There was a chilled air coming from somewhere. There was a whistling sound as if the wind was battering windows; however, this was impossible as the temple was underground. Kane told Polly to go first. He kept touching the walls and tentatively touching the flagstones with his feet to test their sturdiness. The Agents had all pulled their guns out ready for an attack.

At the end of the corridor was another set of smaller wooden doors and as the group approached, this set opened by themselves. The temple and inner sanctum beyond suddenly lit up with candles on the walls. There were candles on indented shelves and chandeliers made from antlers and bones. Directly in front of them was a pulpit and in front of that was a giant silver wrought seal mounted on the floor. In the middle of the seal was a pentagon shaped pillar and on that was a silver chalice with rubies embedded on the outside. Kane held his arm out to halt the troop. He scanned the walls and the ceiling carefully. He then picked up a pebble and rolled it across the floor. Nothing happened other than the silence was temporarily broken by the rolling of the smooth pebble against the rough-edged flagstones. Eventually, he entered the room and told the troops to advance on the Vessel and take hold of it.

Polly put her arm in front of Sam and shook her head to stop him in his tracks. She removed it quickly, lest Kane or any of the others should see the gesture.

Kane stood on the edge of the room by the doors near Polly and Sam. He was watching his troop enter the room. They proceeded very slowly, the same pace as a tightrope walker edging forward with care. They were all tense, shoulders up and on high alert. They formed a line then started moving in on the Vessel.

At first, the shaking was indistinguishable, but as the Agents moved forward the rumbling of the earth was becoming more pronounced. The building started to shake visibly as the troop advanced on the silver seal. Kane gave the signal to keep going and that was when the agent nearest to the vessel started to scream, he dropped his gun and then his skin started bubbling and he was being dragged against his will, towards the Vessel, then another Agent and then another Agent was suffering the same fate and all of the ten agents were being spun around the seal, by an invisible force. A strong wind was sucking them into the Vessel. They were being shrunk and liquified as they were being spun around in the air. Kane was shouting 'retreat, retreat, but none of the agents could pull themselves out of the tornado like swirling force field. The last agent screamed hysterically as he gripped with all his might on to the seal and then his fingers slipped, and he catapulted up in the air and into the vessel. Then an eerie silence fell. The three of them stood there stunned for a while, staring helplessly into the empty space where the last agent had fallen.

Kane quickly understood the vulnerability of his situation and went to draw his gun; but Sam was quicker and grabbed the commander from behind, pinning his arms down and they both fell to the floor. Polly shouted 'don't go near the seal. Only women with the intention of protecting the magical objects can enter here. That's the spell on the door outside'. Sam nodded as Kane was trying frantically to loosen his grip. Sam knew what he was going to do, he had to get Kane to the seal. Polly moved over and placed one foot on the seal. Nothing happened and she let out a sigh of relief. The temple was starting to shake. Bits of stone and rock were dropping from the ceiling onto the floor. She jumped forward and only stepped on the depictions of the White Hart and skipped forward until she came to the Vessel. biting her lips and concentrating fully; she picked up the Vessel with both hands and held it up above her head. She called forth the powers of the Vessel. A full beam of sunlight started to burst forth out of the cup. She slowly edged around while still holding the cup, which took all of her strength to do. She directed the beams at Kane. They bore into his eyes, melting them. He held his hands up and the sun scorched his flesh through to bone. He started stumbling forward and fell on the seal and it devoured him pulling him into the Vessel of Life and he was gone from this dimensional plane.

Polly's eyes had turned a golden colour and there was sun beam vapour emanating from her. Polly's countenance was ethereal and she was looking beyond the temple into the heart of the cosmos, into the unseen void of time. Into the galaxies, the stars and the star makers, the black holes and the expanding universe itself. The purity of life and its ancientness of being. A voice older than time floated in sound waves in this space. The mother of all spoke to her in there and Polly bowed her head and was humble. Polly was then transported back to the temple and her astral form re-joined its body. She stood there transfixed to the floor.

Sam was shouting and trying to shake her out of her trance, while large chunks of rock and stone were falling from the temple structure. 'Polly, I thought I lost you there' Sam said as he hugged her so tight that her feet were barely touching the floor 'where did you go?' he was looking into her eyes, waiting for a reaction. Polly looked stunned then came to her senses. 'I'll explain later Sam, we need to move and fast. You head for the exit, there's something I need to get out of the hidden chamber in the pulpit'. Sam started running back through the doors and Polly joined him. She was carrying an old leather bag across her person. She had drawn her sword and in the other hand, she had the Vessel. Sam had picked up one of the rifles dropped outside of the seal. The hallway was shaking and crumbling too. As they ran through the hallway, they were slipping and sliding about, very unsteady on their feet as the building was shaking apart. They could see the large wooden doors, behind them the rocks started caving in and a dust cloud covered everything and was spreading out through the hallway. Sam and Polly ran through the entrance just as the cloud hit the doors and spread out into the outer chamber where Miles and his personal guard were waiting.

No one could see anything within the chamber, people were coughing and yelling for help. Blinded by the cloud and the darkness as the lights had gone out all around. Polly put the sword of Hestia into her belt and then held the Vessel above her head and asked the

Goddess for the strength to clear their path. A small flicker of light unfurled from the cup and then pulsing, short beams of light shot out of the chalice. The light was dazzling, like looking directly at the sun. The personal guard dropped their weapons and clambered up the rope ladder. Miles watched her for a short while, he made a note on his phone to find out who this girl was as she was powerful beyond anything he had ever seen before and thought to himself, this was the type of power he needed to reshape the world and then he ascended the rope ladder too, barely able to withdraw his eyes from The Chosen One. Polly also saw Miles; she resisted the urge to cut him down. The power of the vessel was unwieldy and required all her attention at that moment. There was no room for error. Miles did not realise how lucky he was.

Eleanora relit the lights with a sweep of her hand. She had used her magic to remove them and she was now putting them back. Polly realised that the threat was over and she recalled the sunlight to the Vessel and slowly put down her arms. Both were weak and she was shaking all over.

Sam made his way over to the Professor and helped Balan lift him up. Eleanora pulled everyone into a circle around Polly and a gale force wind whirled around her. She lifted her hands and stared intently beyond the physical realm and with a clap of her hands they were gone.

Polly and the Tome of Herne

Chapter 20 - Homecoming

The Professor sat up in his bed looking out of the window over the autumnal day. The trees had dropped their golden leaves and the windswept grounds of the castle looked beautiful. Eleanora had taken out the bales of hay for the sheep and some deer were pulling at it. He was reading a magical book about the White Hart and how to track it through the winter. He knew that they would now need to find all of the magical objects before the Company did. It was not enough to have got to the Vessel of Life before the Inner Circle. Each magical object on the list was a powerful magical relic in of itself so who knew if you could complete half of the spell and substitute any gaps with other lesser magical objects – they could not wait to find this out. Magic like this was unpredictable and he did not know what this would do to mutate such a powerful spell as the one to invoke Armageddon. The Vessel of Life was now safely stored in the secret chambers below the castle but the question would be which of the objects should they try to find first? It would need to be the most powerful one.

He mused on this thought for a while and took his glasses off, he placed part of the glasses arm between his lips and pondered this further. There was a knock at the door, but Toni did not wait for a reply. She bounced into the room with lots of energy, her face was carefree and playful, gone were the worry lines and pain; instead, these were replaced with a deep contentment. Polly and Toni had spent a few weeks together in Greece following the aftermath of the event at the Temple. They had both talked, eaten, swam and exercised together but most importantly they had dedicated time to each other to rebuild their friendship away from the pressures of The Chosen Ones responsibilities. Eleanora had not liked the idea but Polly had insisted that she needed to be there for her dearest friend and there was no talking her out of it. Sam, Chris and Balan had all taken turns to nurse the Professor back to good health. They had all made sure he had taken his potions on time and made his favourite foods and read to him from his favourite research books so he did not get frustrated with himself for the time taken to heal from his wounds. A contented domesticity descended over the castle. It was like there was an unspoken need for each person to heal from the events of the last couple of months and support each other to process it and prepare themselves physically, mentally and spiritually for what was to come.

The group were bonding and when Polly and Toni returned, they had entered into a new family of people that had chosen to band together to fight the Inner Circle and stop the end of the world by using their unique gifts.

Today, however, Toni, Balan, Chris with his arms around his dad, Sam, stood at the end of the Professor 's bed, laughing at his stories and making sure he had everything he needed. Eleanora walked into the room and told everyone that Annika had arrived and she was now able to open Portals and pull objects through from other dimensions and Balan had said to everyone in the room that sounded more interesting than watching the Professor fall asleep and snore. They all laughed and then helped the Professor into a wheelchair so he could see the demonstration from Annika too. They all had grown very fond of one another and it was difficult to accept this state of bliss fully knowing that somewhere out there were Miles and The Company, plotting the end of the world.

Mother had not returned from her trip to the French riviera, she had decided to carry on to Paris, then she had travelled to Milan, Florence, Monte Carlo, Croatia, Istanbul and was currently in the windy city of Santorini at a 5-star resort. She was dressed in a tomato red body con dress with diamante Louboutin shoes with a matching clutch. Her red lips were blowing on a set of dice, much to the amusement of the assembled crowd and she continued to shake the dice vigorously ready to throw them down the green table. She rolled a set of threes which was remarkable as that was exactly what she had needed.

No one noticed the man in the tuxedo and the movement of his hands each time Mother won. He was handsome, tall and muscular with black hair and just enough stubble to still be polished but rugged looking too. He sent over a glass of champagne to Mother. She was flattered when the waiter brought it over and waved to the man sitting at a table by himself. The handsome stranger waved at her back and indicated that she should join him by pointing to the empty seat opposite. Mother giggled, took the drink and downed it in one go before galloping over to the seat. It was not the best way to handle such a situation, she was aware, but she had finally asked Father for a divorce and was feeling insecure. Father had vehemently told her from his prison cell that she was old, ugly and obnoxious and he was the only one that would ever put up with her.

Mother was feeling vulnerable so didn't pay attention to the little details of the man in front of her, yet, also she did not seem to be able to notice magic at all. She looked past his occult jewellery, he was wearing a skull ring, she also ignored that he was carrying a glass wand. The most strange detail of all was that he had a glass orb in his top pocket that glowed from within and every time it did so Mother started to feel sleepy and not in control of her thoughts; in fact, she was starting to forget who she was and what she was doing there at all.

The glass knight was picked up by The Lady and delicately put down on a white square, covered by her Bishop and Queen chess pieces, nearby. 'Checkmate' she announced. Miles squinted at the board and his chess pieces. He was looking furtively at his King. There were six of the world's grand chess masters on a screen behind him and they were all conferring in their own languages in the background over the best moves to make or if this indeed was a checkmate situation. Miles waited for them to verify it was indeed a checkmate, even then, Miles stubbornly refused to believe it when they did and consulted his app to see if there was an equation that might help him. Reluctantly, he agreed there was nothing more he could do in the game and placed his King on its side to acknowledge the defeat. The tell-tale signs of anger were there. Miles' lip curled and The Lady enjoyed this small victory over her captor. He then called to one of his private guards and indicated that The Lady should be removed and interrogated further about the girl and the Vessel. The Lady went into her spell induced meditative state and into her inner world for respite. She had started to block out her memories from access even by herself. It was the only way to protect the chosen one and the details of the prophecy. It also meant that she had severed the connection to Eleanora; there was no hope of rescue without it. The guard grabbed her limp body and started dragging her back into The Room.

Each night Eleanora searched for her sister on the ethereal plane but there was no sign of her there. The connection with her sister had been lost. She reeled from the pain and anguish of it. At first Eleanora had thought that this must mean she was dead but Kane had confirmed that the Company had The Lady so this development was confusing. She had started to follow Miles and taken to transmogrifying herself and assuming the identity of a Russian oligarch who was also a billionaire arms dealer, in the hope of ingratiating herself into the company of one of the Inner Circle. Eleanora was desperate to find out the whereabouts of the new location of their headquarters; and finally rescue her sister from their clutching hands. She would not give up until she had found her. There was always the temptation to ask Toni to help but the girl was under strict instructions to not use magic until she had learnt to control it without the use of charged emotions. She was sure that Toni could find her sister and it would only be a little spell. She would talk to her again tonight.

The asteroid was moving at light speed, but Krone had slowed down time so that the environment was stable for him to spend a vast amount of time on the object that hurtled through space. This way he was sure of not being tracked or overheard or traced by magic. He was a very tall powerful demigod, one of the first sons of The Goddess. He had grown up in paradise but an age of getting everything you could possibly want had made him petty, spiteful and bored. He despised the Goddesses' love of creatures and humans and wanted the power to govern them for himself. He sat on his throne looking out at the cosmos and all the wonders of the universe and all he could feel was bored and unsettled, wanting something, anything to happen to create a challenge for him. He wanted chaos, he wanted war, he wanted fear. He wanted his mother imprisoned or better still dead. As he was musing over these thoughts, Nualla the shape shifting shadow creature sashayed into view. She rubbed one of her fingers down his muscular arm and temptingly pressed her lips together. 'I have just come from earth, the temple has been reopened and there was a girl, I think she is your Mother's warrior and she was able to hold the Vessel'. Krone stopped his musings and leaned forward. 'What is happening on Earth that my mother has called forth her champion? Is the Horned God awake? Tell me everything. Do not spare any details' he said in his powerful, deep voice. Nualla playfully replied 'what do I get in return' as she touched his arm again. Krone grabbed her by her neck which looked miniscule compared to his hand and arm 'do not play with me shadow creature, you forget I see you in your true form and it is repulsive to me.' Krone threw Nualla across the asteroid and then he called forth chains that wrapped themselves around her wrists. She looked terrified. He then commanded the chains to drag her to kneel before him. 'Now, begin' he sat back in his throne, ready to hear all that she had to give.

****

Destiny swept through the old forest in St Albans where Polly's story had begun, her first embers of connection to the magic of the natural world. It waited behind every tree she passed, every fauna that sprouted in her path on her way to the willow tree, her beloved. She loved her friends and new family and would do anything for them to keep them safe, but she needed the energy of the forest and of the Goddess herself, this was only given in this hallowed space.

Polly enjoyed the dappled sun on her skin as she walked beneath the canopy of trees. She watched the seeds as they floated on a gentle breeze passing her by, she listened to the birds calling, the squirrels chattering and small creatures scurrying above and all around. The lightness and warmth of the place lifted her soul and made her heart sing. Where Polly's feet had touched the ground, snowdrops sprung up leaving a trail of the tiny flowers in her wake - this signified her symbiont relationship with nature and the harmony of it.

Polly reached the overhanging branches of the willow tree and entered the sacred space of maternal life. This was her temple. Her anchor to the earth, therefore, to herself. Flowers woven loosely in her hair and a white flowing tunic on as homage to her experience with the High Priestess.

She felt at home, at peace, cherished and nourished by the earth and nature. She asked the Willow tree to protect something for her and all living beings. The willow tree obliged by opening its roots to create a chamber deep underground. A vole blinked up at her from its nest with its little pink hairless babies by its side. Polly took the large, scaley egg carefully out of the leather bag recovered from the temple and she kissed it to her lips before giving it to the willow tree to cradle in a snug under the earth. The vole sniffed at it then laid back down and curled up next to it. The willow tree closed its roots back up; moss and foliage crept over the space once more. Polly leaned forward and placed both of her feet in the spot she used to lay in as a small child. It was quite cramped, but she adjusted and laid down once more.

The Willow tree laid its branches over her. Polly, the willow tree and the egg were connected, formed in a circle through the everlasting life force of everything. Below her the egg started to warm in the earth and as it did so, a pulse could be faintly heard in that space underground.

She was everything and everything was her. She understood this now.

The Chosen One would be ready when she was needed, she would be completed by the challenges she faced. She understood her strength and it was her heart. She knew that what was to come would be too much for her to bear at times and some of the costs would be high, but she had no choice, she was driven forwards as the protector of all living things.   It was her destiny.

The End

Polly and the Tome of Herne

To be continued...........

Meanwhile and far away, Polly's rucksack started to smoulder unattended and unseen. The two white feathers given by the dove were changing from soft white strands of plumage and hardening into a metal never before seen on earth. The air stirred around the rucksack and little particles of dust flew away from the objects, pushed by an invisible force. The contents of the bag were moving or a better way to describe it would be that something was coming through.......................

If you enjoyed reading this book and about the world that I have created for Polly and all of her friends; to spring from the pages and come to life, then please start following me on the social media platforms below. I interact with these platforms daily and would love to hear from you and understand what you thought of the book and your views on whether the world wants to hear more about Polly in the form of a second book. It would be an absolute privilege to write it for you.

INSTAGRAM: phillipa_readsbooks

TIKTOK:@peppaaub

Email: peppa.aubyn@outlook.com

Thank you.

Peppa x

Printed in Great Britain
by Amazon

23518447R00155